Contents

ORDINARY DECENT BLAGGERS

JG Neville

BlagVille

First published in Great Britain by BlagVille in 2023

ISBN 978 1 7395711 0 8 (Paperback)
ISBN 978 1 7395711 1 5 (eBook)
ISBN 978 1 7395711 2 2 (Hardback)

To Gary and Dee Dee

1

A Hole in the Ground

At two o'clock in the morning, a car drove up Perry Hill and turned into a side street at the rear of Bell Green gasworks. The headlights came on as it turned again into a narrow lane and approached a fenced off area secured by two steel mesh gates. A tall man in a track suit got out of the passenger side and used bolt croppers to cut off an old padlock. A smaller man, driving, moved the car through the gateway but couldn't get far due to the uneven ground so he stopped, got out of the car and walked back to the gate. 'He'll know someone's been in here.'

The taller man pulled an old padlock from his pocket. 'I'll lock it again with this, could be months before he comes to the site again and he'll just think he's got the wrong key or it's rusted up. Turn the lights off.'

The other man opened the rear door and lifted out a bag with workman's overalls, boots, gloves and balaclavas. He took his shoes off and started to put on a boiler suit but the taller man shook his head. 'You'll get too hot. Take your bomber off and your trackie, then put it on.'

Both men undressed and pulled on the dark blue overalls and old boots.

'Gloves as well.'

The site was strewn with rubble from demolished buildings. Heaps of bricks and other materials were interspersed with corrugated sheets, bits of scaffolding, old timber and other rubbish. Empty oil drums littered the ground and the site was overgrown with scrubby trees, weeds and ivy.

Using torches, they started looking around for a piece of clear ground. As they moved across the site one man tripped over a length of timber and the other walked into a long metal pole jutting out of the ground. 'This place is *lethal*.'

After clambering over some weed covered mounds of earth, they found an area that looked suitable.

'This'll do. It's just earth and we're well hidden behind these heaps.'

Returning to the car they opened the tailgate, picked up spades and walked as quietly as they could back to the chosen spot. Some light from the gasworks faintly illuminated the area but no windows from neighbouring houses directly overlooked them. Removing their gloves to get a better grip of the spades they started digging.

Although the top layer was soft earth they soon encountered loose bricks and lumps of concrete which had to be removed by hand. Thick roots had to be cut by ramming spades down.

'Could've done with some cutters. Hope it's not like this the whole way down.'

'Rest of the site's probably worse. You're not used to this kind of work are ya?'

After half an hour they had dug out a hole, two feet wide, seven feet long and about two feet deep.

'We need another couple of foot, if it's too shallow, foxes'll dig it up.' They continued excavating and after another half hour the sweating men climbed out and returned to the car.

'Let's have a break and a brew, I'll get the flask. Keep an eye out.'

'It's three in the mornin', there's no-one around, we should be OK.'

Remaining silent, they slowly sipped the lukewarm tea, neither man keen to proceed to the next stage. Eventually the smaller one spoke. 'Better get this over with.'

'We need our gloves back on.'

They went to the back of the car and opened the tailgate, both now faintly aware of a bad smell coming from the rope-bound bundle of sacking that filled the space. Each man grabbed a rope and they pulled at the bundle, struggling to get it over the lip of the boot. When it thudded to the ground, a strong faecal smell wafted upwards and both men stepped back gagging, almost throwing up.

Recovering enough to continue, they took an end each and dragged it a few yards away from the car.

'Close the tailgate.'

They tried to lift the stinking bundle but gave up and dragged it across the site tripping over debris every few paces.

When they reached the chosen area they pulled it up over the mound and pushed it down the other side where it rolled towards the opening in the ground. Both men clambered down, pushed it in and shovelled the earth back on top, stamping it down in layers.

'That'll settle down quickly so we need to overfill it by a foot or so. Don't want to leave a dip in the ground for someone to notice. We'll cover it over with rubble and other crap.'

Finished, it looked like any other pile of rubbish on the site.

Torches starting to fade, they had to feel their way back to the car by prodding the ground with the spades.

'We'll need to burn everything.'

'Here?'

'At the yard. I've got a big oil drum and I burn stuff all the time so no-one'll notice.'

Back at the car, work-wear was removed and tracksuits hurriedly slipped on. Overalls and boots were stuffed into a holdall.

While the smaller man got into the car and drove out into the lane, the taller man closed the gates, secured them with the replacement padlock and got in the passenger side. Neither man spoke on the short journey back to the yard.

When they arrived, they took the holdalls from the car and threw them into the oil drum

'What about the tools? There'll be earth and stuff on

them from the site, might link us to it.'

'Hose them off. In fact, do that, *and* put them in the barrel. The handles'll burn.'

With the yard closed up, each man left in his own car. The taller man arrived at his house a few minutes later but parked his car on the driveway instead of putting it in the garage. He got out and closed the door gently then walked to the rear of the house. Opening the back door and creeping into the kitchen as quietly as possible, he was startled to find his wife waiting for him in the dark.

'Been out jogging have you?'

2

Three Weeks Earlier

Thursday 27th August 1981

'You bloody stink mate,' said Lenny, grinning.

'You wot? ... hand me them screws, the free inch.'

'I said you stink mate.'

'Yeah? Well you're fuckin' ugly,' replied Bert, also grinning.

'Don't your wife complain?'

'She does, but not about that.'

'Jill wouldn't let me near her if I smelt like you.'

'What's she like then, this new bird?'

'A bit mouthy. Big arse but pretty, and she can drink. Never seen a bird put it away like that.'

'Watch-it, guv's coming.'

Their boss, Dennis Hattmann, appeared at the top of the ladder and motioned to them. 'Right you two, in the van, now.'

'Thought we was workin' late?'

'It's dog night you cunts. I'm meetin' Crapper later,

so get a move on.'

    'We still goin' to The Duck?'

    'Yeah, but just for a quick one.'

The minibus was in for repairs so the crew had to travel in the back of the van. Hattmann sat in the front and told Lenny to drive. The men made themselves as comfortable as they could in the cluttered confined space and started complaining loudly.

    'Will you lot fuckin' shut up back there, the minibus'll be back next week.'

    'You said that last week, Den.'

    Hattmann didn't reply and the men settled, talking quietly amongst themselves.

    'Sod this for a score a day.'

    'I heard Madden was payin' twenty five.'

    'Yeah? Bonus as well?'

    'Dunno but I'm off soon as.'

The van arrived in Catford about forty minutes later. The crew piled out of the back and ran for the entrance to The Duck, jostling each other to get there first. They burst through the door and marched up to the bar. Hattmann arrived last, and ordered a round for the entire crew as a reward for finding some valuable scrap metal on the building site. He downed half his pint in one gulp and turned to lean against the counter facing the door.

    'How much you get for it anyway?' said Bert.

    'Ninety quid.'

    'An' all *we're* gettin' is a pint?'

    'You can 'ave a smack in the chops as well if you

want.'

The rest of the crew finished their pints quickly and badgered Hattmann to pay for another round but he glared at them and barked, 'That's all you're gettin.'

At the bar, Bert bought a bag of peanuts and offered some to Lenny. 'How'd you pick her up anyway, this Jill?'

'Pink shirt, works every time.'

'Piss off, you cunt.'

'Nah seriously, the best way to pull a bird is wear a pink shirt.'

'Fuck off, how does that work?'

'It's the colour, does somethin' to their brains, makes 'em more amenable.'

'Really. Well you go wearin' a pink shirt in some pubs and it'll be blokes you pull.'

'Oh yeah, what pubs would that be then?' said Lenny, smirking.

'You know the ones I mean.'

'I don't think I do Bert, tell me about them.'

'Fuck off.'

'Is there something about you I should know? I mean I'd never've thought—'

Bert flicked some peanuts at him, and from the corner of his eye, spotted a large man in a dark suit sitting beside a smartly dressed woman at the other side of the bar.

Lenny turned around. 'I saw 'im too, smug lookin' bastard ... are you thinking?...'

'Yeah.'

They turned to Hattmann.

'Guv, wot you reckon?'

Hattmann looked over at the sitting couple and grinned. 'Yeah all right go for it, but make it quick.'

Lenny tapped the apprentice, Young Tony, on the shoulder. 'Fancy a ruckus?'

The apprentice turned round. 'Yeah ... who with?'

'See that big geezer sittin' over there with the blond, to the left of the pillar, yeah? You get a pint and stand in front of 'is table. I'll sneak up behind 'im and when I give you the nod, throw the pint over 'is bird. When he jumps up I'll grab 'im from behind and you thump 'im. Then we all run for it.'

Lenny grinned to himself, he'd seen this before and new-start youngsters were fair game.

Bert moved behind suit-man's table and Young Tony casually positioned himself in front of the sitting couple with a fresh pint.

Lenny kept well back. 'He's fuckin' huge,' he said to the rest of the crew with a broad smile.

The man *was* huge but on the signal from Bert, the young apprentice threw his pint over the woman. It was obviously a deliberate act and everyone around went quiet. The woman opened her mouth wide but no sound came out.

'What the fuck?'... the huge man spluttered, rising to his feet. Bert simply turned away and sipped his pint as if the incident was nothing to do with him.

'Bert,' Tony mouthed, to no effect.

The huge man was now shouting and lashing out. 'Idiot.' He swung at Tony, but missed and fell over the table.

'Bert, Bert for fuck's sake.'

But Bert was laughing hard and moving quickly back to the rest of the crew. The blond threw her wine glass at Tony, hitting him on the shoulder while suit-man had recovered and managed to land a punch on Tony's neck sending him reeling back towards the bar counter. The man tried to punch him again, but Tony, sobering up quickly, avoided the blow and pushed past the other drinkers to get back to his workmates. The crew ignored him as if they didn't know him. Suit-man, now in a furious rage crashed towards them.

Realising that he'd been had, Tony ran for the exit knocking over two underage girls who were cautiously entering. The rest of the crew burst out laughing just as suit-man arrived.

'Wot you fuckin' laughin' at? You know 'im?'

'No mate, never seen him before.'

They all burst out laughing again and ran for the door themselves, knocking the girls over for a second time. Everyone made for the van but there was no sign of Young Tony. As the men scrambled to get in the van, suit-man caught up with them and grabbed Hattmann by the collar but he spun round and punched him hard in the stomach then hit him again in the face. The enormous man staggered backwards and Hattmann climbed into the passenger side of the van. As it sped off Lenny could see the victim doubled over and throwing up. They arrived at the yard a few minutes later and they all got out but Hattmann put his hand up as the men went to leave. 'Whoa, you lot, everyone back here tomorrow. seven sharp.'

'Seven?'

'You bloody heard me, seven. It takes nearly an hour to get to the site.'

Some of the men walked out of the gates and the rest got into an old Allegro and drove off. Hattmann pulled up his T-shirt and blew his nose into it but the snot wasn't really noticeable against the other stains. He spat twice then unlocked his Portacabin and placed a cardboard folder of site drawings on his desk, picked up a copy of the Racing Post then stepped outside and locked the door. He marched across the yard to the entrance and secured the gates with a heavy padlock then walked the short distance to his house and entered by the back door barely acknowledging his wife, Julie. He went straight upstairs to the main bedroom and changed his clothes but didn't wash. Picking up a jacket, he went into the spare bedroom and came out with a hundred pounds in cash which he stuffed into his back pocket. As he came downstairs Julie pointed to the kitchen. 'Your dinner's in the oven.'

'Wot?'

'It's in the oven, I'm just nipping across to Judith's to get my mixer back.'

'Don't want dinner tonight.'

'Might 'ave told me.'

'I always go out on Thursdays, ya stupid cow.'

Julie pulled the front door shut and walked over to her friend's, while Hattmann went around the house, checked windows, locked the back door and switched a light on in the living room. He left by the front door, used a large brass key to double lock it and went to the car. He started to open the drivers door but turned and went back up the steps to the front door of the house. He looked around before turning the key in the lock again and returned to the car.

He drove the short distance to The Black Horse and parked his car on the other side of the road and walked in. Crapper Jim stood facing the bar while his wife Shirley stood to one side ranting at him. Hattmann went to Crapper's other side and ordered a pint. 'I see you brought the dog,' he said.

'I heard that you slag.' Shirley grabbed Crappers arm. 'Just give me the fuckin' keys.' She prised his fingers apart and Jim grinned as he released his grip. Then she turned and stormed off passing Hattmann's friends, Vince Allarth and Ron Gooch as they entered.

Ron caught her eye. 'Hello Shirl—'

'Fuck off.'

Hattmann raised his glass to Ron as he approached the bar. 'Here comes London's worst builder. How's that old Jag, still rumbling along?'

'Better than that pile of scrap you drive.'

'Difference is, mine costs me next to nothin' so I can afford to buy a place in Spain and enjoy myself.'

'So you've blown all your cash then?'

'Hardly touched it. Still got loads. Got a lovely two bed with a balcony and a shared pool near Malaga for nineteen and a half. Fuckin' beat that.'

'Could I use it for a week or two when you're not there?' said Crapper.

'They wouldn't let you on the plane ya drunken git. Anyway I wanna keep it nice, don't want it ruined by any of you lot.'

'How's Julie then? She like it?' said Vince.

'I told her to like it, so she does. End of.' Hattmann turned to Ron. 'How's your missus then? ... still running wild with the cheque book? You should take it off her.'

'She's still gorgeous and well worth the money.'

'Makes fuck-all difference in the dark Ron. You still losin' money on that Croydon job?'

'A bit.'

'Stupid cunt, ya never learn. It's what the customer sees that matters, right. What they don't see don't matter so that's where I make a lot more money. They're not interested in what's in the ground, they don't know what they're looking at, so I use weaker concrete, cheaper bricks, lean mortar. It all adds up and I can make hundreds more on a job, thousands sometimes. If there's a problem, could be years before it's obvious and I'll be long gone, sunnin' myself in Spain.'

He took a large gulp from his pint, then prodded Vince and Crapper on the chest. 'When're you idiots gonna fix my shower?'

'I'm comin' on Tuesday anyway to fix the boiler,' said Crapper.

'Vince nodded, 'OK, I can do that.'

Hattmann looked at his watch. 'Right, Crapper and me are goin' to the dogs, you two comin'? I've got a great tip.'

Ron and Vince shook their heads.

'Suit yourselves, get your arse in gear Crapper, dogs

won't wait for us.'

Crapper finished his pint and left the pub with Hattmann. Ron ordered two pints and sat down with Vince at a table in the corner.

'I don't know why we meet up with 'im. All he does is lord it over us.'

'Always crowing about the money ... he said eighty once after a lot of drinks. D'ya really think he's got it?'

'He told me sixty a while ago then he said eighty. Doesn't spend much, doesn't flash it about. Ordinary gaff, ancient car. Reckons if you don't show off, the tax people leave you alone and go after blokes driving rollers and claiming a loss.' Vince slid his pint aside.

'D'ya reckon it's all from cash jobs?'

'Dunno, there's rumours about him and some big blag from years ago.'

Half serious, Ron smiled. 'Maybe ... so eh ... why don't we rob 'im?'

'It's not enough.' said Vince bursting out laughing.

Neither spoke for a couple of minutes.

'But if you was gonna rob 'im, how would you do it?'

'But I wouldn't—-'

'But say you was ... feoretically.'

'Why you goin' on about this? I ain't gonna do it.'

'But just suppose it could be ... how would *you* do it?'

Vince leaned back and sighed. '*I'd* get someone else to do it.'

Ron persisted, gently pushing and probing but not really breaking down Vince's reluctance.

'Well someone'll do it eventually, bound to. I could do

with the money and I'm fuckin' sick of 'im tellin' me how to run my business.'

'He'd suspect us right away.'

'He's been boastin' for years ... loads'a people know he's got cash. Half the trade in south London knows about it.'

'He's our *mate*, your mate really ... stop goin' on about it you're givin' me a headache.'

'Why won't you do it ... you scared?'

'It's too risky.'

'What's the risk? Wait 'til he's out, turn it over, done. Thursdays would be good, always goes to the dogs.'

'Julie'll be there.'

'OK then we wait 'til they go to Spain.'

'He'll still come for us.'

'Why us? It could be anyone and what's he gonna do? He can't go to the bill.'

'Yeah but we're the closest, he's just told us again.'

'What the fuck's wrong with you, wouldn't you like a share?'

'Course I'd like a share, but I don't want my head kicked in when Den finds out it was us.'

'Well if you won't come in I'll get someone else. I know just the man.'

'Who? ... not Moose?'

'Maybe, and he won't piss about.'

***

The following afternoon, Ron drove to The Gilded Cat in Sydenham and parked at the back. He sat in the car for a while working out a plan to put to Moose but decided not to have a drink. After a few minutes making notes he drove around the corner to a car showroom and parked beside a Bentley. Ted Salter, the Sales Manager was leaving but came over to the car. 'Hello Ron, Kostas is waiting for you in his office. Just go straight in.'

Ron walked in the side entrance and over the marble floor past a Ferrari and a sleek convertible he couldn't identify. Normally relaxed in Moose's company at home, he tended to feel overawed and inferior by the chrome and glass palace Kostas Moustrianos had constructed to display his "Luxury Used Cars". Most of the sales staff were leaving and only Maureen, Moose's PA, remained at her desk. He said hello as he passed her but only got a nod in response so he pushed open the substantial mahogany door, entered the meeting room and went through to Moustrianos' private office and sat down.

His well tanned brother-in-law was kneeling on the floor flicking through files inside the lowest drawer of a large filing cabinet. He got up, smiling. 'Ron ... you're looking a bit glum. Want a drink?'

'Eh ... OK, small one. Brandy if you have it'

'You *must* be unhappy, you had some bad news?'

'The bank's leanin' on me and your sister's spendin' money like water ... yeah I know, you warned me but it's gettin' worse.'

'We've talked about this before Ron, I'm not gonna lend you money, it won't help. You need to cut down your spending and frankly you need to have a serious sit down with Eleni and tell her what's what.'

'I've tried that but it never lasts. She just can't help herself, you know what she's like. Anyway I'm not asking for a loan, I've had an idea, a little venture.'

'Well I'm all ears Ron but building isn't really my line.'

'You've met Den Hattmann?'

Moose nodded. 'A few times. Don't like him. I hope you're not going into business with *him*?'

'Not exactly ... I want to rob 'im.'

Moose said nothing and went to the drinks cabinet and poured two small brandies.

'I'm serious. I really need some money and I'm fuckin' sick of him. He's a cunt. Knocks his wife about an' all. He's got eighty large, in cash, in his house, and I want it, but I'm gonna need help.'

Moose sat down but remained silent.

'I'm really desperate, I could lose the house.'

'I thought you were mates, you went to school with him?'

'Well I ain't mates with him any more. I fuckin' hate 'im. He never stops slaggin' me off. Tellin' me how to run the business. I could stab 'im.'

'This sounds more personal than financial. How do you know he's got the money, I mean eighty grand? There aren't many people out there with that kind of cash under the mattress.'

'He mouths off when he's had a few, been going on about it for years.'

'That doesn't prove anything and if it was true someone would have robbed him by now.'

'That's just it, everyone's heard him braggin' and

no-one believes it, but Jim Smallwood has seen it ... it's real, it does exist.'

'Who's Jim Smallwood?'

'Crapper Jim, plumber that subs for him. He was working at Den's house and had to cut into a ceiling to get at a valve and there it was. It's under the floor boards upstairs.'

'What? He counted it?'

'No he couldn't, but he could see there was a lot.'

'Well five thousand can look like a helluva lot till you count it. Trust me, I handle a lot of cash.'

'He said it went back a long way between the joists, neatly wrapped up in polythene.'

'How did he acquire eighty grand? Did he steal it himself?'

'Don't know. He's mean, doesn't spend, been puttin' it away for years.'

Moose shifted in his chair then leaned forward. 'I take it you want me to help you in person, help you burgle this house? ... Thing is, I've never actually burgled a house, I never saw the point, nicking tellies and stuff, waste of time. You see it's all about risk and reward, and for me, the numbers just don't add up for a burglary and I'd be very surprised if there's really more than a few grand in Hattmann's house anyway.'

'Well no, I was thinking maybe you could fix me up with someone experienced.'

'The experienced someones are mostly in prison.'

Ron finished his brandy and loosened his collar. Moose could see he was sweating heavily. 'Why not just team up with this Crapper bloke? He knows where it is.'

'I'm not sharing with *him*. Anyway he's drunk half the time and he'd cock it up.'

'You could get nicked. Have you thought about that?'

'Of course I've thought about it but it's not as if it's a bank I mean there's no security guards.'

'You need to understand something. If you break into Hattmann's place and nick this mythical eighty grand when the house is unoccupied, then that's burglary. You'll get two or three years if you're caught. But if you break in and there's someone in the house, his wife, and you have to threaten her with a knife or a shooter then that's aggravated burglary or even robbery, you could get fourteen years. If it turns messy you could get life. Are you really willing to risk that for a few grand?'

'I'm telling you it's a lot more. Anyway he's not gonna report it, he can't, he hasn't declared any of it.'

Moose asked more detailed questions about Hattmann's house and business. He particularly wanted to know all about Crapper but didn't commit himself to helping. He smiled and lounged back in his chair. 'I might be starting to like this, a little diversion from my usual activities though I still don't believe eighty. Another brandy? ... Just because it's a house doesn't mean it's a pushover. We'll need to do some serious planning.'

***

'I'm the best car salesman in London and you lot are crap.' Moose picked up a book from the desk and threw it towards Kenny the valuer, but it missed and shattered the glass door on the cabinet behind Ted. Everyone in the room was shocked but remained silent. 'Do I have to come in Sundays to keep the cash comin' in? What am I paying you lot for?'

'Guv—'

'Don't fucking start. That Audi should've flown out the door weeks ago and it's still sittin' there. You fucking bought it Roland, so you fucking sell it. No-one, and I mean *none* of you, is gettin' any commission for anything 'til it's gone.'

As the sales team left the meeting room, Moose caught Teds arm, 'Stay behind, I've got a job for you.'

At the back of the room a door led to Moustrianos' private office and off that a changing room with a walk-in shower, wardrobes and dressing table. Moose went through the door and Ted waited. He tried to brush off some small glass fragments from his shoulder but cut himself and stained his jacket. He took a pen from inside his jacket and started flicking through a notepad. After about ten minutes, Moose emerged having changed from a dark business suit to his preferred pale grey sports jacket, white shirt, black trousers and bright red tie.

'That went quite well I thought, fired them up a bit?' Moose laughed and looked himself over in the mirror. 'What d'ya think? Smart enough for the Casino?'

'They'll let you in.'

'Don't write anything down. Get me a brown Cortina, P reg, a two litre if you can though a one point six will do. Get cash off Maureen from the float.'

The "float" was a code word for under-the-table cash used for purchases and sales of low grade vehicles traded from the "bomber" yard behind the main workshops.

'Who from? ... Fairweather?'

'No, it needs to be clean. Buy a legit ex-company job, invoice to John Smith and make sure it's got a tax disc and MOT. Keep a monkey for yourself.'

Ted understood the drill, he'd hand over the car to Moose and it would never be seen again. He knew better than to ask about it.

'How did it go with the suits?'

'The usual, wanted to know where all my money comes from, I mean they know the business and just can't believe my margins ... if I was them I wouldn't believe my margins either!'

'So they're not gonna give you a dealership?'

'No. The other lot are coming next Wednesday but I think I'll cancel. They're all the same, it's a waste of time.'

'By the way, would you call that Mercedes place in Bexley. A punter wants to trade a De Tomasso and he needs a price.'

'I should charge for pricing.'

'We do all right with the main dealers, we get half our stock from them.'

'True, we take all their white elephants. I'll talk to him, but if he wants us to buy it, it'll have to be cheap. The last one sat around for ages.'

***

Parked outside Hattmann's semi, Vince spotted

Crappers's Cortina carelessly blocking the driveway. He noticed a gash running the full length of the drivers side and the wing mirror hanging off. On the boot lid someone had fingered the words "clean me" into the layer of grime. One wheel trim was missing and one tyre looked soft.

He checked some paperwork then got out and walked up the drive carrying a tool box and a carrier bag. Julie had been expecting him and opened the door just as he went to press the bell. He noticed a faint smell of alcohol as he walked in and their eyes met but neither said anything. Julie raised her eyes upwards then nodded her head sideways towards the kitchen where Crapper Jim was working. He was fitting a control valve to the boiler and the floor was covered in tools.

'Gonna be an hour at least.' said Crapper. 'Then I have to fill it up and bleed the rads.'

'OK, I'll have a look at the shower.'

'Before you start, d'ya want a coffee?' Julie was looking at Vince.

'Later thanks, I'll make a start upstairs.'

'I suppose *you'd* prefer a whisky?' she said, turning towards Crapper.

'Well if you're offering?'

'Just hurry up and finish. You smell bad enough as it is.'

Vince made his way upstairs and Julie followed ten minutes later. She went into the main bedroom, adjusted her hair and touched up her lipstick. Happy with the result, she left the room and looked downstairs before entering the bathroom to talk to Vince. The cover had been removed from the shower and Vince was standing precariously on the edge of the bath trying to disconnect a switch.

'I wish he'd get rid of Crapper, I can't stand him.'

Vince came down off the bath and put his arms gently around her waist.

'Wait until he's gone.'

She pointed towards a bag sitting by the wardrobe in the main bedroom. 'He won two hundred at darts last night so it's going in the hidey-hole.'

'Where is this hidey-hole anyway?'

She pointed towards the spare bedroom 'I'll show you once Jim's gone.'

Vince went back to fixing the shower and Julie went downstairs to find Crapper outside the back door hacksawing a pipe. 'I hope you're not gonna be all day, I'd like my kitchen back.'

'I'm goin' as fast as I can, anyway power'll be off until Vinny's wired it up again.'

Vince came back down. 'OK I've done what I could upstairs ... how long?'

'Another hour more or less.'

'I've got stuff to pick up at the merchant so I'll be back later.' He smiled at Julie and left.

On his return, he quickly connected the boiler wiring and switched on, leaving Crapper to fiddle with the controls. Heading upstairs with another bag and a box he winked at Julie who smiled but stayed put. When Crapper had finally cleared up and been shunted out the front door,

Julie ran upstairs to find Vince sitting on the edge of the bath flicking through an instruction booklet. He nodded towards the bag. 'Not a bad win for a darts night?'

'I suppose he's quite good at it, that and being mean.'

'Does he keep you short?'

'Well I get enough s'pose but we could live a lot better.'

She pointed to the spare bedroom. 'That's where it is.'

Julie took him by the hand and pulled him into the spare bedroom. The room had a spare bed, some boxes and a shelved cabinet unit that fitted into a recess in the wall. Finished in wood, it was well made but didn't look like something you could buy in a furniture shop.'

'Did Den make that, looks like a good job?'

'He didn't want anyone else to know about it. Watch this.'

She put her hand under the second shelf and Vince heard a metallic click.

Gripping the top shelf, she swung part of the unit out from the wall then lifted another catch and slid the lower part across the floor, the entire operation only taking seconds. Then she pulled back the thin carpet to reveal a wooden hatch built into the floor, lifted it, and propping it against the wall, said 'Ta-da,' as she opened her hands out theatrically.

Vince saw several polythene covered bundles packed inside a number of larger bags. Just visible on the right hand side was a grey metal box.

'We should nick the money and run away together.' Julie said, smiling.

It was a standing joke between them. In a quiet way they'd loved each other for years, Julie sick of Dennis. Vince bored with his indifferent marriage to Stephanie. There had been no clandestine meetings and they hadn't slept together. Just the occasional cuddle, a quick kiss.

'Where did he get it?'

'Well most of it he brought home one day years ago and said he'd been keeping it at the yard. He's added quite a bit since then.'

'Did you believe him?'

'Not really but you know what he's like. I wasn't going to risk a slap or a punch.'

'Is it really eighty grand?'

'It's a bit more and it keeps coming in. I don't know when he's ever goin' to spend it.'

'I hope you don't get mice.' He sat down on the bed and looked at Julie. 'Ron's going to rob him.'

'What!'

'I'm serious, wanted me to help him. I turned him down so he's gonna get someone else to help him.'

'Who.'

'Could be Moose.'

'His brother-in-law, that car dealer?'

'I met him once at Ron's house seemed alright, friendly.'

'I heard he was a big-time villain, shot someone?'

'Well he's got a reputation for pulling bank jobs but I dunno, I think it's just rumours. I don't think he's been inside.'

He placed his arm around her middle and made her sit beside him. 'I've been thinking, could you hide the money?'

'Hide it? It's already hidden.'

'Well suppose you moved most of the cash so Ron only gets away with some of it and we keep the rest.'

Julie was baffled and said nothing for a few seconds.

'But ... Den would know, he's in and out of here all the time.'

'From what Ron was saying it's most likely gonna happen on a Thursday night when Den is at the dogs or once you're away in Spain. Well suppose you split it into two separate amounts say eighteen and sixty odds. Every Thursday, as soon as Den goes out, move the sixty somewhere else and just leave the eighteen in the hidey-hole so if Ron comes he'll only find eighteen.'

'Why eighteen?'

'Den's been talkin' about eighty grand for years, everyone's heard about it, but eighteen sounds like eighty. If Ron finds the hiding place with nothing in it he'll know he's been rumbled but if he finds eighteen he might assume there never was eighty. We could get away with the rest.'

'Get away, how? You mean just run off?'

'I don't know. We'd have to do nothing for a while and just wait it out - see what happens.'

'What about Spain? We're off on the eighteenth. Den's sister's stays when we're away and she knows how much there is. She'd put up a fight. She's as bad as Den, nearly killed a woman a few years ago.'

'I don't know what to do about that. We'll just have to take our chances.'

He stretched out on his back looking at the ceiling

and Julie joined him on the bed. 'I don't fancy gettin' robbed. I was in a bank once when it was done over and I was scared to death. Den'll go mental, he'll kill Ron. If I leave him he'll—'

'He doesn't need to know it was Ron, better if he didn't in fact.'

'So what do I say then? Who do I say it was? Crapper? Lenny and Bert? He might think it was you.'

'I'll start goin' to the dogs again on Thursdays, so I'm with him when it happens. In the meantime think about where you could hide the money and practice moving it.'

Julie turned and took his hand. 'I don't know if I can do this, I just don't know. Something'll go wrong.'

'Do you really want this to go on, with Den? I can see that bruise you've tried to cover up and he isn't going to get any nicer. No-one can stand him any more, old mates are avoiding him. He's full of himself, thinks he's seven feet tall.'

'I thought getting the place in Spain he might mellow a bit, relax, but if anything he's worse. I'll think about the cash but I don't know where else to hide it. If Den suspects anything he'll kill me.'

'He might kill you anyway.'

Julie stared at him. 'What do you mean? Does he know about us?'

'I don't think so but he's got it in him. We were driving back up from Addington the other day and this car was trying to overtake and flashing him. We stopped at lights and Den went over and hauled the driver out. Punched him and kicked him, I had to pull him off. He'd have killed the bloke. I'm amazed we didn't get nicked. Anyway the point is he might do something stupid if he gets robbed and then get banged up and that would leave us free.'

'You've thought about this a lot haven't you? It's too complicated. I'm feeling sick.'

'I've thought about *you* a lot, but 'til Ron talked about robbing Den I had no idea what to do.'

'Where am I going to hide the money?'

'Attic or under a bed in another room, it's only until everything dies down then we move it somewhere safe.'

'Does Ron know where it is?'

'Well he assumes it's in the house but I don't think he knows exactly. How about put it in a bag and stick it in the attic? ... I expect they'll force you to show them the hidey-hole so just co-operate. I think they'll do it on a Thursday and won't wait for your hols. They need you here so they don't have to tear the place apart looking for it. They'll want to be in and out fast as possible.'

'So every Thursday I put the sixty in a suitcase or a bag and pop it in the attic soon as Den leaves the house, then—'

'When does he come home after the dogs?'

'About eleven.'

'So take it down about ten just in case he's early. Anyway I reckon they'll be watching the house and as soon as he's gone they'll be straight in. It won't be late so I don't think you should worry about it.'

Julie stood up and started pacing the room.

'You don't think I should worry. I'm going to be robbed and God knows what else and I shouldn't worry.

This is insane, it'll never work. If the robbers don't kill me Den will.'

Vince stood up and held her by the shoulders then pulled her close. 'This is the best chance we're ever going to get.'

The next day Julie used a pole to lower the loft hatch and pulled down the ladder. Then she climbed up and using a torch, searched for a canvas holdall she'd put up there years ago. She found it and dropped it through the hatch then climbed down the ladders and went into the spare bedroom where she opened the hiding place and looked at the cash. Most of the outer bags contained ten bundles of of either tens or twenties and only one bag held fives. Another one was used for day to day cash and had a loose assortment of mixed notes. Only a few were visible, the rest having been pushed along the joist space. They were easily retrieved by pulling the strings attached to the neck of each one.

She placed bags amounting to sixty five thousand into the holdall and took it to the landing. Expecting it to weigh a lot more, she was surprised to have little difficulty in manoeuvring it up the ladder and into the loft. After closing up she returned to the bedroom and secured the hiding place.

She repeated the exercise once more, this time looking at her watch and was amazed that the whole operation took less than two minutes. Later that day Vince phoned her.

'How are you getting on?'

'It's easier than I thought, it's quite quick actually but

it's still a big risk if Den comes home early. Have you seen Ron, has he mentioned anything?'

'Not a thing since I turned him down, but I did pass him this morning as he drove into Moose's showroom, though could have been for work. He's been doing some stuff there on and off.'

'I'll start tomorrow then with the money, have you spoken to Den about the dogs?'

'I did, seemed delighted, says Crapper is too pissed these days. I'm pickin' him up from the yard tonight so I don't expect we'll be back 'til late.'

3

Inside Man

Ted Salter reversed his car into a dark corner at the rear of the Gilded Cat and waited. Chief Inspector George Baslow's Rover appeared a few minutes later and parked about twenty yards closer to the pub. After waiting for a hand signal, Ted walked over to the detective's car and got in beside him.

'So, Ted?'

'We had a visit from two villains trying to punt a Jensen Interceptor, Moose knows about them but won't deal with them. They work out of an old unit in Peckham. They've been round here before trying to flog dodgy motors so you might want to give them a tug. There's a few others on that list worth looking at.' He handed Baslow a sheet of paper with a pencilled list of names and addresses along with some registration numbers and vehicle descriptions. Baslow looked at it and indicated that he knew some of the names already.

'There's also the "bomber" stock behind the

workshops, motors go in and out of there all the time but the sales figures don't tie up with what's happening.'

'You've told me before about the stock behind the workshop. We've checked it several times and there's nothing stolen. So have you got some other evidence that he's got any nicked cars or goods?'

'No.'

'Well then, it's not really a police matter. If he's not declaring cash it's up to the Revenue to argue with his accountant. I'd find you a lot more interesting if you could tell me where he might keep the cash from all the big blags he's supposed to have committed?'

'I don't know, but he's at it, I know he is.'

'What have you got against Moose anyway? You do all right.'

'He bought me out a few years ago but I never got paid the whole amount. Now he treats me like a doormat.'

'Why don't you leave?'

'Don't you want him?'

'Course we want him, but not for something like clocking speedos or dodging tax. We want him for something big.'

'Well he's planning something, asked me to get him a car for cash. An old Cortina. He was very specific, said he must have the car by the fifteenth latest. He wouldn't be seen dead in a car like that so I reckon it's a job.'

'Doesn't sound like a getaway car. Give me the details.'

'Dark brown Cortina, one point six'

'The index number?'

'JJX 689P'

'Where is it now?'

'I left it for him at his arch in Crofton Park. Also he had some new number plates on his desk which I don't think I was supposed to see ... ACC 487P. Here's a photo of the Cortina in the arch.'

'A photo,' Baslow turned to look at Ted. 'You're turning into a regular private eye.'

'I've got a copy of the invoice as well and some details from the reg document.'

'Interesting. Any associates hanging about?'

'His brother-in-law, Ron Gooch, has been around quite a bit recently but apart from that, nothing.'

'Has he done this before? ... asked you to acquire a car, off the books?'

'Yeah, but usually much better faster motors and they disappear. I never see them again.'

'Could he have bought the car for Gooch?'

'Gooch drives a Jag, a classic, I don't think he'd want an old Cortina. Anyway if there wasn't something dodgy going on he wouldn't have hidden it or used a false name.'

'OK, keep an eye on him and hide the photos and stuff somewhere safe. I need to talk to higher-ups back at the station. Meet here again on Wednesday. In the meantime here's twenty, there'll be a lot more if we collar him for something big.'

***

On Monday Baslow waited in the staff canteen reading a paper and occasionally forking some food into his mouth, the usual procedure for meeting Detective Inspector Phil Murris with something new. When he spotted Baslow, Murris made no sign of recognition, but picked up his tray, wandered over to the rectangular table and sat diagonally opposite with only a nodded acknowledgement. To a casual observer they would not appear to be friends.

'What've you got?'

'A snout tells me Kostas Moustrianos is planning something.'

'Well if I believed everything I heard about Moose—'

'Yeah but this one actually works for him.'

'OK, you've got my attention. Anyone else working with him?'

'It might involve one Ronald Gooch, builder. Know him?'

'Don't think so. Has he got form?'

'Occasional brawler, some other minor stuff, he's Moose's brother-in-law.'

'Anyone else?'

'Not so far, but it looks as if Moose is going to use an old Cortina with false plates for a blag. Check these numbers when you get a chance ... I know, an old Cortina doesn't sound like Moose but—'

'OK, meet up tonight usual place.'

At five p.m. Murris parked beside Camberwell Old Cemetery about fifty yards behind Baslow's Rover. He gathered together some paperwork and stuffed it into a briefcase and walked over to the car and tapped the window. Baslow was slightly surprised as he hadn't seen him approach but cleared a map from the passenger seat and let him in.

'Has anyone ever checked Moose's stock, checked if it's above board?'

'It's been done a few times in the past but everything's kosher and we don't bother any more. He's too smart to be nabbed for shifting hot cars.'

'What else do we really know?'

'Very little for certain. A lot of his transactions are in cash and it would be easy to launder the money from blags through the business. He'll be inflating the proceeds of sales. So, while most dealers are understating their turnover, he'll be overstating his and showing handsome profits. As a result paying more tax, but it means he looks clean ... to the Revenue at least.'

'So the customer gets an invoice for five thousand but he puts the sale through the books as six or seven thousand?'

'Exactly, as many of his customers are dodgy and by nature uncooperative, it would be very hard to prove.'

'I get the impression he likes attention from us.'

'He does, revels in it. Likes the successful bad boy image and he's confident because he knows we won't be able to pin anything on him.'

'You quite like him don't you?'

'He's hard to dislike. You go in and he's polite, friendly, cooperative. Compared to some of the villains we deal with ... last time I was in to ask about the Streatham bank job he answered all my questions then insisted I come and look at a "dodgy classic". He showed me this ancient convertible. It wasn't nicked or anything but he reckoned it had been made up from more than one original vehicle, I couldn't shut 'im up.'

'So what now?'

'Well I don't know what's going on but if Moose is up to something it must be big. We need to keep an eye on an arch unit in Crofton Park. Whatever's happening, it'll be after the seventeenth, I can do Wednesday to Friday into the small hours. Can you do Saturday?'

'Yeah, meet here again Wednesday?'

'OK, at five.'

***

On Wednesday Murris parked outside the cemetery and waited as planned. A car he didn't recognise passed him slowly and parked further down the road. Baslow got out of the car carrying a raincoat folded over his arm and walked over to a puzzled Murris.

'It's the wife's, mine's in for a service,' he said, as he opened the door. He sat down and made himself comfortable.

'That Cortina Moose acquired was registered to a company in Deptford. Looks as if they bought it new for a sales rep years ago. They recently sold it for cash to a John Smith ... your informant I assume. Now ... those new plates ACC 487P. They actually belong to a brown one point six Cortina registered to a James Smallwood, known as "Crapper" to his mates, "Crapper Jim". He's a full time nuisance with a big list of previous for drink driving, no insurance, no MOT, et cetera et cetera. Plumber when he's sober ... he was arrested years ago at the same time as Ron Gooch for fighting at a Millwall game.'

'This is gettin' strange. My snout followed Moose after work on Tuesday. Says Gooch was with him and they went over to a Falmer Close in Catford and just parked up for a while. Seemed to be watching the street. Then a Brown Cortina turned up and parked outside number seventeen and guess what? ... Index number ACC 487P. Moose was parked well back in a Merc but moved off quickly as soon as the Cortina arrived. Anyway the Cortina driver got out of the car and went into number seventeen, description sounds like this Crapper Jim.'

'That's not Smallwood's address and a bit late for plumbing work, So—'

'I just don't get it. Moose is a big beast, banks, security vans, big cash businesses. What on earth does he want with Smallwood? ... the man's a liability.'

'We need to have a look at Falmer Close.'

'It's a dead end according to the A to Z, only one way in and out.'

As they approached Falmer Close, Baslow thought he recognised the location. He parked about half way along giving a partial view of number seventeen.

'This place seems familiar, I think I've been here before.'

'Maybe, but all these places are alike.'

'That caravan on the other side squeezed against the wall that doesn't look as if it's moved for years and that extension over there with the green roofing felt, I've definitely been here.'

'Probably day-job stuff, a break in or a domestic. It's a lousy location for a burglary. The houses are too close together and there's no back lane or other access.'

They viewed the road as best they could from the car both reluctant to be seen in daylight. Number seventeen looked pretty much the same as the other semis, a neat enough garden with a blue Triumph Dolomite parked in the narrow driveway at the side.

'I think you need to borrow that dog again and have a wander about after dark.'

'Well in the meantime find out who lives at seventeen.'

That evening, Murris answered the phone at home. He heard the distinctive pips from a call box and wasn't surprised to hear Baslow's voice say 'sorry wrong number'. He put on a coat and left the house, walked to a nearby phone box and called him back.

'Phil, Could we meet again, this evening, about half an hour at the usual place? I could be onto something big.'

'OK.'

Both men arrived at the cemetery at the same time but parked some distance apart. Baslow got out and walked over to Murris' car and got in the front passenger side. A Labrador sat patiently on the back seat as they talked. 'I found out who lives at number seventeen you know where and it's come back to me. I did have a look around there about three years ago. A snout told me this builder called Hattmann had sixty to eighty grand of undeclared cash at home but it was all a bit iffy. No clear idea about exact location and the whole place looked too ordinary. I didn't believe it. All builders have got some secret cash but eighty sounded like bollocks. But if Moose is looking at it then it could be true. So unless I'm completely up the wrong tree, Moose and Gooch are going to rob Hattmann and try and frame Smallwood for it.'

'Where would Hattmann get that kind of money? ... and he leaves it in his house?'

'He could have nicked it himself, there's plenty of unsolved going back years.'

'I'm amazed someone hasn't done him already.'

'Well he's got a reputation for violence and he's a big bloke.'

'So, options? We could wait for them, arrest them in the act and bag a good collar?'

Both smiled.

'Yeah ... sod that.'

'So, we wait for them to do the job and then *we* rob them.'

'I think the two of us could take Gooch afterwards, but Moose? That's a major operation, we'd need help and we might not even find the cash.'

'It would have to be immediately after the job ... surprise them when they're least expecting it, say at the lock-up.'

'If that's where they go afterwards. We still don't know when it's going to happen, we can't hang about there on the off-chance.'

'Maybe we do the job ourselves before Moose and Gooch get there. Wait until mister and missus are out then you could pick the lock and we just nick the money, lock the door again and he might not even notice for days.'

'Yeah, well I've picked a couple of locks but I'm no expert, we might not even get in and we don't know exactly where it is.'

'I'm guessing it'll be well hidden but it has to be easy access, he can't be prising up floorboards every time he wants to put a hundred quid in.'

'What exactly did your snout say?'

'I think he said under the floor not under the floorboards.'

'Could be a floor safe in a concrete floor.'

'In the concrete? Bloody big floor safe to hold eighty odds. I doubt it.'

'The attic's more likely but it could be anywhere, might not even be in the house.'

'What? ... you mean at his yard? ... No, he'll want it close by.'

'We're working blind here. Any chance of speaking to your old snout again?'

'I'd have to find him first. He got twelve months in the Scrubbs for fencing a lorry load of power tools, disappeared after that.'

'We want to be in and out of that house in two minutes flat and the wife's bound to know. We put a gun at her head, she'll cough. I don't see how else we're going to find it quickly.'

'It's too risky, it's a bit open, people coming and going. We could be spotted and if it gets messy inside, a neighbour might hear something and there's only one way out of that close.'

'OK, we certainly can't risk a daylight job but Hattmann must go out at night sometimes, he's a drinker, he must go to the pub at least.'

Baslow started to get out of the car and said 'I'll watch the lock-up tonight and tomorrow and see if anything happens.'

'OK, I'm just going now to have a walk about Falmer Close.'

'Canteen, Friday?'

'I'm tied up with a case review so it'll be one-thirty earliest.'

Murris returned to his car and drove to Catford. He parked a couple of streets away from the target and took his sister's Labrador from the back seat. He put on a green waxed jacket with a matching cap and walked slowly along the main road like an elderly gent. He turned into Falmer Close and walked slowly towards number seventeen. The street lighting was less effective than he'd expected and one lamp was out at the far end making it surprisingly dark. The other houses were identical with only the hedges and gardens showing any variation. A few had cars in the driveways and others were parked in the street. As he walked back up the close on the other side he had a good look at number seventeen. There was nothing to stop access to the back garden and number nineteen to the right was in darkness, had no car, and looked a bit overgrown, possibly unoccupied. The house directly opposite was partially obscured by a pair of large Plane trees. There was no car at Hattmann's house though a light was on in the front room and he noticed movement through the net curtains. Murris walked the dog up and down the close a second time paying particular attention to viewpoints and blind-spots and it struck him that apart from a man under a propped up car fixing something, he hadn't passed a soul in the last twenty minutes. He walked back to his car and made some notes before driving back to his sister's house and returning the dog.

On Friday, the canteen was unusually busy as a visiting party from Hampshire had taken over a large part of it. Murris sat in the corner in the only empty table and waited for Baslow who appeared carrying a bag and a magazine. Baslow left both items on the table, and asking Murris to keep his place, went to the counter and returned with a coffee. Both men then pretended to read but talked quietly, hardly moving their lips.

'It's doable after dark.' said Murris. It's not well lit and very quiet. There's a few trees obscuring the view from the other side.'

'So we park close by and wait for Hattmann to go out?'

'Don't think there's much choice. We don't know when our competitors are going in but it'll be soon. Any movement at the lock-up?'

'Nothing.'

'So a practice run tonight?'

'Sooner the better, let's check the gear.'

***

They met up again after work and drove to the allotments in Baslow's car. Both looked around but apart from a man tending an incinerator at the far side of the plot the place was deserted. Baslow opened the boot and handed Murris a pair of wellies and a spade. 'We have to look the part.'

The plot was badly neglected with knee high weeds over most of the ground and only a small area of neatly tended roses around the gate to suggest that anyone took any interest in it. There were two sheds and the door to the larger was obscured from view by the smaller one and an overgrown trellis screen. The larger shed was whole but dilapidated, with peeling paint, cracked boards and a rusty padlock. The gutters were partially hanging off and a water butt to the side was missing it's lid. They both entered the shed and started moving the assorted tools and pots outside. Even when cleared, it wasn't obvious that the worn and stained floor was actually a false structure covering the original floor underneath.

Standing outside, Baslow produced a metal rod with a slight hook at the end and inserted it into a small hole in the floor close to the threshold. He gripped the rod and pulled the floor upwards enough to get his hand underneath and lifted. Then he pushed the entire panel against the back wall of the shed to reveal another floor. This original floor had a large hatch about six feet by two feet with an inset handle. He lifted this to expose a matching hole about three feet deep which had been shored up with timber boards. 'I always expected it to fill up with water but it's stayed dry all these years.'

Inside the hole were two large holdalls, two smaller

plastic bags and a black polythene bin-liner. They lifted the holdalls out and checked the contents.

In the first one there was black leather gloves and balaclavas, two boiler suits, gaffer tape, rope, iron bars, a crowbar and a knuckle duster. In the second, a very large tent valise had been rolled around a polythene bag which was sealed with tape. Murris opened the bag and checked the two guns by spinning their cylinders. Both were loaded and appeared to be working smoothly. 'I don't trust pistols, give me a revolver any day.'

'Hopefully we won't have to use them.'

They checked the other bags and removed a pair of handcuffs and more rope. Baslow opened the large black bin liner and looked at the neatly wrapped cash bundles inside. 'Money's still here.'

Satisfied, the men repacked everything, replaced the false floor and moved all the gardening equipment back inside, locked up and returned to the car.

'Might as well take a trip over to Falmer Close now, time it, and see if there's any movement.'

Baslow drove and Murris went through a checklist. 'Still can't decide on outfits. What would neighbours expect to see early evening?'

'I reckon dark suits, as if we're salesmen. Instead of briefcases we need something like sample cases which can hold more. We need to get to the back door quickly and mask up, then straight in. One of us close the living room curtains and rip the phone out. The other go to work on Hattmann's wife.'

'I hope the cash is in larger notes, we'll struggle if there's a lot of ones.'

Murris started the stopwatch and nine minutes later they arrived at the close parked up and watched for a while. 'What are we gonna do about wheels?'

'We should break in to Moose's lock-up and nick his Cortina. That would really fuck him up.'

Murris turned to Baslow grinning. 'What? Do the job with *his* car then collar him afterwards?'

Both men laughed.

'I don't think we'd pull that off but it's a nice thought.'

'I've still got the Marina at my unit in Tulse Hill,' said Murris, it's the sort of car nobody notices and we can crush it afterwards at Fairweather's.'

They drove to Catford and parked about fifty yards from Hattmann's house.

A blue Triumph sat on the driveway and another small car was parked across the entrance blocking it in. There was movement in an upstairs room and after a few minutes the front door opened and a middle aged woman left carrying a tray and a bag. She walked diagonally across the street and walked up the side of another house. Shortly afterwards the front door opened again and a man and a woman carried a chair each to the small car and loaded them onto the back seat. They exchanged perfunctory goodbyes and the woman drove off.

'Busy tonight. That was Hattmann alright, he's big isn't he.'

'Friday night, you'd think he'd be out at the pub.'

'There's still plenty of time let's wait and see.'

After another twenty minutes a dark coloured Cortina

passed them and parked outside Hattmann's house. The cars horn sounded several times and after another minute Hattmann appeared from the side of the house and got in. The Cortina then moved into a driveway opposite to do a three point turn.

'Smallwood, no question, we should have brought the gear we could've done it now.'

'There could still be other people in the house, every light's on and we haven't worked out all the details yet. Let's get after Smallwood's car and see where they go.'

Keeping well back they followed the Cortina for about ten minutes in the direction of Dulwich but lost it after being caught at lights.

'We'd better have a back-up plan in case Moose and Gooch get to the money first. We need to figure out where they'll go afterwards. Moose has various properties that we know about but I don't think he'll go to any of them, he's just too careful.'

'They might go to Gooch's though. More likely they'll have somewhere else planned that no-one else knows about.'

'We need to have a closer look at him. Let's check his house now and then go over to his yard.'

They turned around and drove to Beckenham. From there, they turned into Hayes Lane, then turned again into Park Langley. After a complete tour of the area they found Ron Gooch's attractive half timbered villa and parked a safe distance away on the other side of the road. The house itself looked well maintained. The garden was manicured with every shrub expertly pruned, perfect grass and neatly arranged flowers.

'Not the sort of area we normally find villains. The Jag's there. Don't know what the sports car is.'

'Could be a Lancia, maybe an Alpha.'

The houses were situated quite far apart and the wide road and generous pavements added to the feeling of space and light.

'Very hard to get in and out of there without being seen by someone, it's in full view of every house opposite.'

Baslow lowered his sun-visor as a pedestrian walked towards the car and Murris looked down, pretending to read some documents.

'This place makes the Catford house look like an easy hit.'

'Moustrianos used to live around here too but he moved out to somewhere near Sevenoaks. Got a huge place now with a pool and a tennis court apparently.'

'Well we're not gonna learn much more here. Down to Sevenoaks?'

'I'm not sure it's worth it, Moose'll never drive straight to his house and even if he does, do we really want to tackle him there?'

'Don't you ever think that Moose's reputation might just be bullshit? ... Informants link him to every major blag but he couldn't possibly be responsible for all of them. I sometimes think we're being fed rubbish to divert us from the real villains.'

'You're not the only one thinking that but maybe this *is* the real thing. The car and the false plates?

They turned around and headed back to Sydenham to look at Gooch's premises. It was located at the end of a narrow lane only wide enough for one vehicle and several "Private Road No Parking" signs were fixed to trees and posts. They parked the car, got out and walked down the lane. The yard was fronted by two large wooden gates topped with an "R Gooch Builders" signboard. At each side a small section of high chain link fence topped with barbed wire was interspersed with ivy and bind weed making it difficult to see inside. They pulled some out of the way but could barely see anything due to the failing light.

They returned on Saturday afternoon, parked on a nearby street and casually walked down the lane with the Labrador. Peering through the overgrown fence, they could see that a large brick built garage with a steel door was butted on to what looked like an old bungalow. The house also had a lean-to structure attached on the right and further across the yard a huge green shed without an end wall housed some excavators and other heavy site equipment. Two flat bed lorries were parked in front of the house and piles of scaffolding were stacked at various places around the yard along with pallets of bricks and concrete blocks. In one corner, a huge pile of sand, in the other, a very dilapidated oil tank had been propped up on a lattice of timber supports. The yard was surrounded by other properties which backed on to the boundary fence but none were close and mature trees blocked much of the view.

Murris formed a gun with his fingers, pointed and made a shooting sound. 'This is more like it, my money's on here. He'll be using that old bungalow as an office and he's probably got a safe in there.'

'There's no guarantee they'll come here. I'd still prefer to hit Hattmann ourselves.'

'I dunno, it's too risky, too many problems.'

4

Fitted Up

Moose parked his car across the lane outside Ron's yard and waited. He saw the yard lights switching off and shortly afterwards, Ron opened the inset door on the gate and climbed out. He padlocked it, walked up the lane and got into Moose's car.

'All set?'

Ron nodded.

'You sure about Crapper? … if he spots us we're in trouble.'

Ron nodded again. 'He'll be at the The Black Horse all evening, it'll be fine.'

Moose drove to Crofton Park but parked the car a block away from his premises. They got out and walked quickly to the deserted street and slipped inside the arch unit. The Cortina faced the doors. Moose went to the rear and opened the boot. He picked up two number plates and a screwdriver and dropped to his knees and lined up the new plates against the old ones then put the new ones back in the boot. He prised off the screw caps and loosened the screws slightly, and tightened them back up again. He went to the front of the car and did the same. 'All good.'

Ron went over to a large wooden cupboard and lifted out a canvas holdall and laid it on a table. Inside was rope, tape, iron bars, some canvas bags, balaclavas, stockings, gloves and clear safety glasses.

Ron checked the equipment and rehearsed knot tying while Moose went through a door at the rear of the unit and returned with another cloth bag. He reached inside and laid two pistols on the table. After releasing the clip on each one and checking the bullets, he pushed them back in and handed one to Ron.

'I've never used one of these.'

'You point it at the target and pull the trigger. The closer you are, the more likely you'll hit it.'

Both men then stepped into dark blue boiler suits and stuffed balaclavas and rope inside before zipping up. They took tape and other items from the holdall and put them in their leg and side pockets. Moose picked up his handgun and placed it in his chest pocket and motioned to Ron to do the same. Both men then picked up rubber gloves from the table.

'Before and after.' Moose chucked a rag at Ron that smelt of meths. 'Every handle, every knob, every surface. If this doesn't go to plan we don't want our dabs anywhere.'

They carefully wiped down the entire car.

Ron went back to the table and opened a tub of plumbers jointing compound and rubbed some on his hands and then wiped them clean on the front of his boiler suit. He handed the tub to Moose who did the same. Ron then picked up a large empty cardboard box from the table and they loaded all of it onto the back seat of the car. They put on black leather gloves and Moose opened the main doors while Ron got into the car and drove it outside. Moose locked up and got into the passenger seat.

'You ready?'

'I am, let's go.'

Ron started driving carefully in the direction of Catford. They had practised the route already and the roads were quiet but he resisted the temptation to jump the lights at Brownhill Road. He slowed down two streets away from Falmer close and reversed into a narrow lane.

Both men got out and changed the number plates and got back in the car.

Moose started lecturing Ron. 'Remember the runaway train? ... No stopping, no hesitation, be decisive, follow through. Half the battle is making them believe that you *will* kill them. If you hesitate or dither they'll sense it and the games up. Remember, *you* say nothing at all. I do all the talking.'

'Got it.'

'One last thing.' Moose pulled out a quarter bottle of whisky from the glove compartment and handed it to Ron.

'What's this? I don't need it.'

'It's the finishing touch. Take a swig but don't swallow. Spit it out and repeat, then pour some on your overalls.'

'I get it, good idea, but if we're stopped by the bill we'll get breathalysed.'

'If we're stopped by the bill that'll be the least of our problems.'

Both men applied the whisky treatment and Ron set off. He turned the car into Falmer Close and drove to the end. He did a three point turn and drove back up towards number seventeen but switched off the engine and coasted the last fifty yards, stopping across Hattmann's drive. Both men put on safety glasses then got out and opened the rear doors. Ron picked up the box and Moose grabbed the holdall. They quietly closed the doors and marched straight up the driveway to the rear of the house. The back garden was faintly illuminated by an upstairs room but the kitchen was unlit. Ron placed the box on the ground and they both removed their glasses and put on stockings over their heads followed by balaclavas and walked up the back steps to the kitchen door. Ron carefully turned the handle and was pleased to find it unlocked. They quietly walked in, guns in hand. They could hear television sounds coming from the front room and Moose motioned to Ron who ran to the front door and snibbed the latch. Then he ripped the telephone wire from the wall.

Julie, hearing the noise stood up from her chair just as Moose burst into the room pointing his gun at her. 'Get down on the fucking floor NOW!' He grabbed her by the hair and forced her down but another woman suddenly appeared on his right and grabbed his gun arm just as Ron entered the room.

Ron punched her with his left, sending her reeling backwards towards the sofa. He followed through by pointing the gun at her face and made her lie down on the floor. He turned her over onto her front, and ducking down, grabbed the lower edge of the curtains and pulled them shut.

She tried to get up and only stopped when Ron pressed the gun hard into the side of her face and cocked it.

Meanwhile, Moose had pulled Julie back up.

'Get the money!'

She was shaking and tears ran down her cheeks. Moose put the gun at her breast. 'Get the fucking money now or I'll fucking shoot you.'

'It's upstairs, please ... '

Moose grabbed her again by the hair and holding the gun at her back, forced her up the staircase.

'It's in the spare room,' she said pointing at a doorway.

Moose pushed her in. 'Get it for me now.'

Julie opened the cabinet and swung the unit out from the wall. Then she lifted the carpet.

'It's in there.' She said pointing at the hatch in the floor.

'Fucking open it.'

She pulled up the hatch and lifted five clear polythene bags onto the floor. Moose could see there was nowhere near eighty thousand. 'I want all of it.' he said cocking the gun. 'Get it all now or I'll fucking shoot you.'

'That's it, that's all there is.'

Moose punched her in the stomach and she

collapsed to the floor whimpering and sobbing, struggling for breath.

'Where's the rest of it?'

'Please don't ... '

'Fucking tell me now.' He grabbed her arm and twisted it up her back until she howled.

'There was more but he bought a place in Spain. That's all that's left.'

Moose bent down, pulled out a small torch and looked underneath the floor in both directions but couldn't see anything else. He pulled rope from inside his boiler suit and tied her hands behind her back. He then taped over her mouth and pulled a canvas bag over her head, secured it tightly with rope and left her face down on the floor. As he carried the bags downstairs he could hear a struggle going on in the front room. The other woman had tried to get to her feet and Ron was wrestling with her, unable to hold both hands to tie the rope. Moose dropped the bags and helped him, but as he went to hold her she grabbed a tumbler from the coffee table and struck him on the forehead. It shattered on impact cutting through the balaclava causing a deep gash. Both men now held her by the arms and Moose dropped on her back with both knees as she lay on the floor struggling. She let out a muffled groan as the wind was knocked out of her and stopped moving. Ron finally managed to tie the rope around both her wrists, and once secure, Moose taped over her mouth. He fetched a canvas bag from the holdall and pulled it over her head securing it with more tape and motioned to the money bags. Ron put them inside the holdall. They moved quickly to the back door and went outside where they removed their balaclavas and stocking masks. They put their glasses back on, then walked briskly down the driveway and put the holdall and the empty box back in the car, got in, and drove off.

As they hit the main road, Moose exploded, 'Who the hell was that other bird?'

'Christine, Hattmann's sister. She's a wildcat.'

'You reckon? Don't know how I'm gonna explain this to Karen.' He wiped blood away from his forehead. 'Think she might have clocked you?'

'Doubt it, I said nothin' and she couldn't have seen through the masks.'

'There's nowhere near eighty, there's about twenty, tops.'

Ron remained silent.

'It was all a bit down market really, I'm surprised we even got that much.'

They drove back to the lane, reversed in again and quickly swapped the number plates back to the originals. Then they removed their boiler suits and threw everything into the boot.

Arriving at Ron's yard ten minutes later, they quietly opened the gates and backed the car up to the door of the bungalow office. They unloaded the box and bags and took them inside. Ron went back outside and emptied the boot throwing the clothing into a large oil drum. 'I'll burn them tomorrow.'

'See you do.'

Moose emptied the money bags onto a large wooden

desk. There were seventeen one thousand pound bundles and a bag of loose notes of various denominations along with some passports and documents and an envelope with photos of a much younger Julie Hattmann in a bikini. Without checking the thousand pound bundles he quickly counted the loose cash.

'A lot of these are old notes, he's been sitting on them for a while. Eighteen thousand six hundred and forty four quid, not a bad rate of pay for an evenings work.'

'It's not enough.'

'Well it's gonna have to be enough unless you know where to find more.'

'Did you believe her?'

'I did actually. Told you Hattmann would never have eighty grand. Grotty little semi and that Triumph, Jesus, three hundred quid in my bomber yard.'

'Well it'll help but I've still got a big problem.'

'Any more of your mates got hidden cash?'

'Doubt it. Only Hattmann and he's a lying bastard.'

'Stop looking so sad. Apart from Hattmann's sister everything went to plan, we were in and out in two minutes. Believe me it rarely goes that smoothly and so long as Hattmann doesn't go to the law we're scot-free.'

'Wonder if he'll go after Crapper?'

'Well we did a pretty good job of smelling like plumbers and if anyone saw the car it's a brown Cortina they'll describe. Will Crapper tell Hattmann that he'd found the cash and told you?'

'Probably won't remember tellin' anyone, you wouldn't believe how much he drinks.'

They split the money into two equal shares and Moose threw his in the boot of the Cortina. Ron casually flicked through the documents. 'We've got his passports as well so he won't be going to Spain, he'll be furious. He'll kill Crapper.'

'No great loss. Where are you gonna keep the cash?'

Ron pointed up to the ceiling hatch. 'Up there until the heat dies down and then I've got a few debts to settle.'

'What about the mortgage?'

'It's up to date but I took out a couple of other loans secured on the house, that's the problem.'

'Well I have to say you're not bad at this lark and your first time too. Hattmann may have a point about the business though?'

'Yeah I know, I should cut corners at the start of the job not the end. His customers seem to be happy.'

'Go home, have a stiff drink and not a word to anyone. At least we've bought you some time. I'm going straight to Fairweather's – he's gonna crush the car tomorrow.'

***

At about eleven o'clock, Vince and Den returned to Hattmann's House after their night at the dogs.

'Come and look at my shower again, it's still not workin' properly.'

'Den, it's eleven o'clock, I'm knackered.'

'For fuck's sake come and look at it.'

Vince reluctantly followed him up the drive and

Hattmann opened the front door.

'Fuckin' place stinks, what is that?'

Vince came in behind him and and they both heard a muffled groan from the living room. Walking in, they saw an overturned chair and a mess on the floor. By the sofa Christine had managed to shake off the hood and was wriggling furiously.

'Wot? Wot the fuck? Where's Julie? … The money!'

He turned around and pushed past Vince and ran upstairs two at a time into the spare room. He ignored Julie and went straight to the hiding place.

'Who was it? Who the fuck was it?'

Julie was lying in a puddle and was the source of the smell. He pulled the hood off and screamed at her. 'Christ you stink, who was it?'

He ripped the tape from her mouth and she yelled then sobbed.

'You fucking let someone take it.' He checked the hiding place again then went back to Julie and turned her over but didn't untie her. She sobbed uncontrollably.

'Who was it? You must have fuckin' seen them.'

'I don't know, there was two of them.'

Hattmann stepped over her and went back downstairs as Julie cried out for help. Vince had removed Christine's tape and was untying her hands.

'They smelt like plumbers, whisky as well, just like Crapper.'

'Wot? Crapper? I'll fucking kill'im. You just let 'em in?'

'They came in the back door, didn't hear 'em 'til it was too late.'

'What kind of motor?'

'Didn't see it. I tried to stop them, they had shooters. One of 'em forced Julie upstairs. I'd have done the first one but the other one came back down and they tied me up.'

'Who was the other one?'

'Dunno, same boiler suit though.'

'Is Julie OK?' said Vince.

'Spare room.' He pointed up upwards.

Vince went upstairs and found Julie still tied up, wet and stinking.

'I've messed myself.' She said sobbing and shaking. He helped her up and as she walked into the bathroom he whispered in her ear. 'Was it Ron?'

She didn't answer. Hattmann came back upstairs and shouted at her through the bathroom door. 'You stupid cow, how'd Crapper know 'bout the money?'

'Den for Christ's sake, she's in a right state.'

'Eighty fuckin grand. Come with me we're goin' to Crappers.'

'What about Julie?'

'Christine'll sort 'er out.' He ran back downstairs and grabbed a hammer from a tool bag at the foot of the stairs.

'Den this is crazy, can't have been Crapper, he couldn't rob a nursery.'

'Christine said it was a plumber, Crapper with one of his plumbin' mates most likely.' He put the hammer head first into his inside jacket pocket.

They left by the front door and got into Vince's Maxi. He

drove to the other side of Catford and skidded to a halt outside Smallwood's terraced house. A light was on in the front room. Hattmann got out and ran to the front door and started pounding.

'Open the fuckin' door. Fuckin' open it!'

Eventually, Shirley, in a dressing gown, opened the door and Hattmann forced his way in pushing her against the wall.

'What the fuck ... '

'Where is the cunt?'

He checked the front room and the kitchen and ran upstairs looking in each room and opening cupboards and looking under beds. Shirley ran upstairs after him just as Vince came in the front door.

'He's not here. What the fuck are you playing at?'

He punched her out of the way. 'Where is it? Where's my fuckin' money you robbin' bitch?'

'What money?'

'Don't act all innocent, my fuckin' money, the money Crapper just robbed from my 'ouse.'

Blood was now pouring down her face and he grabbed her by the neck and started to throttle her. 'Where's Crapper and where's my money? I'll fuckin' kill you if you don't tell me.'

Vince came up the stairs and tried to pull Den off Shirley's throat.

'Den, leave her, Crappers not here.'

'Well his car's here and he's got my money, the robbin' cunt.' He let her go and she fell to the floor but he grabbed a bunch of her hair and twisted her head up. 'So where is he then?'

'He's in the nick.'

'He's wot? He's taken my money to the bill?'

'He hasn't got your money. He was nicked at the Black Horse for fighting. Bert and Lenny were with'im. They all got nicked.'

'It was fuckin' Jim that robbed my house you fuckin' cow.' He punched her again on the other cheek. 'Christine could fuckin' smell 'im, it was Crapper. If I don't get that money back I'm gonna fuckin' kill both of you.'

Vince tried to pull Hattmann away but he pushed him back and punched Shirley again. She shouted at him, 'The police phoned about half an hour ago said they were keeping 'im til tomorrow so fuckin' get out of my 'ouse.'

He grabbed her again by the hair and dragged her across the floor to the middle of the room. He held on and pulled the hammer out from his jacket and smashed a mirror causing shards of glass to spray across the wall. He threw her down and started smashing the room up. The television imploded when he hit it with the hammer and he pulled a record player from the top of the sideboard and threw it across the room. He shattered a rack of records and then he pulled the sideboard over. When Shirley tried to get up he kicked her in the side.

'I'm goin' to the nick. If you're lying I'll come back and break your fuckin' head with this.'

'For Christ sake Den she doesn't know anythin' about the money, leave her alone.'

'How do you fuckin' know? ... you in on it? Cos if you are I'll fuckin' do you an' all.'

'Den, let's go to the nick and find out.'

Hattmann bent over Shirley. 'Give me the car keys.' She pointed towards the hall and Vince lifted a bunch from a coat hook. Hattmann snatched the keys from Vince and bounded out of the hall to Crapper's Cortina and opened all the doors and checked under the seats. Unable to find anything he opened the boot and scattered tools and plumbing detritus over the tiny lawn. He lifted the carpet expecting to find his cash underneath but there was only a spare tyre and a rusty jack. He looked under the car, then opened the bonnet, slammed it shut and stormed back inside. Vince was helping Shirley to her feet.

'Where's 'is van?'

'Dunno, some mate's fixin' it.'

Hattmann motioned to Vince. 'We're going to the nick.'

Vince drove his Maxi to the police station and they both went up to the desk.

'I'm looking for Jim Smallwood, you got 'im?'

'And you are?'

'Dennis Hattmann, I'm his guv'nor.'

The desk sergeant looked at his watch. 'Night shift is it?'

'No but I need him tomorrow for a job.'

The sergeant ran his finger down the page of a large ledger.

'Yeah, he's here. Do the other two idiots work for you as well?'

'Who?'

'A Leonard Figgs and a Robert Palmer.'

'Yeah, they're mine. When did you bring them in?'

'Seven forty tonight. They were arrested at the Black Horse after a disturbance. They'd been drinking since opening and things got out of hand. We know Smallwood all right, he's a regular though he doesn't normally get involved in brawls. You can have them tomorrow morning. Come back about eight o'clock.'

'I will, don't worry.'

On returning home, Hattmann phoned his sister's partner, Russell Jarrett, explained the situation and arranged to meet him at his yard the next morning. 'We're gonna pick up Crapper from the nick and bring him back here. Find out what he has to say.'

**

The next day they drove the van to the police station and waited for Crapper to emerge. Bert and Lenny walked out first and Hattmann motioned them towards the back of the van.

'It's our new taxi service.'

'Shut it and get in the back.'

As Crapper walked out, Hattmann and Jarrett took him by the arm and guided him towards the van. 'What's goin' on Den? I need to get 'ome.'

'We're givin' you a lift Jim,' and they pushed him in the passenger door and got in themselves, one on each side. 'We're goin' to my yard first to have a little chat.'

'What about.'

'Come off it Jim, you know exactly. I want my money back, all of it'

'I—'

Jarrett pointed a finger at Jim and said 'Save it until we're there.'

They drove the short distance back to the yard and Hattmann left Smallwood in the front seat while he went to the back of the van to speak to Bert and Lenny.

'You two were with him last night?'

'Yeah, we dumped our motor and walked to the Black Horse. Jim was standin' outside waiting for it to open.'

'And you was there all the time 'til the police arrived?'

'Yeah. Crapper was there but he could hardly stand by the time we got into an ruckus with—'

'Right, shut-up. Go and hook up the generator to the pick-up and wait outside, go on, fuck off.'

Jarrett pulled Crapper out of the van and bundled him into the Portacabin. 'Tell me about the money.'

'Wot money? ... The fifty? ... I said I'd give it him on Saturday, got it on me.'

Hattmann barged in, grabbed Crapper by the lapels and pushed him back against the wall.

'Don't act it, I've been robbed by two plumbers and I want it back, every fuckin' penny.'

'I didn't rob you. When was this?'

'Last night when you were locked up.'

'So what's this then, can't have been me?'

'It was someone you put up to it, some plumbin' mates of yours and I want all of it back. What's your share, half? A third?'

'Honest Den I don't know anythin' about it.'

Hattmann kneed him in the groin and he fell to the

floor. Gasping for breath he put his hand out towards Hattmann.

Jarrett said 'Do you want me to—'

'Not yet.'

Hattmann turned back to Jim. 'They should've used new overalls 'cos they smelt like plumbers, whisky as well. Fuckin' obvious they're pals of yours.'

Crapper tried to get up but Hattmann pushed him down again.

'I need names and addresses.'

'Den, I don't know who did it. Is it all gone?'

'They fuckin' robbed the lot, tooled up, knocked the girls about and tied them up. They got all of it, more than eighty grand.'

'Fuck, Den, I don't know nothin'. It's got fuck-all to do with me.'

'Yeah? … Well who else knew?'

'Everyone knows you've got cash Den—'

'Yeah? Well you're the only one who knows exactly where I keep it. So, have a chat with some mates did ya? Three way split?'

'I ain't told no-one.'

'Where's your van?'

'At Judson's garage, valves are shot.'

Jarrett pulled Hattmann over to the other side of the room. 'Look I don't see it, I just don't see Crapper organising this. From what Christine said, they weren't amateurs. I think they've made it look like Crapper to put us off the scent.'

'He must've told someone, how else would they

know?'

'They didn't know exactly where it was, they forced Julie to tell them.'

'Must know my crew and my movements, must've known I was out.'

'Maybe not, they had shooters. I think they expected to find you there. Did anyone see the getaway car?'

'The girls didn't. I could ask neighbours but I'd be surprised. I still think Crapper's involved.'

'Don't make any sense.'

'That was my Spain money.'

They both turned and went back to Crapper who was now sitting up against the wall.

'This is your fuckin' fault Jim. You've talked to someone. If you'd kept your trap shut none of this would've happened.'

'I told you Den, I mean it, I didn't tell no-one.'

Hattmann kicked him in the side and he fell over and curled into a ball wrapping his hands and arms around his head. Hattmann kicked him again then grabbed a crowbar that had been propped up against the wall. 'I'll fuckin' do 'im.' As he swung it back Jarrett grabbed hold of it. 'For fuck's sake Den, you won't get any information if you kill 'im.'

Crapper staggered to his feet and steadied himself against the wall.

'Stick him in the van. We'll take him home and work on 'is wife again.'

They frogmarched Crapper to the van and threw him in the back securing the doors with a padlock. Arriving at his house a few minutes later, they pulled him out of the van and walked him to the front door supporting him on each side as if he was drunk.

'Open up.'

Crapper fumbled in his pocket and pulled out a small bunch of keys. He unlocked the door with a Yale key and as he walked in Shirley stormed out of the kitchen in time to see Jim being thrown on the floor. She noticed Jarrett was carrying a cosh and hesitated.

'What've you done to 'im? He ain't got your money.'

'But he knows who took it.'

'How'd you work that out? Ya fuckin' animals.'

'Cos Crapper knew where it was hidden and he's told someone else, so if he doesn't cough we're gonna hit you about the face with this, although it might actually improve you.'

'Fuck off.' She turned and ran for the back door but Jarrett grabbed her by the hair and pulled her into the living room.

Hattmann kicked Crapper. 'Get up. In there now.' Crapper raised himself and limped into the front room. Hattmann pushed him onto the sofa. Jarrett forced Shirley to the floor and tied her hands behind her back. Making her sit on a chair he secured her to the back. Hattmann held up an iron bar and spoke to Crapper. 'You tell us more or she gets it.'

'Can't tell you what I don't know. Anyone could've robbed you. Why you picking on me?'

'Are we in an echo chamber or some sort of recording studio cos I've heard that exact answer before. You're the only person who's seen the cash so you must have told someone else about it. Maybe you told someone when you were pissed?'

'I don't remember that, nah.'

Jarrett looked at Hattmann. 'Leave it. It's a waste of time. *He's* a waste of time.'

Hattmann turned to Crapper and punched him hard in the stomach then he went to Shirley and kicked her over. She landed on her back and yelped.

'If I don't get that money back I'm gonna kill both of you.'

They left the two accused writhing on the floor and went out to Hattmann's van.

'What d'ya think?'

'I don't know. He's blabbed after a few and someone's pumped him.'

***

On Saturday Vince drove to Ron's yard and parked beside the green shed. Ron looked up from his desk as Vince walked in and pointed to a pile of paper on the floor.

'Got the drawings and the specs for the next stage at Croydon if you're interested?'

'You'll have heard about Den bein' robbed?'

'Yeah, Lenny mentioned it.'

'Nothin' to do with you then?'

'Course not.'

'Funny. You tried to persuade me to rob 'im and when it happens you're all innocent.'

Ron leaned back in his chair. 'What d'ya want me to say?'

'You might want to say sorry to Julie, She's a mess, terrified. You didn't have to hit her. I'm not sure she's gonna get over it. Den smashed up Crappers house as well and really worked him over.'

Ron said nothing, but got up from his desk and went over to the kettle. 'Want a brew?'

Vince nodded. 'He'll figure out it was you.'

'He might think it was you, after all you know his house and you work with Crapper.'

'Well I was with him at the dogs when you and Moose robbed the house so he's not gonna suspect me.'

'Moose as well? You've got it all worked out.'

'There wasn't much to work out since you already told me the plan.'

'So what're you gonna do?'

'I'm—'

They both heard a vehicle with a rumbling exhaust drive into the yard and screech to a halt. The car door slammed shut and a few seconds later Crapper burst through the office door.'

'Divvying up were ya? Ya cunts.'

Crapper had a black eye and cuts around his neck. His jaw seemed slightly misshapen and he looked raw and gaunt. Used to him being slightly drunk and a bit docile they were surprised to see him forceful, aggressive and menacing.

'You been drinking?'

'No I ain't and you cunts can give me a share of Den's cash. I'm not taking a beatin' for nothin'. He's wrecked my gaff an' all so cough up or I'll tell 'im it was you pair.'

'Crapper, we don't know what you're talkin' about.'

'Don't start that, you even dressed up like me. Tell you what, I'll go to the bill. Try and wriggle out of that.'

Ron stood up. 'Don't even think about it.' He picked up a wrench that had been sitting on top of a filing cabinet. Crapper lunged at him but Vince grabbed him from behind and held his arms. Ron raised the wrench to hit Crapper but instead put it down and helped Vince to bundle him out of the door. As they pushed, Crapper tripped on the threshold and and all three fell to the ground. Ron and Vince picked themselves up quickly but Crapper struggled to get off the ground and seemed to be in some pain. Ron kicked him over. 'Go on Crapper, fuck off.'

'You cunts.' He picked himself up and got into the Cortina while Vince and Ron went back into the office and dusted themselves off.

'He's on to you. If he tells Den you're done for.'

'If I go down so do you. Think I don't know about you and Julie? Eleni's seen you together, she's got a nose for it. One word and Den'll chop you up. So both of us'll keep our traps shut. OK?'

Hearing a metallic sliding sound and a click at the door, Vince pushed at the handle but couldn't open it as it had been padlocked from the outside. A smell of petrol wafted in.

'He's pouring fuel!'

Ron rushed at the door and both men started kicking until it flew open. As they went out they saw Crapper holding a bucket and fumbling with some matches.

Ron kicked him as hard as he could hitting him squarely in the stomach. The bucket went flying, splattering both of them with petrol. Crapper straightened himself up and Ron punched him upwards hitting the underside of his nose and causing him to fall backwards and hit his head on the edge of a dumper truck. His head shook violently for a few seconds then went still. Vince had picked up a shovel and was ready to swing at Crapper but lowered it once he saw he wasn't moving. He looked at Ron then pushed the motionless body with his foot. 'He's out cold.' said Ron.

'I think it's worse than that,' said Vince. He felt for a pulse – nothing. He put his ear to Crappers nose. 'He ain't breathing.'

'Can't be, I only punched 'im.'

'Look at him. There's blood comin' out the back of his head.' Crappers nose seemed to be pushed back inside his face. 'He's hit his head on the dumper, I think you've killed him. He's dead I'm tellin' you, he's bloody dead mate.'

'Christ, he was trying to burn us alive.'

'You're covered in petrol, get those clothes off before you catch fire.'

'What are we gonna do?'

'Close the gates before anyone else appears. I'll get the body covered up. He went over to a pallet of concrete blocks, tore off the tarpaulin and spread it over Crapper's body. Ron went quickly to the gates and locked them.

'Should we take him inside?'

'No, we don't want blood in there.'

'Fuck me.'

'Christ, you idiot, why'd you try and fit up Crapper?'

'It was Moose's idea, thought it'd send Den on a wild

goose chase.'

'Yeah? Well Crapper worked it out easily enough. At the moment Den thinks it was some of Crapper's pals but his new mate Jarrett is with 'im. They'll work their way through everyone they know and it won't take them long to get to you. Don't suppose Moose told you how to get rid of a body and cover up a murder?'

'It was self-defence, he'd 'ave killed both of us.'

'We need to hide the car, move it behind the bungalow.' Vince grabbed Ron's arm, 'Wear gloves, you don't want your fingerprints on the car.'

Ron went to the car but the keys weren't in the ignition so he went back to the body and fished them out from a trouser pocket. 'Will I take his wallet as well?'

'I dunno, why?'

'We could plant it on Den.'

'How?'

'Dunno but I'll keep it. I'll hide it.'

'Bit of a risk. You don't want it here.'

'I'll think of something ... It's gonna be harder to get rid of the car than the body.'

'Oh you mean you expect me to help you bury a body?'

'You're part of this whether you like it or not.'

Vince shook his head. 'We need to sit down, have a brew, have a think.'

They went inside and collapsed onto chairs. Neither spoke for a few minutes, then Ron got up and opened a cupboard door revealing a row of spirit bottles. 'You want a stiff one?'

'Booze is the last thing we need. I can't believe this. How the fuck? ... What were you thinking?... I said you'd never get away with robbing Den and now you've made it ten times worse.'

'If we can hide the car and the body then Den'll think Crappers scarpered with the cash.'

'It's a big if. You got a Cortina sized hole somewhere?'

'It's not as if I couldn't dig one.' said Ron, pointing outside at the excavator. 'We could go to Bell Green.'

'Bell Green?'

'Yeah, Den's got a plot behind the gasworks. He's not working it at the moment. Place is overgrown with trees, rubble everywhere, looks like a bomb site. So bury the body there and if it's found, Den'll get the blame.'

Vince sipped his tea but said nothing.

'We'd have to wait until it's dark of course but we could manage it.'

'What about the car?'

'We could get it crushed but someone's bound to blab. Better to dump it somewhere like an airport, make it look as if he's gone abroad with the money.'

'No-one's gonna believe Crapper could manage that, Shirley least of all.'

'Got a better idea?'

Vince looked at the floor and blew out a long breath. 'Maybe ... Newhaven.'

'Newhaven?'

'Yeah, Me and Steph have been on the ferry a couple of times to Dieppe. There's a big open car park beside the docks. Nobody checks anything, we could leave the car there.'

'That might do, we could drive down there now.'

You gonna tell Moose?'

'Definitely not, God knows what he'd do. He might kill me, you as well if he knows you're involved.'

'Does he know you talked to me about robbing Den?'

'No and it's better for both of us if he never finds out.'

Vince stood up and started pacing the room. 'Shirley'll notice Crapper's not around and it's her car. So she'll go to the bill and tell them about Jim getting a kickin' from Den and shouting about money.'

'Then maybe this'll work out for us. You might get Julie to yourself after all.'

'I can't believe I'm involved in this ... you got an alibi for the robbery?'

'At home watching TV.'

Will Eleni back you up on that?'

'Moose has already spoken to her, she knows the rules.'

'What about this mess?'

Ron pulled a pack of cards from his desk and laid them on the table. 'We can cover each other. We were discussing the Croydon job then we had a few drinks and played cards. Anyway you were with Den on the night of the blag, what're *you* gonna say?'

'To who, the police? What can I say? I was with Den so I didn't rob him, that's it.'

Ron dealt out some cards and it struck Vince that Ron was remarkably calm and collected. Not phased by the past half hour at all, as if it was simply a minor problem to be solved. He leaned on his elbows and rubbed his forehead with both hands then looked up at Ron. 'How much did'ya get anyway?'

'Eighteen odds.'

'Each?'

'Nah, all-in.'

'So much for the eighty grand then.'

'Yeah, the lying cunt.'

'Does it solve your problem?'

'Helps, but I'm still in trouble.'

'S'pose we'd better get on with it,' said Vince tilting his head towards the door.

'Let's drag him over to the corner of the yard. There's a pile of rubbish there, we can cover him up until we get back.'

'Better check his car for petrol. We don't want to stop on the way.'

5

Too Late

'George, for fuck's sake answer.' Murris swore at the call box handset, put it back and tried again. A woman's voice answered, 'Chief Inspector Baslow's phone, WPC Meacher speaking.'

'Sorry wrong number.'

She put the phone down as Baslow entered the room. 'Just a wrong number.'

Murris waited inside the call box for a couple of minutes and grabbed the handset as soon as it rang. 'Is that you, we need to talk now, immediately.'

'Usual place twenty minutes.'

When Baslow arrived he found Murris pacing up and down the narrow roadway. He coasted to a halt and wound down the window.

'We're too late, it's been done. Hattmann's been robbed, pros by the sound of it, so most likely Moose and his in-law, maybe a driver.'

'Fuck, though I didn't really fancy doing it ourselves.

When'd it happen?'

'Thursday, Hattmann's dog night.'

'Who told you?'

'One of Hattmann's men. A Bert something, has been telling anyone that'll listen so I picked it up from one of my regulars. Got messy apparently. Hattmann went after Smallwood which is obviously what Moose and Gooch wanted. The upshot is Smallwood has been beaten up and had his house trashed.'

'We have to hit Gooch right away before he gets rid of the cash.'

'May already be gone.'

'Today?'

'Let's go to his yard for about five and hit him when his crew have gone home.'

Baslow went back to the station but left early and met up with Murris again at the allotment. They loaded robbery gear into Murris' Marina and drove to Sydenham, parking in an adjacent road that gave them a view of the entrance to Gooch's yard. They waited until all Gooch's men had left, then masked up and and drove slowly through the entrance. Baslow got out, shut the gates behind him and walked to the bungalow as Murris rolled forward quietly. Together at the doorway, they pulled out their revolvers and rushed inside.

Gooch, taken completely unawares jumped back, startled by the guns and the men's appearance.

'You know why we're here so don't fuck about.'

'I don't—'

'We want Hattmann's money that's all. Hand it over

and we'll leave you alone.'

'Don't know what you're talking about.'

Baslow hit him across the face with the butt of his revolver and he staggered backwards, stunned, but didn't fall over. Murris forced him onto a chair and tied his hands behind his back. Then he went out to his car and returned with two large holdalls. He laid out the contents on Gooch's desk.

'I suppose you think that if you keep schtum you'll get away with this? Well you won't. I could say to you, tell all and we'll let you keep you some money, maybe even join our firm? You'd do that, wouldn't you?'

He picked up a large wrench and moved closer to Ron. 'Well that's not how this works. As you can see from all the gear,' he said pointing at the polythene sheets, power tools, gloves and overalls, 'you might not be leaving this room in one piece.'

'The only question is how long it takes. Co-operate and it's all over quickly, you walk away. Piss us about and it could go on for hours, days maybe and you wont even be able to crawl out of here ... we've got a hole already dug ... so?'

Ron began shaking violently, his right leg pulsing up and down. He was both freezing and sweating with a hollow sensation in his stomach and chest. A wet patch appeared on his trousers and a puddle formed on the floor. Baslow and Murris went into the other room and started switching on power tools.

'Might've overdone it. He really thinks we'll kill him.'

'Should spill then.'

Entering the room with a wrench, Baslow held it to

Ron's face. 'Where's the eighty grand?'

'There wasn't eighty it was only eighteen.'

'Don't fuck me about, he had over eighty. You must —'

Ron screamed 'We thought it was eighty, honest, wouldn't have done it for eighteen.'

'So where's your share then?'

Ron flicked his head up towards a loft hatch.

Baslow moved an old wooden stepladder under the hatch and climbed up. Using a torch to look around he saw that the joists had been floored and the rafters panelled. He manoeuvred himself through the opening and stood up.

There was no obvious hiding place and it appeared empty apart from a box of old cassette tapes and two black bags propped up against the gable wall. In one bag, bundles of used notes - nine grand seemed about right, also some passports, some documents and photos and a purse with jewellery. In the other, a balaclava, gloves and a filthy boiler-suit. Baslow dropped the bags through the hatch and climbed down.

'I don't believe you Ron, where's the rest?' He picked up the wrench and slammed it down hard on Ron's thigh. Ron sucked in hard, eyes watering. 'There isn't any more, I told you. For fuck's sake just take it.'

'What about Kostas? He's got the rest hasn't he?'

'He got nine, same as me.' Gooch's nose started to bleed.

'Your frightened of him aren't you. You should be, he's a very bad boy, cut you up if you cross him.'

'I'm telling you, we both got nine. It's all there was.

He knocked her about, she was pleading with him, said there was more but they bought a place in Spain.'

'OK, so where has Kostas stashed his?'

'I don't know, he hasn't told me, why would he?'

Murris placed a canvas sack over Ron's head and they both went back into the other room.

'Think he's lying?'

'Dunno, maybe.'

'We might actually have to use this gear,' said Murris nodding towards the power tools.

Baslow rummaged in the bag and saw a will, an old vehicle reg document and a life assurance certificate. 'Have a look at these passports.'

Murris flicked through the pages quickly. 'Mr and Mrs, he's got two sets ... duplicates ... so?'

'Look at the names in his ... one's Hattmann and one's—'

'Wilson, Reginald Wilson? ... That name's familiar. It's bloody good, what's he up to?'

'Good? It looks genuine, I think it is genuine, it's the real thing, must've used Wilson's details to get it. Anyway we'll keep them along with the cash, might be a useful bit of leverage.'

They both walked back into the main office. 'We're gonna take this as a down payment, a deposit. What you have to do is get the rest of the money back here. If you don't, we've got a lot of options. We could tell Hattmann or we could tell the law but the one we prefer is we shoot your fucking head off and cut your wife up. Understood?'

Ron nodded. Murris slammed the wrench down on Ron's knee and Baslow forced his gun barrel into the prisoner's mouth. 'We'll be back next week.'

They left Ron groaning on the chair and walked out carrying the bags and all their gear.

After they'd driven off, Ron got up from the chair and managed to rub the rope against the sharp end of a shovel until it frayed. He limped over to the toilet, removed his trousers and pants, cleaned up and slipped on a pair of overalls then poured himself a whisky and phoned Moose.

'We've got a problem, not on the phone, I need to come over it's serious. I'm really—'

'OK calm down. I'll wait for you. I was gonna work late anyway, the door'll be open. Just come in. I'll tell Maureen.'

He drove to the showroom and parked his car beside Moose's Bentley. The lights were still on but there was no sales staff around. Maureen glared at him as he limped towards her desk and insisted he wait. She buzzed through to Moose and told him his brother-in-law was at the desk, then simply flicked her finger in the direction of Moose's office. He walked in to find Moose holding up a Rolex.

'Like it? I swapped it for an old Lotus that had been sitting about for a while. What's up? You're limping. What the hell's happened to your face?'

'I've just been robbed. Two men in Balaclavas and guns, just like us. They know about the blag and they took my share. They want the rest—'

'Slow down. Who were they? Was it Hattmann?'

'No. I don't know who they were, they might be

coppers.'

'Why d'ya say that?'

'I dunno, they seemed very sure of themselves as if they knew everything. They know you were there.'

'How the hell could anyone else know about it? Moose stood up. 'Who did you tell?'

'I didn't tell anyone, and that's the other thing they were expectin' eighty. I told them there was only eighteen but they didn't believe me. They're comin' back next week for the rest or Eleni gets it as well as me.'

'Fuck.' Moose sat down again and held his head in his hands.

'There's more.'

'For fuck's sake what else?'

'We've got a problem with Crapper.'

'I'd say he's the one with the problem.'

'Crapper got himself nicked that night, Den even picked him up the next day from the police station so he knows it can't have been him that did it. They took him back to Den's yard, gave him a kicking.'

'Who's *they*?'

'Jarrett and Den, Russell Jarrett.'

'Jarrett? When did he appear?'

'I thought you knew. He's been out for months. Got a share in Christine's bodyshop from what I heard.'

'Christ, this is getting worse. Did you know about him being in business with Christine before the blag?'

'I only just heard.'

'So if Crapper blabbed, Den might be on to you. Could he know about my involvement?'

'Don't know but he might figure it out. Another

thing, Den's saying he lost eighty not eighteen.'

Moose sighed. 'That's interesting, who's been talking anyway?'

'I heard it from Lenny, one of Den's chippies.'

'I'll put some feelers out, see if I can find out who's after us. In the meantime go home and not a word to Eleni.'

6

Missing

Detective Inspector Ralph Maidencoombe stood in the doorway of the main office and made eye contact with Vic Sandwell, his Detective Sergeant. Sandwell got up from his desk and went out to the corridor.

'I keep hearing about some big blag in Catford, but nothing's been formally reported?'

'Yeah, I've heard it as well. A snout told me some builder called Hattmann may have been robbed of eighty grand, but didn't have any clear details.'

'Half the station is talking about it but no-one's actually doing anything'

'Could be a wind-up.'

'I'm sure that name's come up before.'

'Could be something trivial and the story just grew legs.'

'Well if someone's been robbed and not reported it, then it only means one thing ... it's dodgy cash.'

'Nothing from upstairs?'

'Baslow told me to ignore it. So either it's rubbish or

he's keeping it for himself.'

Sandwell nodded, '*Can* we look at it? I mean it's just a rumour at the moment.'

'Ears open, mouths shut, lets see what turns up.'

Later that day Maidencoombe was standing in the foyer talking to another plain clothes officer as Shirley Smallwood walked into the police station and approached the desk. The constable looked up and smiled.

'You got my 'usband 'ere?'

'Mrs Smallwood, so nice to *s-e-e-e* you again, it's been *s-u-u-u-ch a* long time.'

'You got 'im or not?'

He sniffed the air. 'I don't think so, can't smell him but I'll check the ledger.' He made a comical play of checking the custody record book and then declared, 'Surprisingly, Crapper's not in the cells. You might want to check the local gutters and derelict buildings.'

Maidencoombe overheard the conversation and raised his eyebrows at the constable who stopped his witty sarcasm and took some details. 'Last time we had him, a Dennis Hattmann came in looking for him, picked him up the next day. Have you asked *him*?'

'He ain't seen him.'

Maidencoombe left the other officer and joined the conversation. 'Constable, once you've taken this lady's details show her up to the interview room. I'd like a quick chat if you don't mind,' he said, looking at Shirley.

'If you want.'

'Sir, this blokes a regular drunk, it's a waste of time.'

'Just do it.'

Five minutes later Shirley was shown into an interview room. She glared at Sandwell and sat down opposite Maidencoombe with her arms folded.

'How did you get those bruises?'

'Walked into a door.'

'Twice?'

'Fell down the stairs an' all.'

'I see. A bit clumsy are you? Or had you been drinking?'

Shirley looked away but said nothing.

'So why have you waited so long? It's been two days since you saw him and you're only now reporting him missing, what's going on?'

'He's done it before, disappears for days then comes back stinkin' of booze, no phone calls, nothing.'

'OK, so he goes on a bender ... where?'

'I don't fuckin' know do I? Could be anywhere, I don't care about him but I need the car.'

'What does he do?... building trade?'

'Plumber.'

'Who does he work for?'

'Himself mainly, I dunno, he doesn't really tell me.'

'So he's self-employed?'

'Yeah, for years.'

'Has he got money troubles? Anyone chasing him? Banks?'

'Don't think so, gives me cash when I ask 'im. I mean he's not loaded but ... I dunno.'

'Anyone he could be staying with? Friends, relatives?'

'No-one can stand'im when he's having a session. Anyway I've already phoned round everyone I know. No-one's seen 'im.'

'How's your marriage?... I mean are you happy, any problems?'

'He's the fuckin' problem. I'm sick of 'im disappearin' and boozin', never know when he's gonna show. He'd fuckin' pissed himself last time.'

'I have to ask you this, could he be seeing someone else?'

'You mean another woman? Doubt it, but if he is, she's welcome.'

'OK, lets start again at the beginning, you last saw him on Saturday ... when?'

'About twelve, didn't want any lunch, he just went out, the pub probably ... where else would he go?'

'You tell us and which pub?'

'He didn't say anythin' so I don't know.'

'Where does he normally drink?'

'Everywhere local, but he's been barred from the Admiral in Grove Park.'

'Has he got a favourite.'

'The Black Horse, I used to go there with 'im.'

'Did he take the car?'

'Well it's gone.'

'Did you actually see him take it.'

'Who else would take it?'

'Did you see him get into the car and drive off?'

'No.'

'When did you notice it was missing?'

'Sunday morning, he hadn't come home. I looked out the window and it wasn't there.'

'All right, what kind of car?'

'Cortina, Ford Cortina.'

'And?'

'And what?'

'Colour, reg number ... how long's he had it?'

'It's brown. He's had it for a couple of years. ACC 487T.'

'Does he have any other vehicles, a van for instance?'

'Yeah he's got a van, but it's knackered. Hasn't used it for weeks. Some mate's supposed to be fixin' it. I don't know where it is.'

'OK, we'll come back to that.'

'Who does he drink with, friends? Workmates?'

'Anyone. Sees Den quite a bit.'

'Den?'

'Dennis Hattmann. He's a builder, does a lot of plumbing for 'im.'

'Is he a drinker too?

'A bit, not as bad as Jim. Goes home at night.'

'Where do they go and when?'

'Could be anywhere. Sometimes goes to Wimbledon dogs on Thursdays with Den. Used to go to Catford 'til he got barred.'

'Gets barred a lot doesn't he?'

Shirley said nothing and fumbled in her bag.

'Who else?'

'Any of Den's crew, Alf, Lenny, Bert Palmer and the rest of 'em. Bunch of animals.'

'What about relatives.'

'I told you already, none of them's seen 'im.'

'OK. Give all the details to my colleague here. I'll need everything, addresses and phone numbers, the lot.'

Maidencoombe left the room and Sandwell squeezed what he could from a truculent Mrs Smallwood. He walked back into the main office twenty minutes later and popped his head around his superior's door. 'Funny that Smallwood should disappear just after this Hattmann bloke is supposed to have been robbed.'

'Where would Hattmann get a load of cash? Have we anything to connect him with any robberies or major crimes?'

'He's got a bit of form but it's minor really, brawling, D&D. He did sixty days for punching a bloke in a pub but that was nearly ten years ago. A few speeding tickets, a drinker and a bit of a fighter. Doesn't look like a big player, but he was questioned in seventy four about the Rotherhithe security van job, you know the one where that guard lost an eye. A gang from Deptford went down for it and he knew one of them. But nothing came of it and he hasn't been linked to anything else. He doesn't seem to be on anyone's radar.'

'Any of them out?'

'Only one, a Reg Wilson and he's in a hospice, leukaemia. Only a few weeks to live.'

'OK, log the Cortina as missing and notify neighbouring forces. Get John to look for his van. Also, look into known associates if you can'

***

96

The next day Maidencoombe arrived early and was surprised to see his detective sergeant already at work. 'Any news on Smallwood?'

'His Cortina's turned up, Sussex police found it at Newhaven docks.'

'That was quick. Any idea how long it's been there?'

'No-one has a clue, the parking's free so there's no tickets but one tyre is looking soft so may have been a while. Strong smell of petrol from the boot.'

'So? Leaking can?'

'They don't say but they did find a receipt for WH Smith and they think he may have bought a map before he parked up, a French map but can't be certain.'

'Smith's sell French maps?'

'They do in Newhaven apparently, for the ferry traffic, but again can't be certain. The receipt was two pounds sixty, same price as all their French maps.'

'So he buys a French map, leaves his car but takes the map ... gets on board and sails off like Lord Lucan? Why buy a map if he was leaving the car?'

'God knows.'

'So he's on a ferry to Dieppe, then what? Falls off? Disappears in France?'

'Or, he didn't get on the ferry at all and we waste a lot of time trying to get the French police to look for him.'

'What about the ferry people, don't they have a list of travellers?'

'It's called the "passenger manifest". They do but it's not reliable. Lots of day trippers on foot, half-cut both ways. Only those travelling with cars are properly logged, and yes, I have asked. No Smallwood. Lot's of Cortinas booked on since he disappeared but they've all showed up and no reg numbers to match our man.

'We need to shake up Hattmann a bit, see what falls out.'

They walked out to the staff car park and got into Sandwell's Fiat.

'Before we head off, Baslow's been asking about Hattmann and Smallwood.'

'Thought he wanted us to leave it.'

'Well he obviously realised we were looking at it on the QT. Very little gets by him.'

'What'd you tell him?'

'Just the outline ... Hattmann robbed ... Smallwood gone. Assumption, Smallwood probably inside man ... disappeared with his share. I told him about the Cortina being found in Newhaven but gave him very few details. Judging by the questions I think he already knows quite a lot from other sources.'

'I don't know how he keeps track of all these sources of his.'

Another thing. I've seen Phil Murris from the Regional Crime Squad with Baslow in the canteen several times over the last few months. They sit together but pretend not to talk.'

'Pretend?'

'I'm quite good at obs. They were pretending.'

'If they're mates, why hide it?'

'I don't know what's going on.'

Hattmann's yard was locked up so they drove the short distance to his house. It looked like a very ordinary semi. Like so many others in the area, nondescript, average, boring.

'Must be a million houses like this in London, doesn't look like the home of a major blagger.'

A woman opened the door. Not bothering to introduce himself, Sandwell flashed a warrant card and said 'We want to talk to Dennis.'

'What about?'

They walked past her purposefully and went into the living room.

'He's not here, he's in Plumstead on a job.'

'Well perhaps you can help? James Smallwood has disappeared, last seen on Saturday, that's five days ago.'

'Probably drunk, I don't know why Den uses him. Doesn't show up half the time.'

'When did you last see him?'

'Dunno, couple of weeks ago. He was fixing our boiler.'

'And you haven't seen him since?'

'No, and I don't want to either.'

'Dennis keep a lot of cash here?'

'No he banks it, doesn't like it lying around.'

'Ever been robbed, burgled? ... here I mean?'

'Had tools nicked from the shed once but nothing else.'

'You didn't report that ... we don't have any record.'

'I don't remember.'

Maidencoombe placed a card on the table.

'When your husband comes back tell him to call us,

we need to have a chat.'

The two officers left quickly and said nothing until both car doors were shut.

'Notice the marks on her neck and the bruising around her wrists?'

'I did, but she seemed calm enough.' said Sandwell.

'He could just be knocking her about, but to me that looked as if she'd been tied up.'

'So maybe Smallwood *has* robbed Hattmann and run off to France? Anyone else I might believe it but the mans a drunk, he's useless, I don't think he's capable.'

'It *is* hard to believe and we still don't know for certain that anything's been nicked. Hattmann hasn't reported it and I just can't see him having that kind of cash.'

'Maybe he's old school, won't grass.'

'Or maybe he's got more than cash to hide. Money robbed, a furious Hattmann catches up with him ... Smallwood disappears. Crapper Jim might have stopped breathing.'

'I don't see this as a one man job, someone else must be involved.'

'Well one thing's for certain, blaggers can't keep their mouths shut. They just can't help boasting and showing off, it's in their blood. Something will leak out.'

7

Charity Work

The next day Moose drove his Bentley to the showroom and parked carelessly at an odd angle. He marched up to the entrance and barely acknowledged Maureen as he walked past and into his office. Once inside, he made a few phone calls but getting no clear answers he started pacing the room. 'All this for nine fucking grand.' He tried phoning Ron again but got no reply.

The buzzer sounded and Maureen told him that Detective Chief Inspector Baslow and Detective Inspector Murris wanted to see him.

'Tell them about five minutes, offer them a coffee.'

He went straight to his ante-room and looked in the mirror. 'So it's *that* pair,' he muttered, as he did up his tie. After brushing his hair he splashed some water on his face and put on a fresh jacket. '*Relax, breathe slowly, give nothing away … big smile.*' Pressing the intercom button on his desk, he said 'send them in.'

The two policemen walked in and smiled warmly at

Moose who put down a bundle of papers and stood up from his desk. They shook hands.

'George, Phil, How are you? It's been a while.'

'I think we're both very well thank you. Yourself?'

'Never better. I've got a twelve year old Macallan here, special edition, fancy a nip?'

'It's a bit early, but tempting ... go on then, a small one.'

'Phil?'

'A small one, very small.'

Moose poured the drinks and the officers sat down on the comfortable leather chairs.

'So gentlemen, to what do I owe the pleasure? Not the Streatham job again? I've really tried on that one but I've got nothing more. Contrary to rumour I don't control all major crime in London.'

'We know that Kostas,' said Baslow, 'but we think you can help us with a more recent robbery.'

'Go on.'

'A builder by the name of Dennis Hattmann was robbed last Thursday of eighty thousand in cash. Or rather his wife and sister were robbed. He was out at the dogs and came home to find them tied up and the money gone. Now the robbers are clearly pros who know their way about a blag. They've dressed themselves to look like plumbers. In fact they've made it look like Hattmann's plumber mate, a certain James Smallwood, has carried out the robbery. They've made him a patsy ... don't you just love these Americanisms?'

Murris leaned forward and continued the story. 'Hattmann's immediate reaction was to charge round to

Smallwood's house. But after beating up Mrs Smallwood he discovered that Crapper Jim, as he's known to his mates, was actually in the nick the night of the robbery having been arrested for drunken brawling in the early evening. So now he knows that Smallwood wasn't present at the actual robbery but thinks that some of Smallwood's mates have done the job and that Jim has helped them in some way. So he picked him up the next day from the nick and interviewed him with his fists and other implements but can't find the cash and doesn't know who Smallwood's mates are ... you following?'

Moose nodded.

'So far so good. Hattmann suspects Smallwood but doesn't know who the actual robbers are and even he seriously doubts that Crapper Jim could have organised something like this. If nothing else had happened then the whole affair would have fizzled out. At the station we hear rumours about the blag early on but Hattmann can't officially report the loss as it's dodgy cash to start with.'

'I don't think I can help you with this.'

'Bear with us because this is where the robbers plan starts to unravel.'

'On Saturday, Smallwood left his house at lunchtime and a couple of days later his wife reported him missing. She's well known at the station. She has to collect her drunken husband regularly and no-one takes her too seriously but one of my more alert and inquisitive colleagues overheard her saying that her husband works with Dennis Hattmann. Having also heard rumours about the raid on Hattmann, he interviewed her. She didn't mention the robbery and was only interested in getting her car back, apparently indifferent to Mr Smallwood's whereabouts. It was found the next day at Newhaven ferry terminal but no sign of him.'

'So this is really a missing persons enquiry? ... You want me to help you find Smallwood?'

'Well yes and no—'

'Surely it's obvious. Smallwood's involved with the robbery somehow and he's legged it with his share, got on the ferry.'

'That's what someone wants us to believe. But we think that for some reason the real robbers have found it expedient to "disappear" Smallwood. Maybe they got nervous. Maybe Smallwood realised who'd fitted him up and demanded a share. More likely he threatened to tell Hattmann, and, given that man's propensity for violence the real robbers probably thought it best to shut up Smallwood for good. I'm speculating, we'll probably never know exactly what happened or why.'

'What have you got to back up this theory?'

'There's no evidence that Smallwood bought a ticket or got on the ferry.'

'That doesn't prove anything. He might just have left a false trail to throw Hattmann off the scent.'

'Well that could've have worked but we have evidence that the real robbers bought an identical car to Smallwood's with matching false plates to carry out the robbery. We have a sales receipt from a firm in Deptford for a Brown Cortina made out in the name of John Smith. We have a Polaroid of it being stored at a unit in Crofton Park and we know that it was crushed at Fairweather's the next day.'

Moose shifted uncomfortably in his chair.

'Now if Smallwood hadn't disappeared none of this would make much difference but now that he's vanished it opens up into something very much bigger. If that evidence should come to light then the real robbers could be in the frame for murder as well as the blag.'

'Stop a minute, there's a lot of holes in this whole story. Firstly, I know Den Hattmann a bit. He's a builder, so some cash-in-hand jobs? Probably, but eighty thousand? Come off it. He's never seen that amount of cash in his lifetime. Secondly, why would supposedly professional criminals risk drawing attention to themselves by killing someone they've framed for the robbery and then make a bad job of staging his disappearance?'

'Well Hattmann didn't get that cash from building work. It's probably the proceeds of an earlier crime and as to the disappearance? Even pros make mistakes, miscalculate, get over-confident.'

'What evidence have you got that Smallwood is dead?'

'We've got no evidence that he's alive.'

'Surely then, the disappearance points to Hattmann. If he believes Smallwood robbed him then he's got an obvious motive?'

'He's certainly capable but there's no evidence that *he's* responsible for the disappearance and a lot of first class evidence linking Smallwood to the real robbers.'

'I don't see how I can help you with this.'

Murris leaned forward. 'Well as you know the Met is struggling with an army, a plague almost, of rapists, muggers, druggies and perverts contaminating the city. Resources are stretched to the very limit. We believe that the police force should be concentrating on fighting this kind of low life and not inflicting unnecessary grief on ordinary decent blaggers, who're only trying to make a living and have a bit of fun.'

'Well I'm with you on that but I'm still struggling to see how I can help.'

Baslow took over, 'Many officers are hoping for an early and comfortable retirement. They carry out their duties enthusiastically and pursue villains with the utmost vigour. They hope for just rewards but sadly their retirement funds don't always enable them to live as well as they deserve. Our charity helps those officers by providing rewards immediately so that they're better motivated to focus on the really disgusting end of the criminal market, and not on the classier and better organised white collar operators who do very little harm to the ordinary public and in fact often contribute to the well-being of society.'

'You'd like a charitable donation?'

'That would be very much appreciated, I'm glad you understand.'

'And how much of a donation would help you to focus your efforts on the lower end of London's criminal population?'

'Seventy one thousand pounds will incentivise our best officers to focus their efforts lower down the scale ... in a timely and efficient manner.'

Moose guffawed and sat back in his chair. 'I think you must be confusing me with someone who has that kind of cash and such a specific figure too.'

Baslow leaned forward. 'Oh, we're sure if you ask around, talk to business associates you've worked with before, you'll be able to gather up that amount. We'll pick it up next week and our bankers will only accept tens and twenties, nothing smaller or larger, or too old or too new. They're very particular.'

The two policemen stood up and Baslow extended his arm to Moose who got up and reluctantly grasped the detective's hand. Baslow held on tight. 'It's been very nice talking to you again and the Macallan was superb, I must get a bottle of that myself. Until next week.'

The two detective's turned and left the office. Moose sat down and thumped the table. 'Damn and fuck.' He picked up the phone and called Ron's yard but only got a crackly answering machine. He left a quick message and then phoned Ron's home. Eleni answered. 'Get Ron to call me as soon as he gets in. It's urgent, very urgent.'

'Nice to hear from you big brother, bye.'

After an hour of phoning, Moose gave up waiting and drove over to Gooch's yard. He arrived just in time to see him opening his office door. The Bentley skidded to a halt and Moose got out and walked quickly up to him. 'Ron we've got problems.'

'I know that already.'

'Well they just got worse. You were right, those men that robbed you *were* coppers. I already know them, though I hadn't realised they were bent. They came to the showroom bold as brass. They know about everything including the car. So what I want to know is, who did you talk to and where the hell is Smallwood?'

'But—'

'And they want seventy one thousand or else they fit us up for Crappers disappearance. So tell me, where the fuck is he?

Ron said nothing.

'You're hiding something, I know you. What's going on?'

Ron shook his head. 'I ain't got a clue.'

'Everyone believes it was eighty so why did we only find eighteen?'

'Maybe there really was eighty and Crapper's cleared out most of it before we got there and now he's vanished with it.'

'Well those bent coppers are after the whole eighty and if we don't do as they say, they'll give the car evidence to their mates and we're stuffed.'

'How'd they find out about the car anyway?'

'The bloke that sourced it was working for me but he walked off in a strop a couple of weeks ago so maybe he told them. The point is they know about it. Paperwork and everything.'

'What are we gonna do?'

'Well now I know who they are, I might be able to scare them off. I know a few other coppers higher up the chain and one of them owes me a big favour.'

8

Interrogations

'Dennis, glad we caught up with you at last.'

Hattmann looked up from his desk as the two detectives entered his Portacabin. Maidencoombe sat down opposite Hattmann and Sandwell walked around the office looking at wall planners.

'You know why we're here so I won't waste time. Where's James Smallwood, Crapper?'

'Wish I knew. Let me down on a job. Had to get someone else and it cost me.'

'Is Jim cheaper then?'

'A bit, it all adds up.'

'When did you last see him ... exactly?'

'Friday morning. Picked 'im up from the nick and we went back here to talk about a job. Dropped 'im off later at his place. Got an earful from 'is wife.'

'What time was that?'

'Don't remember. Mid-morning sometime.'

'And you've had no contact since, no phone calls?'

'Nothing.'

'How long has he worked for you?'

'On and off about twenty years.'

'So he's on your books at the moment then?'

'Not exactly. He's self-employed so he gets paid for each job rather than a wage.'

'So he works for other builders as well?'

'A bit, mostly works for me.'

'So cash then, cash in hand?'

Hattmann rocked his head from side to side but didn't reply.

'Look Dennis we're not interested in tax dodging. He's a missing person and we need to find him.'

'Wot's all the fuss about? He's always doin' this. Disappears for days then comes 'ome. He'll turn up. He's an alky.'

'Yeah we know all that but this time his car's been found in Newhaven and no sign of him.'

Hattmann leaned back and his head tilted to one side. 'He's never driven that far in 'is life.'

'Sure he doesn't have any work down there, any customers, other builders?'

'Nah, never goes out of London.'

'What about relatives, family or friends?'

'Far as I know they're all in London. I dunno ... you'd have to ask 'is wife.'

'Any other men missing, anything suspicious?'

'I had to let a couple of them go last week but they're not missing'.

'Did you see him on Saturday?'

'No. Told you already. I dropped 'im off on Friday and that's it.'

'His wife said he went out about lunchtime on Saturday and she hasn't seen him since.'

'Well I usually work here on Saturday mornin', to catch up with paperwork, but me and the wife went over to New Cross to help her sister move 'ouse. If he did come to the yard, it'd have been shut.'

'No messages on your answering machine?'

'He never leaves messages on the machine. I'll check it again, but I'm pretty sure there ain't.'

He went to the machine and pressed play. A succession of suppliers and an angry customer had left mostly garbled messages but nothing from Smallwood.'

'Ever had a break-in, stuff nicked?'

'Yeah, now and again. Round here everything walks if it's not nailed down.'

'We don't have any reports.'

'If I make a claim it knocks up my premium so I don't bother for small stuff. Had a trailer nicked last year though.'

'And you didn't report it? Not exactly a small item.'

'No need, I knew who'd done it so I went straight round and got it back. Last time they'll try that on me. I get kids climbin' over the fence and damaging stuff sometimes but nothin' too serious.'

'Anything in this office worth nicking, do you have a safe?'

Hattmann pointed at a cupboard. 'Have a look at it if you want.'

Sandwell opened the cupboard and examined the tiny

safe. The door was open but there was only some documents and a small cash box.

'Got some power tools worth pinchin' in that other cupboard but apart from that not much.'

'What do you know about Jim's personal life?'

'What d'ya mean?'

'Girlfriends? Bit on the side?'

Hattmann guffawed. 'I ain't aware of anything, I'd be amazed. Used to go to the dogs with 'im but I gave up, he's too pissed.'

'Anyone he doesn't get on with? Enemies?'

Hattmann smiled. 'His wife … gets on with my crew OK far as I know.'

We'll need a full list of all your men, addresses, phones the lot. Also a list of anyone who's worked for you in the past year but moved on. Lastly I need a list of all your sites that Smallwood worked on over the last year. Oh and also other builders that he works for.'

'D'ya think something bad's happened?'

'We're keeping an open mind as they say but I've got an uneasy feeling about this one.'

The two officers returned to their car.

'Nicely played,' said Sandwell. 'Don't think he suspected anything.'

'He tried a bit too hard to look relaxed.'

'Not a bad performance though, considering he may have lost a fortune.'

'Notice anything in the office?'

'Not really, did you?'

'I reckon some blood might have been cleaned off the

wall beside the door. Wiped back but I think there's still a trace.'

'Got the impression he was genuinely surprised about the car.'

'Me too.'

'If his alibi checks out, where does that leave us?'

'Could be other people involved, he's got mates. A bit too convenient don't you think? Usually at the yard on a Saturday but on the very day Smallwood goes missing he just happens to have a prior engagement elsewhere, with presumably lots of witnesses.'

'Maybe we should be looking at Smallwood's wife. If he's nicked the money then maybe she's spotted an opportunity to get rid of him and grab some cash at the same time?'

'Think she's that smart?'

'Maybe she's got another bloke. She'd have needed help to move the car and so on.'

They returned to the station and sat down in the canteen.

'OK, let's talk to Smallwood's wife again. We'll turn up at the house and give her a hard time. Grab your notes. Let's play it as if we think she's killed him and she might spill something useful.'

***

The phone rang and Julie answered cautiously. 'Five seven five one.'

'It's me.'

'You took your time. Why haven't you called? Den's

going mad.'

Vince looked around and put another ten pence in the slot. 'I don't want to make him suspicious. Is he out?'

'Yeah, but he'll be home soon. He's in Plumstead again tomorrow, come round in the morning.'

The next day Vince parked outside Hattmann's house. Carrying a tool box, he walked towards the front door which opened as he reached the steps. Julie, in a dressing gown, let him in. She looked dishevelled and frightened.

'How are you?' he asked.'

'What d'ya think? I might have broken ribs. The way Den's going I'll be dead soon.'

'Does he suspect anything?'

'Still thinks Crapper's involved but doesn't really know who else.'

'Where's the cash?'

'That's really what you're here for, you don't care about me. I thought I was gonna die.'

'The money's for both of us. We'll wait until things calm down.'

'Den's never going to calm down. If he doesn't kill me it'll be someone else.'

'What's he sayin' about Crapper?'

'Nothing, I don't ask him. He's makin' my life hell though. He's really knocking me about.'

Vince pulled her close and she winced. 'Don't, it hurts. You need to to take the money today. Where are you gonna hide it?'

'My cousin's got a safe at his garage in Sydenham. I'll park it there for a while.'

'Then what?'

'I think Cyprus might be safest.'

'How you gonna do that?'

'Dunno, don't worry about it for now. I'll think of something.'

'Where's Crapper anyway, d'ya know?'

'No idea, ain't seem 'im since that night.'

'Was it Ron and Moostri' whatever 'es called that robbed me?'

'I thought Ron was gonna do it but now I'm thinking it might have been Christine.'

'What?'

'I spoke to Ron and he says he was at home with Eleni that night. But Christine has taken up with this bloke called Jarrett. He's got some involvement in her bodyshop.'

'I've heard of him, I thought he was inside?'

'He was, just got out last year. He did seven years for robbery. So maybe Christine has organised the whole thing with Jarrett and they've tried to make it look like Crapper.'

'Police were here looking for Crapper. Wanted to speak to Den, they got him later at the yard.'

'Did they ask about the robbery?'

'No, they were just looking for Crapper. They asked if we'd any break-ins or stuff.'

'What did Den say to them?'

'Dunno, he didn't really say much to me. If Jarrett did the job why on earth has Crapper run off?'

'Maybe he hasn't, maybe he's been sorted.'

'Sorted?'

'Yeah, maybe Den's caught up with 'im and you know ...' He tilted his head to one side and clicked.

'D'ya think? Maybe that's why he's so edgy. He hasn't got the money back though.'

'If he has done 'im in, the coppers'll catch 'im. He won't get away with it.'

'I'll get the cash down. You got a box or something?'

'Better be careful, neighbours might see.'

'Your car's here all the time, don't think they'll notice.'

Julie climbed into the attic and dropped the bags through the hatch. Vince went to the car and came back with a holdall. He loaded the cash and returned to the car. There was no-one around.

Instead of going to Sydenham, he drove through Bromley and Orpington and out into the Kent countryside for twenty miles taking a circuitous route to a heavily wooded area near Westerham. He parked his car at the rear of a large half-timbered hotel and restaurant called the Four Way House and sounded the horn twice. A few minutes later, Matt Melshott, a tall moustachioed man in his early fifties wearing a double breasted suit walked over to the car.

Vince wound the window down. 'Matt, everything OK?'

'Yes, come in, no-one's around.'

Vince got out of the car and carrying the holdall, followed the man into the lounge bar. They walked through a door marked private and a narrow staircase took them down into the basement. Beer barrels and other supplies were neatly stacked on one side and an empty wine rack covered much of the rear wall. Melshott went to the side of the rack and lifted a box out of the way. Then he slid the rack to one side. Using a key he unlocked a flush door built-in to the wall and led Vince into a tiny windowless room.

'Is this it?'

'It is. Put the bag inside that barrel and then we'll stack these other boxes on top. Vince opened the lid. 'It's full of crap.'

'I know. Just empty it and put the bag in then pile it all on top.'

'Is this really safe?'

'It's perfect. I slide the wine rack over to hide the door. I'm the only person that knows about it.'

'I suppose I should tell you—'

'Don't tell me anything. It's better that I don't know.'

***

The following day, instead of heading off early as usual, Hattmann made his entire crew wait in the yard. They stood as if on parade as Hattmann marched up and down the line. 'You all know I've been robbed and Crappers disappeared so most likely he's involved. I'm gonna talk to you one at a time and you're gonna tell me what you know. The men looked at each other and noticed that Russell Jarrett was padlocking the gates shut. He was accompanied by two other men they didn't recognise.

'It's got nuffing to do with us.' said Bert, 'and anyway he was with us at the pub, couldn't have bee—'

'Save it.' Hattmann pointed at Lenny. 'You first ... inside.'

Lenny walked into the Portacabin and was surprised to see Hattmann's sister sitting at the end holding a hammer. Hattmann and Jarrett walked in behind him and locked the door.

'Sit down and tell us what you know.'

'I don't know anythin'. Last I saw Crapper was Friday when you picked us up from the nick.'

'You seen Crapper talkin' to anyone, sneakin' off anywhere, acting suspicious?'

'Crapper? Come on Den. He drinks, he does plumbin', that's it. I ain't seen him with anyone unusual.'

'Where were you on Saturday?'

'Don't remember but I didn't see Crapper.'

Christine got up from her chair and walked up to face Lenny. 'You'd better be telling the truth or I'll fuckin' do you with this.'

Jarrett intervened. 'Lenny, Crapper's car's been found in Newhaven. What do you know about it?'

'I don't know nothin'. Where's Newhaven?'

'On the coast, there's a ferry to France.'

Lenny looked baffled.

'He's never mentioned Newhaven or France to you?'

'All Crapper talks about is dogs and plumbing.'

Jarrett and Hattmann looked at each other. Hattmann shrugged.

'Go outside and tell Bert to come in.'

Lenny left the office and gestured to Bert, 'You're next.'

Bert walked in and looked around. 'Hello Christine.'

He noticed the hammer and didn't wait for an answer. 'What is this?'

'You can't keep your fuckin' mouth shut can ya? Tellin' every cunt about the robbery.'

'Den—'

'Tell us where Crapper is.'

'I ain't got a clue.'

'Where would he hide if he had to?'

'Honest I've got no idea.'

'I think we should cut his fuckin' tongue off,' said Christine, who was now holding a pair of scissors.

Jarrett waved his hand at her.

'Has he got any family or friends on the coast, near Newhaven for instance?'

'Dunno, he's never said. Why don't you ask Shirley, she'll know?'

'Oh, we will, don't worry,' said Jarrett.

'Right, fuck off and tell Sid to come in.'

They repeated the exercise with everyone except Young Tony who was made to wait in one of the vans.

'We're not gettin' anywhere, they don't know anything.'

'What about Shirley? Maybe she organised it. I could talk to her,' said Christine.

Hattmann shook his head. 'The bill ain't gonna let this go. They'll find out I've been robbed and if Crapper doesn't turn up I'm in trouble.'

Jarrett stood up. 'I think this is bollocks. I've said it already, the robbers were pros. I reckon Crapper has tipped them off about the money and been promised a share but they've done the dirty on him and fitted him up for the blag. He wouldn't fit himself up would he? Then they've killed him to shut'im up.'

'We should go and see Shirley anyway, make sure she doesn't tell the old bill nothing about you gettin' robbed.'

***

Sandwell left the station, went out to the car park and started his Fiat. Maidencoombe got in a few minutes later. 'Got all your paperwork?'

'Everything.'

Sandwell drove the short distance to Crapper's street but parked about a fifty yards down from the house. They left the car and walked quietly up to the front door. Maidencoombe pushed the bell button but heard nothing so after a minute he knocked gently at first and then harder. Shirley opened the door with a towel wrapped around her head, her bruises still visible. 'What do *you* want?'

'You know why we're here,' said Sandwell and both men shunted her into the living room. As they entered they saw the smashed television, the remains of a mirror still hanging on the wall, a sideboard with one leg missing and propped up with a box and a curtain torn at the lower edge.

'Bit of a party here, got out of hand did it?'

She went to the window and drew the curtains fully open.

'Sit down and tell us what happened to your husband.'

'I told you already.'

'As you know your car's been found in Newhaven but no sign of Jim. It's being brought back here for the forensic boys to look at. So you're going to tell us what you did with Jim and what you did with the money.'

'What money?'

'The money Crapper robbed from Dennis Hattmann, the money you helped yourself to once you got rid of him.'

'I don't know nothin' about Den's money and I don't know where Jim is.'

'Do you think we're blind? This place has got *"crime scene"* written all over it. There's been a struggle in here, a fight and Jim's disappeared. How'd you kill him?'

'I didn't kill 'im but I will if I find 'im.'

'The forensic boys will go over this place, they'll find the evidence, they'll find blood.'

Sandwell took over. 'Ever been to Newhaven, got on the ferry?'

'No.'

'Got any family or friends down there or anywhere in Sussex?'

She shook her head.

'You've been helped, got another bloke haven't you? I wouldn't blame you but you didn't have to kill Jim. You could've—'

They heard a loud knocking at the front door. Sandwell started to get up but Maidencoombe motioned to him to remain seated. Shirley went to the front door and as she opened it Hattmann and his sister pushed their way in.

'Get out you cunts.'

Christine grabbed Shirley by the hair and dragged her into the kitchen then Den forced her to the floor and they both stood over her. In the living room, Maidencoombe put his finger to his lips and both men stood up and moved quietly to the door.

'Where's Crapper?' Hattmann said as he kicked her in the side, 'and why's 'is car in Newhaven?'

'I don't know.'

'You'd better not tell the old bill about me gettin' robbed.'

'You keep your fuckin' mouth shut or we'll fuckin' kill you,' said Christine, as she grabbed Shirley's hair again and held a knife to her face.'

'Hello Dennis,' said Maidencoombe, 'having a little catch-up?'

Startled, both Hattmanns turned round to see the two policemen. Sandwell was holding up his warrant card.

'Who's the lovely lady then?' said Maidencoombe.

Neither answered.

'Well it isn't your wife so I assume this is your girlfriend, definitely your type judging by the aggressive behaviour.'

'I'm 'is sister.'

'Name?'

'Christine Hattmann.'

'Ever been married?'

She shook her head.

'Why does that not surprise me?' He turned to Sandwell, 'Vic, use that phone in the hall and get a car here with a couple of uniforms. He turned back to face the Hattmann siblings. 'Right, you're both nicked for assault, threatening behaviour and carrying an offensive weapon. Hand over that knife ... don't even think about resisting.'

Maidencoombe took the knife and both policemen pulled out handcuffs.

'Put your paws out ... you as well.'

The duo looked at each other but said nothing. They cuffed both of them and Maidencoombe pointed to the living room. 'Both of you in there now and sit down,' he said, as he pulled Christine forward by the shoulder. Sandwell helped Shirley to her feet. 'About fuckin' time.'

In a loud voice Sandwell said, 'Shirley Smallwood, I'm arresting you on suspicion of murder.'

In the living room, Dennis and Christine stared at each other, astonished.

Sandwell forced Shirley back onto a chair. 'I ain't touched 'im, he—'

'Shut up. You can talk at the station.'

A panda car drew up outside and two constables walked up to the house as Sandwell opened the door. 'We've got three. You take those two in the lounge and we'll take *this* piece of work ourselves. Separate them once you've booked them in.'

'That your car out there?' said Sandwell, looking at Hattmann.

'No comment.'

'For crying out loud, we aren't even at the station yet. Give me the keys and we'll drop the car off at your house and let your wife know you've been nicked.'

Hattmann awkwardly retrieved the keys with his cuffed hands. Sandwell snatched them away and handed them to the other detective. They drove both cars the short distance to Hattmann's house. Maidencoombe parked on the driveway, got out and went up to the front door. Julie Hattmann opened the door and immediately recognised Maidencoombe.

'He's not here—'

'He's been nicked, I've just brought your car back.' He handed her the keys.

'What's happened?'

'Assault and threatening behaviour on Mrs Smallwood.'

'Shirley?'

'Yes, and she's been arrested on suspicion of murder ... her husband. We'll be back tomorrow to have another chat with you. Sleep well.'

She closed the door and went straight to the phone.

Maidencoombe went back to Sandwell's car and got in the front.

'This is fuckin' crazy,' said Shirley, 'I haven't killed Jim. Den nearly killed *me*.'

'You can tell us the whole sorry story back at the station. Until then shut up.'

As the policemen drove away Julie picked up the phone and dialled Vince's house but Stephanie answered so she put the phone down without speaking. That evening Vince phoned her from a call box. 'Did you call this afternoon?'

'Yeah—'

'Steph's gettin' suspicious. Don't call me at home, I'll call you from phone boxes.'

'Have you heard about Den?'

'No, what's happened?'

'He's been arrested for assault, Christine as well.'

'Who did they assault?'

'Shirley Smallwood. That's not all. Shirley's been arrested for murder.'

'What! Whose murder?'

'Crapper.'

Vince let out a long breath. 'I can't believe this. I thought Den might be in the frame for killing Crapper, but Shirley?'

'They must have some evidence.'

'Don't s'pose they'll share it with us.'

'Did you hide the money?'

'Yeah, it's safe but we need to be careful, we can't do a thing at the moment. Did you get the passport photo.'

'Not yet.'

'Well get it soon and post it to me at the flat and keep a suitcase packed. You need to be ready.'

***

On Friday, Baslow entered Moose's office and sat down. All pretence at friendliness and civility had ceased and the two men stared coldly at each other. Murris walked in a few seconds later.

'My information is that the robbers only found eighteen thous—'

Baslow put up his hand. 'Stop. Even Hattmann is shouting about eighty, everyone is. It's only you that's talking eighteen.'

'If you'll let me finish? I reckon this Smallwood bloke isn't as stupid as everyone thinks. He's got wind of the plan somehow and cleared out most of the cash before these mysterious blaggers hit Hattmann's house. Now he's run off with it, sixty odds. I agree he probably didn't get on the ferry but that doesn't mean he's dead. He'll turn up and then you can interview him and return the money to Hattmann or donate it to your little charity.'

'No-one believes Smallwood could have pulled this off. He's never sober two days running.'

Murris stood up and started flicking through papers on Moose's desk. 'Look Kostas we have to stop dancing around this. We know you acquired a Cortina in the name of John Smith and robbed Hattmann with your brother-in-law Ron Gooch. We know you made it look like Smallwood. We know you crushed the car at Fairweather's.'

'You can't prove any of this,' said Moose, struggling to control his anger.

Baslow took over. 'We have a witness, John Smith, or should I call him Ted. He's used a number of names over the years to acquire cars for you under the table. All the time he was working for you he was also working for us … quite a few collars over the years. Nothing big but worth the informant payments. And the detailed records he's kept? Gold dust. You really should have paid him the full amount when you bought him out. He bears a grudge and he's happy to take you down. Can't wait in fact.'

Moose remained silent.

Murris pointed at him. 'You're going down for murder, you and Ron Gooch. Smallwood's under the ground on a building site and not in France or anywhere else. So cough up the rest of the money and then you, Ron, Karen and Eleni can sleep peacefully at night, secure in the knowledge that all the evidence linking you to Crapper Jim will have vanished.'

'Your partner has already donated nine grand to our little project as he understands the situation. You however, have become a bit dense since our last meet—'

The door from Moose's private rooms opened suddenly and Chief Superintendent Rodger Pilling walked in. 'George, Phil.'

Both men froze. Pilling pointed to the empty chair and Murris sat down. Pilling sat down on the other chair beside Moose. 'I do a bit of consulting work for the South London business community. Moonlighting really, but then we all do a bit of that, don't we gentlemen?'

Baslow noticed the bulge of a shoulder holster.

'Kostas has explained the situation to me and I think we really have to wrap this up and move on, don't you? There's no real evidence that Hattmann ever had eighty thousand but in the interests of peace and stability and acting on my advice, The Moustrianos Motor Company is willing to donate four thousand pounds to your charitable operation.' He paused for a few seconds and stared at Baslow. 'In return, the charity will focus it's energies on finding the most likely solution to this case, Mr Smallwood, and discard any unreliable evidence connected to my client it may have acquired. Are we agreed?'

Pilling raised his eyebrows and looked at each man in turn.

'Do we understand each other?'

'Sir.'

'Sir.'

'Good, then that's settled.' He turned to Moose. 'Do call me if any further issues arise.'

He got up and left the room. Moose lifted a shoe box out from under his desk and pushed it across to Baslow. Glaring at Moose, he opened it, took out four bundles of cash and passed two to Murris. They stuffed the money into pockets and stood up.

'That's the way out,' said Moose, pointing at the door.

The two corrupt officers left the room, returned to the car and drove off in the direction of Dulwich.

'I knew he was one of us but I hadn't realised he was also, you know ... one of *us*.'

'I suppose it's possible that Moose really did find eighteen so if Hattmann has lost eighty then that does leave Smallwood as the likely thief.'

'But why not take the lot, why leave eighteen?'

Baslow shrugged. 'We've no evidence Smallwood is actually dead, it was a bluff really, we haven't got a body, Moose knows that.'

'At the moment we're up thirteen and if we keep looking we may come a cropper.'

'Sixty's a lot to walk away from and although we've been warned off Moose, he pretty much told us to keep looking for Smallwood.'

'So he must think he's alive.'

'Maybe Pilling wants us to find Smallwood then he'll muscle in and take a share?'

'Exactly what I was thinking.'

'So what are we left with? Smallwood nicks most of the cash before Moose and Gooch get there so they only find eighteen. Then Smallwood disappears. So if Moose didn't catch up with him who did?'

'It points to Hattmann.'

'But it doesn't look as if he got the money back.'

'We're going round in circles.'

'Hang on a minute, there is another possibility.'

'What?'

'Hattmann has faked the whole thing.'

'Why would he and why would he still be looking for the money?'

'Suppose there really was eighty originally but he's been spending it instead of keeping it for the Deptford firm. They'll be getting out soon and expecting their share so he stages a robbery and says "*Sorry guys I was robbed*".

'Smallwood's disappeared so it looks as if *he's* run off with the cash.'

'And Hattmann makes a big show of looking for him and the money.'

'He could've killed him.'

'Maybe. He'll be desperate. If the Deptford crew reckon he's just spent it they might kill *him*.'

'So his sister's part of it?'

'Maybe, maybe not.'

'His wife as well?'

Murris shrugged.

'Or how about this. There was more than one hiding place and the rest of it is still in the house or hidden somewhere else.'

'Too many options. I can't decide if Hattmann is more stupid than we think or a lot smarter. I'll let Ralph keep digging then take over if he finds anything.'

'Want to sit in with him, when he's talking to suspects?'

'No, I'll leave him to it, don't want to appear too interested.'

***

Sandwell and Maidencoombe entered the interview room and sat down opposite Shirley Smallwood.

'Did Dennis say how much he'd lost?'

'He said eighty grand.'

'Who was Jim working with? We know he was locked up here so who did the actual robbery?'

'Don't know, nothin' to do with me.'

'So *you* don't know anything? The problem is, Jim has disappeared, your living room is a bomb site and you're covered in bruises. Look, we understand you've had to put up with Jim's antics all these years. You've fixed up someone else to rob Hattmann, give you a share. They've made it look like Jim was one of the robbers but Jim's figured it out and now they've killed him and tried to convince everyone that he's run off with the cash.'

'How'd ya know he's dead?'

'Years of experience tells me he's not alive.'

'You don't seem to realise the trouble you're in. You've got motive means and opportunity and you own the crime scene.'

'Tell us what happened in your living room.'

Shirley moved in her chair and folded her arms again but didn't reply.

'Do you want to spend twenty years in Holloway?'

'Den'll kill me.'

'What exactly do you know? ... begin on Thursday.'

She hesitated and looked down at the floor. 'Jim came home from work 'bout half past four. Didn't want dinner, said he was meeting Bert and Lenny at the Black Horse. He went out about six. Next thing I gets is a phone call from your lot tellin' me he's been nicked along with the other two.'

'Then what?'

'I watched telly and was just goin' off to bed when I heard bangin' at the door. I opened it and Den barged in started knockin' me about and shoutin' that Jim had tied up Julie and Christine and robbed 'im. I told him Jim was in the nick so it couldn't have been him that done it but he kept punchin' and kickin' me. Then he smashed up the telly and the rest of it. Said he'd kill me and Jim if he didn't get the money back. Then he went off.'

'What time did Dennis arrive?'

'About half eleven.'

'What car was he in?'

'Dunno, didn't see it.'

'So Jim came home the next day?'

'Den picked him up from the nick on Friday and took

'im back to his yard and gave him a hiding. Then they brought him to the house. They tied me to a chair.'

'Who's they?'

'Den and Russell Jarrett, Christine's bloke. They tied me up and Dennis kept hittin' me and threatening to kill me but I don't know nothing.'

'Then what?'

'They left and Jim untied me. We tidied up a bit and I asked him what's goin' on but he said it weren't anythin' to do with 'im. We stayed in and I asked him again later about the money but he denied everything.'

'So you stayed in on Friday evening, didn't go out at all?'

'Yeah and Jim didn't drink a thing. He usually gets pissed on a Friday night but he didn't touch a drop and he didn't go out.'

'So the next day, Saturday, What happened?'

'On Saturday he went off like I already told you. That's the last I seen 'im.'

'You didn't ask him where he was going?'

'No.'

'Was he sober when he left the house?'

'Yeah, and he was in an angry mood, don't often see 'im like that.'

'Did he take tools, equipment?'

'Dunno, stuff's usually in his car or his van. Doesn't bring much into the 'ouse.'

'And you still don't know where the van is?'

'No idea.'

Maidencoombe ended the interview and a WPC took Shirley back to the cells.

***

'We'll go in my car to Julie Hattmann's,' said Maidencoombe. Sandwell followed him to the car park and noticed Baslow and Murris deep in conversation at the far corner of the car park.

'What are those two up to?'

'Don't know, but I don't like it whatever it is. I get the feeling sometimes that everything we do is being undermined by some sort of invisible hand and they're behind it.'

'They've got special powers you mean?' Said Sandwell, starting to laugh.

'I think they might be bent.'

Sandwell turned to look at him.

'Get in the car and I'll explain.'

Sandwell stopped smiling and got in the passenger side. Maidencoombe opened his door and leaned over to place his briefcase on the back seat then he sat down and turned to Sandwell.

'Baslow has this huge network of informers that feeds stuff to him but there's not that many actually on the books. I know a bloke in finance. He says Baslow puts in a few claims but nowhere near enough for the amount of information he gets. Think about it, all the snouts he refers to, dozens of them.'

Sandwell pursed his lips and looked puzzled but said nothing.

'Why would all the villains he deals with pass him information for nothing? ... It's hard enough getting them to talk for cash.'

'Maybe he's forcing them … has compromising information … threatens them, tell me or else.'

'Well that's bent in my book and it suggests he could also be withholding evidence. How many times have we thought we were going to crack a case only for it to fizzle out?'

'And Baslow is always there, like a vulture, watching everything.'

'Exactly. Swooping in at just the right moment.'

'Money. Can't see why else he'd do it.'

'Worse, the information exchange might be two way, he could be feeding stuff back.'

'Maybe the villains have got stuff on *him*?'

'He's a bit too relaxed and confident, cocky almost, so I don't think it's that.'

What do we do?'

'Nothing at the moment. We have to concentrate on the Hattmann robbery and Smallwood's disappearance but once that's over let's work out a plan for looking at him.'

Maidencoombe started his old Volvo and reversed out of the parking space. He drove around to Falmer Close and parked at Hattmann's house. Julie Hattmann was looking out of the window as they got out of the car and she opened the door as they started to walk up the drive. Sandwell noticed a neighbour staring at them from the adjacent garden.

'What now?'

'I told you we'd be back, can we come in? He didn't

wait for a reply but kept walking up the steps. Julie led him into the lounge and Sandwell closed the door behind him.

'Mrs Hattmann, Julie, please sit down. You've met my colleague here Detective Sergeant Sandwell.'

'What's this all about? I didn't see Den assault anyone and I didn't do anything.'

'It's related to the assault charge. We want you to tell us everything about the night you were robbed, Thursday the seventeenth.'

Julie's eyes opened wide but she said nothing.

'You need to tell us the details Julie ... Dennis is in a lot of trouble ... Jim Smallwood is missing, probably dead and you have information that can help. If you think keeping quiet will help Dennis you're wrong, it'll only make things worse and you could be charged yourself with a whole list of offences. So tell us what happened.'

She looked down at her feet and started to cry. Sandwell handed her a hanky. She sniffed and wiped her eyes.

'You were robbed, you and Christine, when Dennis was out at the dogs?'

'Yes.'

Go through it, slowly.'

'Two men came through the back door with guns.'

What time was this?'

'Maybe eight o'clock, not sure.'

'Did you notice anything about them, did you recognise them?'

'They were in boiler suits like workmen.'

'Do you know who they were?'

'No, they had balaclavas on, stocking masks as well. I don't know who they were.'

'Go on.'

'One of them forced me upstairs and made me open up the hidey-hole.'

'The hidey-hole?'

'It's under the floor in the spare bedroom.'

'Go on.'

'He hit me and tied me up, I thought I was going to die.' She started to cry but Maidencoombe pressed on.

'What about the other one? Where was he?'

'He was downstairs with Christine. She put up a fight but they both held her down and tied her up.'

'Did you see Christine being overpowered?'

'No she told me afterwards. I was upstairs on the floor, he'd taped over my mouth'

'But you could hear a struggle?'

'Yes.'

'Then what?'

'We were both tied up for ages until Dennis came home and found us.'

'What time exactly?'

'Don't know, he usually comes home about eleven from the dogs.'

'Then what?'

'Christine told Den what happened and how she thought they they were plumbers and one of them might have been Crapper. He went off in a rage, took a hammer with him. Christine helped me to clean up and and I went to bed. Den came in about an hour later and said Crapper had been in the police station all evening so it couldn't have been him but he was sure he was involved somehow. Thought the robbers were some of Crapper's plumbing mates.'

'Did you think they were plumbers?'

'I don't know, I couldn't tell. Christine told me they were. Said they smelt like Crapper.'

What does Crapper smell like?'

'That oily putty smell that comes off plumbers. Usually smells of whisky as well.'

'Did you smell any of this?'

'I didn't notice. I was too frightened, I don't remember.'

'How much money was taken?'

'Over eighty, eighty thousand. I don't know exactly.'

She started to cry again and Sandwell got up, went into the kitchen and started making tea. Once she had composed herself Maidencoombe continued. 'Where did Dennis get eighty thousand?'

'He brought a pile back from the yard years ago and he's been adding to it ever since. When he gets a cash job he puts it in the pile. Takes money out sometimes to buy stuff but mostly it just sits there.'

'That doesn't quite answer the question. You said Dennis brought back a pile from the yard.

'How much exactly?'

'I don't remember, it was thousands.'

'So he'd been accumulating money from cash-in-hand work and storing it at the yard?'

'I don't know, I didn't ask him. He gets angry if I question him and he hits me.'

'Does he hit you a lot?'

'Sometimes, he's got a short temper.'

'Did you see a car, the robber's car?'

'No.'

'Going back to the money, who else knew it was there?'

'Only Christine I think.'

'What about Crapper Jim?'

'I don't know, it's possible. He's done a lot of work on our heating system. He might have found it when he had the floorboards up.'

'Are you sure no-one else knew Dennis had a lot of cash hidden somewhere?'

'I don't think so, no one ever mentioned it.'

'Was that all of it? Does he have any other cash hidden somewhere else, back at the yard for example?'

'It wouldn't be safe there, kids break in all the time.'

'All right, show us the hidey-hole.'

9

Big Silver Merc

Maidencoombe sat down at his desk and started going through notes in his pocketbook. The phone rang and he picked it up.

'Ralph, I hear you collared someone in relation to that plumber that's disappeared?' Baslow's voice sounded a little anxious, agitated.

'I was just about to phone you. I want to have a get-together in the briefing room this afternoon and also I'll need some more men. I think we're now looking for a body.'

'I'll check with Pilling but that should be OK. I'll come down in a minute and you can fill me in.'

Sandwell and Meacher set up the display boards at the end of the briefing room and started pinning on photographs and bits of paper, along with a map of the local area. Half a dozen other officers walked in and sat down followed by Maidencoombe carrying a large bundle of folders which he placed on the desk at the front. He turned to Sandwell. 'Everyone here?'

'Just waiting for Chief Inspector Baslow.'

'He's up to date already, so I'll start.' Maidencoombe turned to the assembled officers. 'You've all heard the rumours about a big blag in Catford but no official complaint from the victim. Well for once the rumours are true. On Thursday the seventeenth of September, one Dennis Hattmann, a local builder, and all-round brute, was robbed at his house of a very large sum in cash. He was out at Wimbledon Dogs and so wasn't at home but his wife Julie and his sister Christine Hattmann were in the house watching television. Two men burst in the back door, assaulted and tied up both women and cleared out cash from a secret hiding place in the spare bedroom. When Hattmann returned about eleven pm he found his wife and sister tied up and the money gone. The wife in particular suffered quite a vicious assault. Hattmann immediately jumped to the conclusion that his friend and sub-contractor James Smallwood, also known as "Crapper Jim", was one of the robbers. This assumption was based on his sisters observation that the men were plumbers.' He pointed to the photograph of Crapper. 'A less likely robber than Jim Smallwood is hard to imagine, but anyway, Hattmann charged round to Smallwood's house and according to Mrs Smallwood, on failing to find him he attacked her and smashed up the house. She managed to persuade him that her husband wasn't there and can't have been one of the robbers, because he was in custody here at the station, after getting involved in a brawl at a local pub. Hattmann then came here and enquired about Smallwood but was told to come back on

Friday morning.' He paused to take a drink and re-arrange some papers.

'So, convinced that Smallwood was involved in the robbery somehow, Hattmann picked him up from here on Friday and took him back to his premises with the help of this man,' he said, pointing to the board, 'Russell Jarrett, a well known blagger from the seventies. They knocked him about quite badly, then took him home and continued with the beatings, threatening to kill both mister and missus if the money was not returned. On the following Monday, Shirley Smallwood, came into the station and reported her husband missing but didn't mention the visit from Hattmann. She says he left the house on Saturday about midday and she hasn't seen him since. This is not unusual behaviour for Crapper Jim, a habitual drunk, but she needs her car back and crucially she mentions that her husband works for Dennis Hattmann.'

'So ... having heard the rumours about Hattmann we talk to her and take it a bit more seriously. Information is circulated to neighbouring forces and Sussex police very quickly spot his vehicle in the ferry car park at Newhaven but no sign of the man himself. There's no evidence that he got on the ferry or even bought a ticket ... he's simply disappeared.'

'Our initial assumption was that Dennis Hattmann had caught up with him, possibly killed him and tried to make it look as if Smallwood had sailed off to France. However, that theory has now been dismissed as Hattmann and his charming sister Christine have been terrorising Mrs Smallwood, demanding to know the whereabouts of Mr Smallwood and the money. They also threatened to kill her if she blabbed to us about the robbery. Myself and DS Sandwell caught them in the act yesterday and collared them.'

A junior officer raised his hand. 'Do you know how much was taken?'

Maidencoombe glanced at his notes. 'Various figures have been bandied around but Mr Hattmann's now co-operative wife, Julie, has said over eighty thousand.'

Several officers whistled.

'Where did this cash come from?'

'I'll cover that later as I want to focus on what I think is more important right now, the whereabouts of James Smallwood. I think it highly likely Crapper Jim is dead. It also seems very likely that although he didn't personally take part in the robbery, he and his wife are involved somehow. The robbers went to considerable lengths to make the victims believe they were plumbers, in fact made it look as if Smallwood was one of them.'

Sandwell flipped the display pad over to a fresh sheet and Maidencoombe continued. 'So now we have a number of possibilities. We think the most likely scenario is that Smallwood tipped them off about the hidden cash but they fell out, perhaps over share-out ... the usual reason blaggers fall out. The robbers have tried to fit-up Smallwood for the robbery so it's reasonable to assume that the disagreement happened before the the event took place.' He paused for a drink of water and motioned to Sandwell to turn the pad over again. 'The next possibility is that that Mrs Smallwood heard about the cash and she organised it with the blaggers and arranged for them to fit up her husband but that is extremely unlikely, and frankly, I don't think she's that smart or has the connections.'

Baslow quietly entered the room but stayed at the back and raised his hand. 'Do we have any idea who the actual robbers might be?'

'None at all but likely to be experienced operators.'

'Where do you think Hattmann's money came from?'

'It's possible but not certain that much of it came originally from a robbery in Rotherhithe back in nineteen seventy four.'

Chief Superintendent Pilling had entered the room without anyone noticing. 'Have you had a proper look at that job?'

'We've skimmed over it a bit. A firm from Deptford were sent down and are still inside but the money was never recovered, one hundred and twenty thousand. We're pretty certain that Hattmann wasn't one of the robbers but he was questioned at the time as he appeared to know one of the crew. It's possible he's been storing the cash for them. It's also possible that Hattmann *stole* the cash from the Deptford gang and they've arranged for someone else to steal it back, but if that's the case, why on earth bother with the fake plumber charade? We think the robbers may in fact be close to Hattmann and his circle and they've adopted the plumber outfits to divert attention from themselves. There's also the remote possibility that Mrs Smallwood has accidentally or deliberately killed Mr Smallwood and got rid of him, but we think that very unlikely.'

A uniformed sergeant raised his hand. 'What about Christine Hattmann? I've arrested her for violence before and she could have set the whole thing up, she's an evil piece of work.'

'That's possible and we'll be looking at her very closely but we're going to focus on Mrs Smallwood for the time being as she's being a lot more co-operative than Hattmann's sister and I think is more likely to crack. She's told us a lot already but as always, not everything.'

Maidencoombe walked over to the display boards and pointed at the blank spaces. 'There's characters missing from that board, the two robbers and probably a driver. I want you to go to Hattmann's address, Falmer Close, and talk to neighbours. We want to find out what cars were seen on that Thursday, in fact any unusual cars in the area in the preceding weeks. Was anyone spotted entering or leaving number seventeen that evening? Next, I want you to go to Smallwood's address and do the same. Crucially we want to know everything that happened between Hattmann dropping him off on Friday and Mrs Smallwood's appearance here on Monday.'

Another hand went up.

'Isn't it possible that Smallwood's disappearance is completely unconnected with the robbery, that he's just blind drunk in a ditch somewhere?'

'Anythings possible of course but there's just too

many things linking the Smallwoods to the Hattmann robbery. We're working on the assumption that something sinister has happened to him and the robbers are the most likely suspects. DS Sandwell has prepared copies of the action plan, pick one up before you leave, and I want preliminary reports back here by five pm today.'

Pilling and Baslow nodded to Maidencoombe and left the room as the junior officers collected their paperwork.

***

Vince left the site in Croydon telling his two men that he had a doctors appointment. He drove a short distance and stopped at a telephone box. It stank of urine.

'It's me, can you talk?'

Julie answered. Yeah, there's no-one here.'

'What's happened?'

'The police have been here again.'

'What did they want?'

'They know I've been robbed, Shirley must've told them so I couldn't get out of it. I had to tell them most of it.'

'You didn't say I was with Den?'

'No and Den hasn't told them either. His solicitor told him to say nothing.'

'What about Christine?'

'She's the same.'

'Did they ask how much was taken?'

'Yeah, so I told them eighty odds.'

'What else?'

'I said it came from cash-in-hand jobs. Don't know if they believed me.'

'So they don't know about me yet?'

'Don't think so but they've started asking neighbours so someone might mention you or the car.'

'This is gettin' messy. Has Den said anything about me?'

'Nothing at all, he just grunts. Thinks the police are listening in.'

'Get those passport photos, black and white.' He ended the call and went back to the car for his notebook. He flicked through it until he found Matt Melshott's number then he went back to the phone box and called him. 'Can you go ahead with that transfer, thirty?'

'Will do ... I take it you'll be needing the passports then?'

'Soon as I've got the photos I'll bring them over.'

He put the phone down and went back to his car. He drove back to the building site and parked beside Ron Gooch's site hut. As he got out Ron walked over, 'I've just heard that those coppers have been back to see Julie.'

'Who told you?'

'Eleni, she arrived just as they were leaving.'

'Julie doesn't know anything about Crapp—'

'And neither does Eleni but she's not stupid, we need to be careful.'

'When can I start on the top floor?'

'First fix'll be done by Thursday.'

***

Sandwell walked into Maidencoombe's tiny office and suggested a coffee at the canteen. They took the stairs to the second floor but said nothing until they were seated at a corner table, out of earshot of canteen staff and other officers. Maidencoombe leaned forward. 'So where are we with the door to door?'

'One neighbour mentioned a bit of a disturbance at around the time Mrs Smallwood says Hattmann appeared. She saw a dark coloured car drive off but thought it was a domestic and didn't bother about it. Shouting and door slamming are regular events at the Smallwood household and neighbours often see loud arguments in the garden ... mostly missus shouting at mister. Several other neighbours seem to know the Smallwoods quite well and aren't in the least surprised that he's disappeared. They fully expect him to turn up and no-one mentioned the robbery or cash. The brown Cortina is a normal feature and no-one can remember it coming or going on Friday or Saturday. No-one has seen any other unusual cars or seen anyone acting suspiciously so we've nothing so far to contradict Shirley's account.'

'Hattmann?'

'Quite a bit more there. The brown Cortina is a regular visitor outside Hattmann's house. One neighbour in particular constantly irritated by it using his driveway to do a three point turn instead of using the turning circle. Also complained about a white van doing the same but that hasn't been seen for a while - presumably Smallwood's Transit.

'Did he or she see anything that night?'

'No, but another neighbour saw a large silver Mercedes with two occupants loitering near the entrance to the close a few weeks earlier and no-one around there owns anything so swanky … no reg unfortunately. Another neighbour spotted a man walking a dog after dark a few weeks ago. Struck her as odd because she didn't recognise him and he walked around the entire close twice and seemed to be looking around a lot. Thought he might be a burglar casing the area. She wrote down some notes. Described him as dressed like an old man with a cap, a stick and a Labrador. He had a short length coat or jacket possibly tweed—'

'Dressed *like* an old man?'

'When she first saw him he was walking like an elderly gentleman but on the second time round he was walking more like someone younger and fitter. Also, she thought the clothes were a bit *posh* for the area. Hasn't seen him before or since.'

'Great things net curtains.'

'Two others mentioned a beige Maxi parked outside Hattmann's from time to time and a white van regularly parked in the same spot. No reg number but they described Jim Smallwood to a tee.'

'OK, we need to ask Julie Hattmann about the Maxi and probably more important, find Smallwood's van but the really interesting stuff is this Merc and the dog walker. Re-visit the neighbours and clarify as much as possible.'

'One other thing, the neighbours are well aware that our builder friend knocks his wife about. One in particular is a regular visitor and has seen Julie distressed on a number of occasions. All of the neighbours are a bit frightened of Hattmann.'

'Well if nothing else we can get him for wife beating as well as assaulting Shirley Smallwood. We can have another go at Julie Hattmann later … back to Shirley?'

'We've nothing to contradict her story so far but we should press her on the van, might open up something useful.'

They returned to the main office and Maidencoombe phoned the custody suite. 'Bring Mrs Smallwood up to room three.'

'How long you gonna keep me here?' Shirley pushed away the tea proffered by the young WPC.

'This has become a murder investigation Shirley and you don't get to walk away without giving us a lot more information.' Maidencoombe sat down. 'Would you like a solicitor?'

'Yeah, if you've got one that does divorces.'

'Tell us about the van.'

'What about it? I ain't seen it for weeks.'

'Exactly when did you last see it?'

'About three or four weeks ago, he said it was knackered and he had to use the car instead.'

'You said before that some mate was fixing it, who exactly?'

'I don't know.'

'Shirley, think hard. Where does he normally get his vehicles fixed or serviced?'

'There was a place in Norwood but that was a long time ago. I think he fell out with them. Jedson, Jebson maybe.'

'Judson's, I know it.'

'Might be there s'pose.'

'OK, we'll check them out. Tell us more about the van … a white Transit?'

'It's a heap. Time he got rid of it anyway.'

'What exactly was wrong with it?'

'Engine. There was blue smoke pourin' out the exhaust and wouldn't do more'n twenty.'

'So he doesn't normally use the car for work?'

'No.'

'Has he got premises or a yard?'

'Used to use an old garage years ago but he sold it when he got rid of his men.'

'Got rid of, you mean fired?'

'He had half a dozen men and loads'a work but he couldn't handle it so he sacked 'em all. Now he just works on his own.'

'When was this?'

'About five years ago.'

'Anyone take it badly. Any threats?'

'They were glad to get away from 'im.'

'Tell us about Russell Jarrett.'

'I know he's a villain.'

'Well everyone knows that. How well do you know him?'

'Hardly know 'im, he was with Den when he came round but he didn't hit me. It was just Den.'

'Before that when did you last see him?'

'Months ago, maybe at the pub. He's sometimes

there with Den.'

'Has Jim ever talked about him?'

'Don't think so, don't remember.'

'Shirley, there's a big problem here. You say that Jim didn't leave the house from Friday until Saturday lunchtime and that his car was parked outside all that time.'

'Yeah'

'We've talked to all your neighbours, they have a clear view of the house and no-one, not a single one, can remember seeing his car there. Nobody saw him drive off on Saturday. So we've only got your word for it. Dennis Hattmann clearly hasn't any idea where Jim is or he wouldn't be hounding you. You're the last person to see him alive and in my experience that's usually the person responsible.'

'Responsible?'

'Responsible for hiding or killing the missing person.'

'People go missin' all the time, they ain't all dead.'

'True, but when you add up the circumstances it's hard to believe he's still alive.'

Sandwell opened a folder and looked at some notes. Then he showed Shirley some photographs of the Cortina. 'Going back to the car, our forensic boys have been all over it and they say there's been a lot of petrol spillage in the boot. Any explanation?'

'Forgets to fill up and runs out so he keeps a gallon in the boot.'

'There was no can anywhere in the car.'

'I don't care about fuckin' petrol I just want out of

here.'

Maidencoombe ended the interview and Shirley was taken back to the cells.

'We're not really getting anywhere with her and we don't have a body. A solicitor will make mincemeat out of us, we'll have to let her go.'

'One more go at the Hattmanns?'

'They'll stay no comment. We could charge them with the assault on Shirley Smallwood but I'm wondering if instead we just bail them. They're not going to give up looking for Smallwood and the eighty thousand and if we keep an eye on them, they might lead us to both.'

'Worth a try.'

'I'll run it past Baslow. Tell me more about Jarrett, I'm aware of him but not the detail ... his record please, and the rumours.'

Sandwell leaned forward as another officer sat at an adjacent table. 'Early forties. Got seven for robbery in seventy four, bank job in Southwark. Wouldn't admit his guilt so no parole. Released earlier this year.'

'So not around for the Rotherhithe job?'

'Definitely not and no obvious connection other than his current association with Hattmann.'

'Violence?'

'About average for the type. Uses it as a means to an end. Never been collared for anything other than theft or robbery but believed to have been involved in at least one murder and several violent incidents in prison.'

'Known associates?'

'Some of the South London robbery firms. No-one's watching him apart from us as far as I know.'

'Is he on the Flying Squad special list?'

'No, which is surprising considering his record.'

'So if Hattmann has involved Jarrett in his search is it just muscle?'

'Dunno, maybe he owes Hattmann for something.'

'We're getting bloody nowhere. We still haven't a clue who the robbers are and there's no sign of Smallwood and nothing firm enough to link anyone to his disappearance.'

'I'll go back to Falmer Close right now and press the neighbours on the Merc and the dog walker.'

'Big silver Merc?'

'There's hundreds of them in London.'

'Most of them owned by villains I'll bet.'

10

Bit of a Clear Up

Moose approached the counter and manoeuvred himself onto a bar stool. Chief Superintendent Pilling was already at the bar and nodded an acknowledgement. Moose ordered a half of cider. 'Never thought I'd take up golf but here I am.'

'You'll meet a lot of very useful people here. We'll get you into chequered trousers eventually.'

'Not without a fight.'

'As to that other matter, they should leave you alone but it might be an idea to tidy up loose ends, just in case.'

'Tidy up?'

'I won't be able to help you if that bloke surfaces. Do you have anyone who can help?'

'One or two.'

Pilling turned to leave. 'See you at the medal on Saturday.'

'I'll be propping up the bar.'

Moose finished his drink and left the clubhouse. He

walked towards his Mercedes which was now hemmed in by two Range Rovers. The driver of one gave him a big smile. He didn't recognise her but thought she looked classy. He drove away from the club and stopped in Dunton Green to use a phone box. 'It's Moose, I need a bit of a clear-up.'

'How urgent?'

'Five grand urgent.'

'Details?'

'Not over the phone, let's meet up.'

'That nice place on the way to Sevenoaks?'

'Perfect, I'm close.'

Moose arrived at the pub and outlined the situation specifying some very strict conditions.

'Can't do it, too risky. He's an informer and he's linked to you. The pair that came to you won't let this go. I'm surprised you asked me.'

'Ten.'

'It's not a question of more money.'

'You do owe me a favour, a very big one.

'I'd be putting both of us inside ... it's crazy.'

'Do I have to do it myself?'

'Don't even think about it. Have you got anything on him, anything compromising?'

'Not really, he's done some finding and sourcing for me, but if he blabs about that he's puttin' his own neck on the block as well as mine.'

'Family?'

'Divorced. Teenage daughter lives with the ex but spends time with him, weekends and so on.'

'That might work.'

'How?'

'You owe him money?'

'Well he thinks I do but it's bollocks.'

'Get the five grand together and we'll pay him a visit. Where does he live?'

'Gipsy Hill.'

'That's sort of Norwood isn't it?'

'Rents a flat there, grotty area but his wife got the house when they split up so it's all he can afford.'

'You free now? It'll be dark soon.'

'Yeah, but what exactly are we going to do?'

'Go back to the showroom and swap your flash motor for something that won't stick out. Pick me up in Beckenham, that little back street from last time.'

They drove towards Gipsy Hill in an old Vauxhall and discussed the new strategy for dealing with Salter which Moose accepted was much safer. He parked as close as he could to Ted's flat and switched the engine off but as he started to open his door he felt a hand on his arm.

'Wait a minute.'

'What are you doing? What the hell is that? ... cocaine? That stuff'll rot your brain.'

'Keeps me sharp, razor sharp. Always do a line before a job like this.'

Moose shook his head and they both got out of the car. The road was litter strewn and the hedge on the property was overgrown and stuffed with crisp packets and bottles. The whole area had the feel of a once respectable area gone badly downhill. Bedsits, dingy flats, run down shops, peeling paint and dog dirt everywhere. The house itself was a huge Victorian semi of three storeys that had been divided up and it wasn't clear how many dwellings had been created from it. There were two groups of bell pushes but some were hanging off and they didn't all have names. Moose pressed the button marked Salter but there was no sound and nothing happened. He pushed again and held it down. After a couple of minutes Ted opened the door, dishevelled in loose trousers and an old shirt. He hadn't shaved for a couple of days.

'Good you're in.' The two men pushed Ted back into the hall and closed the door.

'I don't work for you any more so get out.'

'Ted, even by your standards you're being short-sighted,' he held up the bag, 'I've got something for you, so take us upstairs and and pour us a drink. By the looks of it you've had a few already.'

'I'm not—'

'My friend here will become very unpleasant if you don't co-operate.'

The other man said nothing but opened his jacket to reveal a cosh. Then he pointed upstairs. They tramped up the staircase taking care to avoid the stains and damp patches on the mangy carpet. Moose put his hand on the banister but quickly removed it from the sticky surface. 'Christ, this place is filthy.'

They entered the tiny flat which comprised only a single room with a bathroom and a kitchenette through an archway.

'This is worse than I thought Ted. You're gonna be

glad we came.'

'I doubt that.'

Moose's accomplice pointed to an armchair and Ted sat down.

'Who are *you* anyway?'

'Right now I'm your friend, but that can change.'

'I've got a lot of money for you Ted, but before I give it to you I need assurances and answers to a few questions,' Moose paused for a few seconds, 'what made you start working for Baslow?'

The blood drained from Ted's face.

Moose snorted. 'Yeah, we know. He told me you've been working with him for years, helping out, making notes in that little black book you always carried. He found you quite useful.'

'OK, he paid me but I never gave him stuff about you. Just about dodgy guys in the trade. I was a proper informer.'

'Well yes and no. Baslow paid you all right and he collared the odd villain from time to time but you were never official.'

Ted looked puzzled.

'What I mean is, you were never on the books. The Met has no official record of your work, no reports filed, no payments made. They've never heard of you.'

'But—'

'You were being paid unofficially. Off the books, under the table, whatever you want to call it.'

'But—'

'Stop butting me, just listen. Baslow is bent. He's as bent as they come, along with his sidekick Murris—'

'I don't know anyone called Murris—'

'He paid you out of his own pocket and he can afford it believe me. He's helping himself all over the place. He's being paid by villains to lose evidence, to turn a blind eye. He even gets paid to fit up innocent people. He charges for protection. In short he's a gangster with a warrant card and there's virtually nothing he won't do. He's got his nose in every trough in South London and here's the problem, your problem. One of his schemes hasn't worked out as planned. He miscalculated. He tried to squeeze me with information you provided but it's backfired badly and he could fall into his own trap.'

Salter stood up but Moose's accomplice shook his head so he sat down again. Moose coughed and continued. 'You told him about my little enterprise with the Cortina?' Moose raised his eyebrows. 'A man connected with that car has disappeared, probably dead. Nothing to do with me I assure you, but Baslow *is* involved and the only thing connecting him to the car and the missing man is Ted Salter. So now you've gone from being useful to being a liability, one that could put him away for good. He needs to shut you up. Get rid of Ted ... problem solved.'

Salter slumped back in his chair.

'Now of course I don't want to get dragged into any of this. Nothing would stick but it would be a serious distraction and very bad for my reputation with the trade and the punters. So what I want from you is all the records you kept, photographs of the Cortina and my arch unit, those little black notebooks, the John Smith invoice, the lot. I want the camera as well.'

Ted was half listening and half watching the other man searching through his possessions. A small case was dragged out from under the bed and the contents tipped onto the duvet. 'Looks like it here.' He passed a bundle of photographs to Moose.

'Where are the notebooks?'

Ted pointed to a bookshelf. 'Behind the books.'

'Now I've been thinking about our previous dispute and you're current predicament. I'm going to give you five thousand pounds on condition you keep quiet and move out of London. You're from Nottingham aren't you? Up there would be fine.'

'And if I don't want to play your little game?'

'My friend here will shoot Melanie's legs off and make you vanish. She'll spend the rest of her life in a wheelchair wondering why her dad disappeared.'

'You bastard.'

'That's a very ungrateful response to a gift of five thousand pounds and we're saving your life too. Baslow will kill you and if my information about Murris is accurate it won't be a quick death.'

'I need time to think about this.'

'Just think about Melanie, you've got five minutes. I'll pour you a drink.'

Moose's accomplice found a Polaroid camera and an Instamatic with no film in it. He held it up looking at Ted.

'Doesn't work.'

'Where's the negatives?'

'In a folder up there. I didn't use the Instamatic for any of this stuff.'

'Is that absolutely everything?'

Ted nodded and turned back to Moose. 'Baslow might track me down anyway.'

'Look Ted, we're giving you a head start and enough cash to start afresh somewhere else.'

'You owe me a lot more than that.'

'I'm not going into all that again. The offer is, take the money and move away or we cripple Melanie. You don't have a weak hand Ted, you don't have any cards at all. Face it.' He opened the bag and laid out the cash on the table. Salter glared at him.

'Don't be a fool Ted, take the money.'

Salter picked up the bundles and flicked through them, then got up and put them under the mattress.

'What photos did you give to Baslow?'

'None, I showed them to him and he made some notes but he told me to hold onto them and keep them safe.'

'Hmm, makes sense.'

The other man nodded and started smashing the cameras. Moose stood up. 'Ted, move out of here now, tonight. Just go before Baslow gets here, and phone your ex. Tell her you got a new job in Devon or somewhere else far away ... you don't want to be reported missing. Same story to your landlord and neighbours.'

The visitors left the flat and walked down the grubby staircase carrying a bag each of notebooks, documents, photographs and negatives.

'Is that bloke really dead?'

'Maybe, nobody knows.'

'All that stuff about Baslow, quite creative.'

'Well it's about half true from what I know.'

11

Bailed

Detective constable Akerman knocked on the open door of Maidencoombe's office before walking in. 'Sir, the Maxi.'

'The Maxi?'

'The beige Maxi reportedly seen outside Hattmann's house on several occasions. I've got an update.'

'Go on.'

'OK, the car belongs to a Vincent Allarth, generally known as Vince or Vinny. We've talked to him and it's interesting.'

Maidencoombe flicked his fingers impatiently in a circular motion. 'Come on, come on.'

'He's an electrician and works for Hattmann and several other building firms as a sub-contractor. He only works for the building trade and doesn't normally do domestic work but he does however sort out Hattmann's house as required and has been there recently fixing a shower and an issue with the boiler. He's apparently known Hattmann for years and gets work from him on a regular basis.'

'So he might have known there was cash hidden at the house. Where was he on the night of the robbery?'

'He was with Hattmann all evening at Wimbledon Dogs.'

'Hattmann's wife didn't mention him.'

'They came back to the house about eleven and Hattmann persuaded a very reluctant Vince to come inside to have another look at his shower. Place was in uproar when they entered, Christine Hattmann tied up on the floor. So Allarth knows all about the robbery and it was him that drove Hattmann round to the nick that night.'

'So what else do we know about Vince?'

'Seems to be clean. Small business. Has two men that work for him full-time. They do electrical work for building firms all over South London. No convictions, no arrests, no intelligence linking him to any villains or to any crimes, nothing.'

'But he socialises with the local caveman?'

'I asked him about that and he's known Hattmann since way back. Used to like him all right but says he's become more and more difficult over the last few years. Very aggressive with everyone but Vince needs the work and doesn't want to fall out with him. He said that Hattmann nearly exploded when he found out he'd been robbed.'

'What about Mrs Hattmann, did he see her that night?'

'He says no but Hattmann's sister told him what

happened and said it was probably Jim Smallwood that robbed them.'

'What did Allarth make of that?'

'He couldn't believe it. Said Smallwood is always drunk these days and not reliable to work with.'

'Did he say exactly what state Christine was in?'

'Said he untied her but she seemed quite composed considering what she'd been through.'

'Did you believe him?'

'No obvious reason to doubt him. Got the impression he wishes he wasn't involved. He wanted to leave right away but Hattmann pretty well forced him to drive round to Smallwood's house.'

'What d'ya think?' said Maidencoombe turning to Sandwell.

'Hmm ... Allarth gets work from Hattmann but he's also scared of him? Seems unlikely he's part of the robbery.'

'Let's keep him on file for the time being.'

'John, hang on ... is this Vince *mates* with Smallwood?'

'He says not really, he's just one of many tradesmen he has to work with from time to time.'

'Anything on the Mercedes or the dog-walker?'

'A resident on the main road has reported seeing a silver Merc parked near the corner a couple of times but unable to provide dates. So far no-one else has seen the dog-walker but we haven't managed to get to all the neighbours yet, so there's still a chance.'

'OK John, keep at it.'

Akerman left the room and Sandwell shut the door

behind him. 'Well Vince Allarth is new but apart from that, seems to confirm what we've already been told.'

'Wonder why Julie Hattmann didn't mention him being there on the night?'

'Is your nose twitching?'

'Not sure. Have another chat with her, a gentle chat.'

***

The custody sergeant opened Shirley Smallwood's cell, informed her she was being released on Police Bail and took her to the desk. 'You have to report here again in seven days.'

'You found 'im then?'

'No idea. Sign this and hop it.'

'I'm fuckin' sick of this.'

'We're fuckin' sick of you. Go on, piss off.'

She left the station and started in the direction of home but changed her mind and walked towards the shops. 'I've had enough of this, I've fuckin' had enough.' She bought some vegetables, a piece of meat and some other groceries then went into a chemist's and bought some hair products and some painkillers. She bought an address book from a stationers and headed for home.

On the way, she stopped at a phone box and made three calls. Using a pencil, she made notes on the back of an envelope then left the box and continued towards home. When she opened the front door there was some mail on the mat and a hand-written note from a neighbour to say that some more policemen had been asking questions while she was at the station.

She flicked through the letters but placed them back on the mat without opening any of them and hung her handbag on a coat hook in the hall. She walked around the house and surveyed it. Nothing had changed since she was arrested.

The damp clothes and sheets smelt like dirty rags when she opened the washing machine but she decided to dry them anyway, hanging the larger items outdoors and the smaller ones on a clothes horse which she carried upstairs to the spare bedroom.

Back in the kitchen she drank a cup of tea and ate some biscuits before going back upstairs to run a bath.

Taking her clothes off she looked in a mirror and examined all the bruises and marks around her body. She shook her head and got into the bath and lay there rubbing cream on all the parts of her body she could reach. When the hot water ran out, she got up and dried herself off and looked in the mirror at her long hair. 'That'll have to go.' She put on a dressing gown and stood on a chair to pull down a suitcase and an old red handbag from the top of the wardrobe. She laid them both on the double bed. Searching through the wardrobe and a chest of drawers she pulled out clothes that hadn't been worn for years and placed them in the suitcase. She tried on boots and a red coat last worn about ten years earlier and was surprised to find they still looked good and fitted well. She folded the coat carefully and put the boots in a carrier bag then placed both on top of the other clothes in the suitcase and packed in some toiletries.

Back in the kitchen she read the instructions on the hair dye bottle and gathered together towels and jugs and headed back up to the bathroom. She spent the next few hours becoming a blonde. Inspecting herself in the mirror she thought it an improvement overall and pulling her hair back in a pony tail was surprised and pleased at her new look. She went back downstairs and made a single phone call then made a sandwich and some more tea. As the afternoon wore on she sat in the living room copying out her old address book into the new one. Most entries were copied and she also reproduced the alterations and deletions but purposely omitted four entries altogether. She used a mixture of different pens and pencils and creased the pages and rubbed on some dirt in places.

She placed the new one on the coffee table, put the original in her red handbag and went back upstairs and gathered together all the hair dye packaging, placed it in a carrier bag and put that too in the suitcase. She washed down the bath and the sink, cleaned out the plug hole and made sure there was no traces left anywhere. She took particular care to remove stray blonde hairs and vacuumed the upstairs twice emptying the bag at the back of the garden. Satisfied, she returned to the living room and sat at the window peering through the net curtains watching her neighbours coming and going.

At about six o'clock she went upstairs and put on make up and tied back her hair, dressed herself in the same clothes she had come home in, and tidied the bedroom. She carried the suitcase downstairs and left it in the hall near the door. Then she tidied up the kitchen and laid the table for two with a glass of wine at each place. She cut up the vegetables and placed them in saucepans and put them on the cooker but didn't turn on the heat. She prepared the piece of meat, covered it in foil and placed it on a roasting tray at the side of the cooker and turned the oven on. She opened a cupboard and took out a packet of custard powder and mixed some up with milk in a bowl then left it at the side of the hob beside two dessert plates. She opened the fridge door but didn't shut it. She turned the heating up much higher and switched on the kitchen light. Going back into the hall, she put on the same dark blue anorak she had being wearing earlier and sat in the living room looking out of the window. At about half past six, satisfied that all her neighbours were inside and probably preparing dinner she switched on the television, turned on the light and went into the hall where she took her house keys out of her anorak pocket and hung them on a coat hook. She went back into the living room and pulled over a chair then went into the kitchen and tipped over another chair. She tried to break it but only managed to bend one leg slightly. She grabbed at another coat and tore it off the hook and threw it down on the floor. She pulled over a small shoe rack scattering the footwear. Back in the kitchen, she retrieved two bundles of cash from behind a false panel under the kitchen sink, wrapped them in cling film and put them inside the red handbag. She went to the other handbag she'd hung up earlier and took only her driving license which she placed in the red one. Leaving her purse, chequebook and everything else in the original bag, she returned it to the hook.

Then she pulled the anorak hood over her head, picked up the suitcase and went through the front door pulling it shut quietly.

Keeping her head down, she walked quickly down the path, along the street and around the corner to the main road. She passed a few people as she went along but no-one she recognised. She had planned to change her clothes at Catford Bridge station but now decided it was too risky so when she reached the town centre she hailed a cab. The driver helped her with her case and she slumped back in the seat. 'Sydenham station please.' She flipped back her hood and untied her now blond hair. The driver noticed.

'Sorry which station was it love?'

'Sydenham. I'm catchin' the train to Southampton for my sister's hen party.'

'Very nice.'

The cabby talked continuously but she didn't really listen and only muttered the odd response. When they arrived, she paid and gave him a generous tip then walked into the station and found the ladies. She went into a cubicle and struggling in the confined space, managed to swap her shoes for boots and her anorak for the red coat. Flustered and hot she freshened up at the wash hand basin, applied much brighter red lipstick and went back into the station where she purchased a return to London Bridge. Twenty minutes later she was heading towards the capital and on her arrival she made another call from a phone box then headed for the tube station. She arrived at Russell Square twenty minutes later and walked the few streets to a small hotel in Cartwright Place where she had booked a single room in a false name.

She didn't feel like eating and went to bed early after watching some television. Following a restless night on an unfamiliar bed, she left early the next day and walked back towards Bloomsbury until she came to Spirelli's Hair Salon. 'Sorry, I haven't got an appointment, can you fit me in?'

'It's OK, we're quiet anyway. Have a seat ... what would you like done?'

'I'd like it as short as possible without looking like a man,' she pointed to a photograph on the wall.

'Are you sure? You've got such a lovely head of hair and you've dyed it recently, I can feel it.'

'I know, but it's too much work keeping it this long and I can't be bothered any more.'

The stylist worked quickly, efficiently removing the long blond hair, making Shirley look and feel a lot younger. She thanked the woman and her assistant, paid, picked up her suitcase and walked to Kings Cross tube station where she made a call from a phone box then bought a sandwich and a ticket for Liverpool St.

'I can sound a bit posh when I try,' she thought.

**

Chief Inspector Baslow walked in to the main office and stuck his head around Maidencoombe's door. 'Where are we with the Hattmanns?'

'Just about to call you actually. They've said nothing at all. We could hold them for threatening Mrs Smallwood but not for Mr Smallwood's disappearance. So if you're OK with it I'll bail them and keep an eye on them. They might find Smallwood for us.'

'D'ya think he's still alive?'

'My gut says no but there is a chance. If he is, he'll probably have some of the money.'

'Any clue as to the robbers identities?'

'No, to be frank. Vic's team are having a thorough look at the Rotherhithe job and the Deptford firm that went down for it, but apart from one of them, they're all still inside.'

'Who's the one?'

'Reg Wilson but he's dying, he's in a hospice so he can't have been one of them.'

'Reg Wilson? I collared him years ago when I was up at the river. Might go and have a chat. Which hospice?'

Maidencoombe gave him the details and Baslow left the office. Sandwell appeared at the door and raised his eyebrows.

'Baslow's getting a bit more involved. He's going to talk to Reg Wilson.'

'Don't think he'll get much out of him, he's nearly dead. Could it have been someone working for the Deptford gang?'

'Personally I doubt it but who knows. Anyway, go and bail the Hattmanns and set up someone to watch Dennis. Let's see what he gets up to.'

Sandwell walked down to the custody suite and handed the sergeant the required paperwork then followed him to the cells. They escorted both Hattmanns back to the desk.

'You're being bailed to appear here again in seven days. In the meantime stay away from Shirley Smallwood. I mean it. Both of you, leave her alone.'

'Thanks for nothing.'

The pair collected their belongs from the desk, signed the forms and left the station.

'What's going on?' said Christine, as they crossed the road.

'They've got nothing on us about Jim. They ain't got clue where he is. They ain't got a body.'

'Shirley'll be back home, do you wanna ...?'

'Not yet, let's see if they're watchin' us.'

They walked the short distance to Hattmann's yard and surprised his wife Julie emptying a bin.

'*You*, inside NOW.'

'She went into the Portacabin. Den and Christine followed.

'D'ya want a tea or a coffee?'

'Sit down.'

Julie looked apprehensive.

'I told you never to say anything, to keep quiet, but you've blabbed about it ya stupid cow.'

'Den—'

They know 'bout it. The eighty thousand, the blag, everything.'

'Shirley told them. I couldn't deny it. They're not idiots.'

'Keep your fuckin' mouth shut, all right ... has anyone

phoned about work?'

'Nothing new. I sent the men to work on the Plumstead job. Norman seemed to know what needed doing.'

Christine made some tea and they all sat around the desk.

'What're we gonna do?'

'I ain't got a fuckin' clue.'

'The passports are gone as well, we can't go to Spain.'

'I fuckin' know that. We're skint anyway.'

'There's about three thousand in the bank.'

'Yeah but the merchants are chasing me and I need to pay the lads. Go back to the house.'

Julie left the cabin quickly and drove off in the Triumph. Christine stood up and started pacing the room. Den picked up a coin and started flipping it. 'Who else does Jim know? Who else could he have got to do it?'

'Vince was with you so can't have been him so what about Ron?'

'Doubt it, he ain't got the bottle.'

'Have the police talked to 'em?'

'Dunno, they didn't say.'

'Does Jules know about the Rotherhithe job?'

'Dunno, maybe. Think she suspects but she's never asked straight out.'

'Might have been mates of Reg's firm. Crapper knows them somehow and he's helped them.'

'The only one that knew I had the cash is Reg. Why would *he* organise robbin' me? It was him that gave it me in the first place. I can't believe he told the rest of the firm, they'd 'ave killed 'im.'

'How come Reg got it?'

'All I know is he got it from Cake Kanavan somehow and he asked me to keep it for him till he got out. Asked me to look after 'is wife an'all. I used to bung her a hundred now and again but she got herself another bloke and divorced Reg. When he realised he was dying he told me to keep the money. He's got no kids so it's mine now, or at least it *was* mine.'

'Where did Kanavan go?'

'Reg said Spain.'

'What about the rest of the firm?'

'They think Cake took *all* the cash to Spain. The police never knew about him, but now they know I had eighty grand, they're never gonna leave me alone.' He kicked a chair over. 'Where the fuck is that cunt Crapper?'

A car drove into the yard and Russell Jarrett appeared at the door.

'Who told you I was out?'

'Julie, five minutes ago.'

Christine stood up. 'I've gotta get down to the workshop,' she looked at Jarrett, 'see you down there.'

'Stay away from Shirley.'

She left the cabin and drove off.

12

Decapitation

Moose drove his Bentley into Ron Gooch's yard and parked beside the old bungalow. He got out and stretched before putting on a coat and walking in the front door. Ron looked up from his desk. 'Moose—'

'This is a fucking mess. It's cost me the whole nine grand to pay off Ted and those bent coppers and I'm out for the Cortina as well. So you owe me.'

'Sorry Moose, I was sure there was eighty.'

'I think there was too but someone else got there first, maybe your mate Crapper. I take it you haven't heard from him?'

'No-one has. Den's goin' mental lookin' for him.'

'Eighty?'

'Yeah, he's lookin' for eighty.' Ron stood up and went over to the sink. 'Want a brew?'

'No.'

Ron made himself tea and went back to his desk. He held up a sheaf of papers. 'I'm back to square one. It's gettin' worse.'

'Ron for fuck's sake, your cash flow problems are the least of it. I've gone along with this caper to help you out and now I've got bent coppers on my case. Crapper's vanished and might even be dead so the final demands you've been getting just don't cut it.'

'Couldn't I help you on another job?'

Moose sat down. 'Look you did well on the night, I accept that, but it's just too risky at the moment. Right now I want to avoid us getting arrested.'

'D'ya think they'll leave it, the bent coppers?'

'Probably, but if their straight colleagues dig deep enough *they'll* get to us anyway. Fucking Crapper. I've never even met the bloke and now I'm a suspect in his disappearance. What happened? Go over it again.'

'It was your idea to fit 'im up, just too clever. If we'd just done it straightforward it wouldn't be a problem.'

Moose glared at him. 'Yeah, I know ... start at the beginning.'

'He went to the Black Horse and met up with Lenny and Bert. They got into a brawl with some bloke at the bar and got themselves collared so they were all locked up during the blag.'

'Then what?'

'Den and Jarrett picked up Crapper from the nick on Friday morning and took him back to Den's yard and gave him a kicking then took him home and smashed up his house. Punched Shirley about as well. On Monday Shirley reports Crapper missing and says she ain't seen him since Saturday. Phoned round his mates before she went to the cop shop.'

'What about his car?'

'It was found in Newhaven. Den and Christine were arrested on suspicion but released. That's all I know.'

'What do *you* think has happened?'

'I dunno, but with Jarrett involved anything could've happened. How well d'ya know him anyway?'

'Got to know him a bit years ago, quite liked him. Matt Melshott put us in touch. He had a good track record and we were planning a couple of jobs together then he got arrested for a previous bank job, someone grassed. Got on all right with him. Seemed professional, smart. I thought he was hard-case but not a nutter. I had a run-in with his brother though, a few years ago.'

'What was that about?'

'Stephen's a dealer like me, and he bought a load of ex-fleet cars, cleaned them up and clocked them. Offered them to me. I'd done quite a bit of business with him, no problems so I trusted him. As soon as they were delivered it was obvious they were dodgy but he wouldn't take them back so I had to muscle him. You wouldn't believe how much he screamed when I used a nail gun on his foot, it was embarrassing.' Moose laughed and shook his head.

'Will it come back to bite you?'

'Stephen won't, he's learnt his lesson and the brothers don't get on but if Russ finds out we robbed his new mate Hattmann then who knows, maybe.'

'How's your alibis?'

'Karen'll be fine she's used to it, but we're getting off the subject. What happened to the rest of the eighty grand? Who took it and where's Crapper?'

'I don't know anything else. If Den's found Crapper he didn't find the money.'

'Well someone has got to that money before us. How could Crapper have known we were coming? And how the hell could he have got that money out of there without the wife noticing?'

Ron shrugged.

'When did Crapper tell you in the first place?'

'Ages ago but Den has let slip a couple of times after a few drinks.'

'Did Crapper talk about nicking it?'

'No.'

'And you didn't suggest taking it?'

'No.'

'Who else could he have told?'

'Anyone I suppose but there's always been rumours about Den's cash.'

'Are you sure you didn't talk to anyone else about robbing him?'

'Course not.'

'Didn't mention it to Eleni?'

'No.' Ron walked over to the door and shut it.

Moose spun round on his chair. 'That door's a mess. What happened, you get a break-in?'

'Some kid got in. I didn't notice and I locked him in so he kicked his way out.'

'How'd you not notice?'

'I was up the back of the yard so he must've come through the gate and sneaked inside. I padlocked the door and was just gettin' in the car when bang, the door flies open and this kid runs out. Fuckin' nuisance but he didn't get anything'

Ron sat down and poured tea into two cups. He pushed one across the desk but Moose shook his head.

'She'd have to have been out of the house. Would she leave Crapper there alone?'

'Unlikely but there's someone else we're forgettin' about, Den's sister. She looks after the house when they go to Spain. In fact she's round there all the time.'

'The one you had the fight with?'

'Yeah, fuckin' wild bitch.'

'But how could she have known we were coming?'

'Maybe she didn't, just a co-incidence. But another thing, she's gone all lovey-dovey with Jarrett.'

'What?'

'Yeah, he's been stayin' at her place since he got a share in the business.'

'Fuck.' He sighed, leaned on the desk with his elbows and held his head with both hands. 'There was space for a lot more under the floor. So she's cleared out most of the cash, just left the visible stuff, the eighteen that I found?'

'Looks like it, fuckin' cow.'

'Smart move. Might have been ages before Den noticed. Doesn't explain Crapper's involvement though, they didn't need him.'

'Maybe he rumbled them and they had to shut him up.'

Moose blew out a long breath. 'Are the police onto them, the regular police I mean?'

'Dunno.'

***

At Hattmann's yard the men packed into the van as best they could. The minibus had been repaired but the garage wouldn't release it until Hattmann paid the bill. The complaints began but Hattmann cut them short. 'Don't fucking start.'

Lenny climbed in with a black Labrador in tow.

'Aw, not that fuckin' dog again it stinks.'

'Why don't you leave it at home?'

'I can't, it's too old, need's let out.'

'Well keep it at your end of the van.'

The men were even more uncomfortable than usual due to the large quantity of materials being carried and the strong September sunshine rapidly increased the temperature in the unventilated cargo bay.

'It's overloaded, it'll pack in.'

'Then he'll have to get the minibus back.'

Traffic was slow moving and the journey was mostly stop start in second gear.

'We could've walked faster,' said Alf.

Hattmann turned round and shouted through the bulkhead hatch, 'Well fuckin' get out and walk then.'

Alf didn't reply and the men lowered their voices to grumble.

'He's on edge today.'

'Worse than usual. Not surprising though, he's lost the lot.'

'How much?'

'Eighty I heard.'

'He might go bust.'

'I've had enough anyway. I'm bloody sick'a this van.'

A few hundred yards from the site the traffic slowed to a halt and the dog started moving about as if looking for a way out. Young Tony turned to Lenny 'That dog needs to pee.'

Hattmann turned round and shouted at Lenny. 'If it pees in here you're fuckin' fired.'

Lenny was half asleep and seemed oblivious. The van started to move again slowly and the dog became more and more agitated but no-one paid much attention. It turned around and started whimpering quietly. Normally Lenny would have recognised the signs but he was too sleepy to notice. The dog tried to push into a corner but was shoved away by Sid. The traffic speeded up again and the dog started spinning around frantically. 'I'm telling you that dog needs to pee.' said Young Tony again. But the dog had peed a copious amount before they set off and no-one had considered the obvious alternative. A motor cyclist suddenly cut in front of the van causing Bert to swerve violently. 'Fuck's sake.'

As the van lurched to the left a generator slid across the floor and hit the dog squarely on the side. Unable to control himself any more, the elderly dog's back-end exploded and sprayed diarrhoea over half the floor hitting several men on the legs. All the men woke up and were immediately overwhelmed by the smell. Hattmann turned round. 'What the fuck is goin' on back there?'

'Lenny for fuck's sake.'

Gasping for breath, the men shouted to Bert to stop the van.

'I can't stop in the middle of the road, we're nearly at

the site.'

'Just fucking pull over.'

'Bert just stop.'

'That fuckin' dog.'

Eddie threw up over Alf. Steve was struggling to breathe and started to retch, slowly at first then he vomited an orange spray with lumps. Bert struggled to maintain control of the van as nausea overwhelmed him. The dog, now terrified by the men shouting and flailing about sat down in the mess and was sliding about as the van lurched from side to side. Hattmann grabbed at the wheel to steady it as Bert turned the van into the site and came to a sudden halt, causing the men to tumble into each other. They all crowded to the rear doors but couldn't open them as the catch was broken and Hattmann had padlocked it from the outside. They tried to kick it down.

'For fucks sake Den, open the door.'

'Fuckin' open it.'

Hattmann had come round to the rear of the vehicle and was fumbling with a bunch of keys as the men kicked and battered the door. Bert fell out of the drivers seat and threw up at the side of the van. Just as Hattmann finally got the key to work, the men made a concerted push and the doors flew open hitting him on the forehead, causing a deep gash. The men fell out tumbling over each other, retching, sweating, coughing and swearing. Some fell to their knees to vomit. Others were wiping away sick from their clothes and fighting over the tap on the water bowser. Hattmann picked himself up, oblivious to his head injury and the blood pouring down his face. 'I'm gonna kill that fuckin' dog.'

The Labrador was cowering behind the generator but jumped out as Hattmann approached. He grabbed a shovel and hit it on the back. It yelped but kept moving. He kicked it several times and the dog howled as it's back leg fractured. It tried to limp away but Hattmann swung the shovel hitting it on the neck then he kicked it in the face shattering it's jaw.

The dog cried in pain but still tried to get away. He jabbed at it with the shovel and an ear flew off, then it fell down as it's front legs buckled. Hattmann jumped on it's head several times but it still moved, so he stood over it and rammed the shovel down on it's neck. The dog stopped moving, but it took three more thrusts to sever the head completely.

Lenny had stopped vomiting and stood watching, horrified and paralysed with fear. Hattmann called out to Norman. 'Get rid of this.'

Norman came over and exchanged glances with Lenny but said nothing. Hattmann turned to Lenny. 'You're fuckin' fired, I told you. Go on fuck off.'

Lenny stood still. 'That's my dad's dog, you're a fuckin' lunatic.'

Hattmann turned away and walked towards the men. 'There's a box of new overalls in the hut. Use them. Get the van cleaned out and get a move on, we're way behind.'

Lenny turned around and left the site. He walked in a daze for about a mile to Croydon Station and caught a train to Sydenham, other passengers repelled by his appearance and smell. From there he caught a bus to Catford and went home to his tiny flat. He couldn't face washing his jeans so he threw them out and put on another pair. Then he washed his T-shirt in the sink and hung it up to dry. He put on a fresh T-shirt and a jersey then opened a can of beer but only drank about half before pouring the rest down the sink. Pacing the room he tried to think of the best way to inform his dad about the dog but couldn't think of any way to tell him without upsetting him. He gave up, left the flat and walked towards the shops. He stopped outside a bookies but didn't go in. On the other side of the road a pub was just opening up and he crossed the road intending to go in but changed his mind and instead walked back down the road to the police station. The desk sergeant looked up.

'I've got information about a missin' man, Jim Smallwood.'

***

'Guv, glad you're back. A joiner called Leonard Figgs walked in to the station and said he knew stuff about Jim Smallwood, the missing "Crapper Jim".'

Maidencoombe raised his eyebrows. 'John, let me get in and get my coat off.' He walked towards his office. 'And get me some tea.'

Akerman returned a few minutes later. 'First of all, he says Hattmann has been going mad interrogating all his men and threatening them. His sister and Jarrett also present. The upshot is Hattmann is still looking for Smallwood. Also, he lost it at one of his building sites and killed a dog belonging to Figgs.'

'A dog?'

'Yeah, it was horrible according to Figgs.'

'What about Smallwood?'

'Figgs hasn't seen him since that Friday morning and neither has any of the rest of the crew but he's convinced Hattmann will kill Smallwood when he catches up with him.'

'When was this?'

'The dog? Today.'

'No, the interrogation.'

'About a week ago.'

'We already knew about Figgs, you talked to him, didn't you?

'Yes—'

'So is there really anything new here?'

Sandwell came in and sat down, Akerman continued. 'Well it does show Hattmann's willingness to use extreme violence.'

'Not sure if the dog thing will help or hinder us with regard to Smallwood but we could use it to hold him if need be.'

***

At the pre-arranged time, Vince went to the call box on Baring Road and waited. He picked up the handset as soon as it rang.

'It's me.'

'Are you OK?'

'Not really.'

'I got the photo, you look different in black and white. I'm going to the passport guy now.'

'You really think we're gonna get away with this?'

'We have to.' The pips sounded. 'Same time tomorrow.'

He put the phone down and went back to his car. He took a road map from the glove compartment and looked at routes to Westerham. He decided this time to go via Sevenoaks.

When he arrived, the car park was unusually busy and he noticed that nearly all the cars were Vauxhall Cavaliers in plain colours. He parked at the far end and walked to the small private door he'd used previously but found it locked, so he went round the front to reception. The foyer was packed with animated young men in suits standing together in small groups laughing and shouting. He was just about to hit the bell when Melshott tapped him on the shoulder. 'I've got a function on, sales conference, we'll need to be quick.'

Vince followed him down the narrow passageway to the private office and handed him an envelope as he sat down.

'These're good, they'll do fine.' Melshott looked up and Vince handed him another envelope. 'Two up front as agreed.'

'Perfect, they'll be ready in a couple of days.' He unlocked a filing cabinet and retrieved a foolscap envelope. He handed it to Vince. 'That's your new bank account in Spain. I've transferred thirty thousand for you and the statements are there.' He laughed. 'In Spanish but all you need to understand are the numbers.'

'I wanted to ask you about a villain called Jarrett that might cause me—'

'Vince I never talk about anyone else even if they're not clients.'

'So you do know—.'

'Vince, this business works because everyone trusts me. I'm a middle man but I keep you all in separate compartments.'

'But I—'

Melshott raised his hand. 'Vince don't ask ... if person A introduces person B to me, I don't tell A what I did for B or vice versa. Everyone knows I keep my mouth shut, I don't pry, I only ask for information really needed for the job in hand. I don't gossip. If I leak information then the business is finished and apart from needing a bodyguard I'd lose lot of income which I'd never make up doing half board for sales reps and the occasional function.'

'Sorry I asked. Can I see the rest of the cash now? I need five for some unexpected expenses.'

'Of course.'

Back in the car he flicked through the bundles of tens then headed back to London. He stopped in Beckenham and used another phone box to make some more calls then he drove home.

13

Mix it up

Baslow left the station and drove to the Royal St Mary Hospice in Greenwich. He showed his warrant card at the desk and asked to see Reg Wilson. The suspicious receptionist asked him to wait while she checked with the Sister. A few minutes later, a tall elderly nun appeared and without introducing herself, directed him into a side office.

'Mr Wilson is in the very last days of his life. Our job here is to make his final days as peaceful and comfortable as possible. I cannot allow you to torment him.'

'I fully understand. I wouldn't normally dream of doing this but I think you will be aware of Mr Wilson's past? He's linked to a murder investigation and I believe he has information that could help us not only solve an old crime but also prevent harm to a very vulnerable woman. I only need to ask a few quick questions.'

The nun sighed and tapped the desk. 'Let me see your

identity papers.'

He handed over his warrant card. She examined it carefully and made notes on a pad before handing it back.

'A few minutes is all I'm prepared to allow but I'll have to ask him first. Wait here.'

She returned a few minutes later. 'Five minutes only and if he is in the slightest bit stressed or upset I will stop it immediately. Do you understand?'

'Perfectly.'

He followed her along a corridor and through another door to an annexe that wasn't visible from the road. She went through double doors on her right and they came to a nurse's station surrounded by more doors. Opening the first one on the left she signalled Baslow to enter

Wilson was partially propped up on pillows and his blotchy shrivelled arms lay on top of the blanket. A drip stand stood at his left and on the other side an oxygen cylinder. A tube was connected from that to his nose and if that hadn't been present, Baslow would have thought him already dead. He barely recognised the old criminal.

'Mr Wilson, this is Chief Inspector Baslow.'

Reg opened his eyes and managed a weak smile. 'Cunt.'

'It's been a few years Reg. I see you haven't lost any of your natural charm.'

Reg coughed and his oxygen tube fell out. A nurse who had come in behind them re-attached it quickly and propped up his pillows.

'What happened to the Rotherhithe money?'

'Cake got it.'

'Cake?'

'Cake Kanavan.'

'All of it?'

Reg nodded.

'Where is he?'

'Spain.'

Reg coughed again violently and Baslow noticed the bucket beside the bed. The young nurse said she thought he was about to be sick.

'Enough.' The sister took Baslow by the arm and led him out of the room and past the nurses station.

'Is it possible I could visit him again?'

'Out of the question. He really is at the end and I'm going to ensure he dies in peace. Leave now.'

Baslow left the building and drove to the cemetery to meet up with Murris.

'He's only in his mid fifties, felt sorry for him, he looked terrible. If I get that ill, shoot me.'

'I want your money first,' said Murris laughing. 'What'd he say?'

The Sister wouldn't let me ask him much but he told me Cake Kanavan had all the money from the Rotherhithe job and had gone to Spain. You know Kanavan?'

'Kevin Kanavan, quite well actually. I knew him as Cake too. He wasn't one of the Rotherhithe boys though. Do you believe Wilson?'

'No. I'm sure he gave the money to Hattmann to look after. He's playing games right to the end. He was one of these blokes in the game for the fun as much as the money.'

They walked along the path with collars upturned.

'But check out Kanavan anyway. Find out if he really did go to Spain.'

'Will do.'

'It's pretty clear Hattmann doesn't know where Smallwood is so how about we offer to help him for a finders fee?'

'Worth a try.'

'He may be willing to co-operate if we offer to steer the enquiry away from the Rotherhithe money and bluff him a bit about Kanavan. My gut tells me you're not gonna find any trace of Kanavan in Spain or anywhere else.'

'You mean he might be dead?'

'If I was to place a bet—'

'What about Pilling and Moose. They could be watching us?'

'All they'll see is us doing our job.'

'Together?'

'I think I'll go on my own. Less intimidating, he might open up.'

***

At the station, Sandwell burst in to Maidencoombe's office. 'Ralph, neighbours have reported something at Smallwood's house. Lights on for days but no movement. One of them peered through the letterbox and said there was a bad smell and flies, looked like a disturbance in the hall.'

'Surely not?'

'Looks like it. I told the uniforms to break in immediately.'

Maidencoombe grabbed his coat and they raced to the crime scene.

Several police cars were parked randomly outside the house and clusters of neighbours were gathered in adjacent gardens. A uniformed PC stood guard at the front door.

'Is it bad news?'

'There's no-one in there, no body.'

'What's the smell then?'

'It's food.'

The house was very hot and they had to step over the mess in the hall. In the kitchen the smell was worse. A piece of meat was putrefying on a plate and the fridge was wide open. Some milk in a bottle had turned to a cheese-like curd with blue mould. Flies buzzed everywhere.

'Christ it's warm in here.'

'It's like the Marie Celeste, tables been laid, food's out and the oven's on. It's obviously been days.'

A uniformed PC walked in to the kitchen. 'Sir, a neighbour has reported a bit of noise on Tuesday evening. Said she saw a woman banging on the door about seven thirty. Also saw a dark coloured hatchback parked outside. Didn't pay much attention as there's been lot's of disturbances over the years. Didn't see her leave. A large woman in her forties she thought.'

'Christine Hattmann?'

'Sounds like it.'

They spotted Shirley's handbag on the coat rail and checked the contents.

'Her purse is here and her chequebook. Cash as well, forty quid.'

'Check those keys on the hook I bet they fit the front door.'

'They do. Uniform said the door was only on the latch. Mortice hadn't been locked.'

'So ... she's been abducted? Where's the blue anorak she was wearing at the nick?'

'She's been expecting someone for a meal by the looks of it. Doors and windows haven't been forced so she's just let them in. She must have known them.'

'Right, pick up Christine Hattmann and I'll get a team over to the brother, might catch him at his yard.'

***

Baslow drove his Rover into Hattmann's premises just as the men were leaving. A Saab 99 was parked at the side of the Portacabin. He suspected it was Russell Jarrett's. He parked up and within a minute Hattmann came out of the cabin and over to the car. 'Help you mate?'

Baslow held up his warrant card.

'Your pals just let me out. What d'ya want?'

'I know, I'm their guv'nor. I'd like a little chat, off the record.'

'What's that mean?'

'Take me inside and I'll tell you.'

Hattmann turned and flicked his head towards the cabin and Baslow followed him. As the Chief Inspector walked through the door he came face to face with Jarrett. 'Hello Russell.'

Jarrett looked surprised and suspicious. He met Hattmann's eyes.

'Russell, I'd like a chat with Dennis off the record. D'ya mind sitting out in your car for ten minutes?'

Jarrett looked at Hattmann and shook his head.

'Yeah he would mind. If you've got somethin' to say you can say it in front'a Russell.'

Baslow sat down. 'OK. I'll outline some ideas I have about your situation ...'

'Get on with it.'

'My colleagues are giving you a hard time about Smallwood which is your own fault as you keep attacking him and his wife. Personally I'm not surprised. If someone had robbed me of eighty large I'd want to kill them.'

Hattmann said nothing and Jarrett sat down on a chair to his left.

'Dennis, I know you got the Rotherhithe money from Reg Wilson. All that stuff about Kanavan and Spain is rubbish, but the thing is, I can make my team look at that, and away from you. Reg is gonna die any day now so he won't be around to contradict me.'

'So what? Don't know what you're talkin' about.'

'Dennis don't be obtuse, this is unofficial. I'm not writing anything down. We're just having a friendly chat.'

'What'd ya you actually want?'

'Russ. I'm just trying to clean up this mess for everyone's benefit.'

'I don't trust him Den.'

'Russ, please, give us five minutes alone.'

Hattmann looked at Jarrett. 'Russ?'

'Up to you. I've got stuff to do at the shop but I know this cunt, don't fuckin' trust him.' He picked up his jacket and a small tool box and left the cabin.

'Hear me out. I know where the cash came from. I know you were robbed of the lot. My boneheaded DI doesn't think you've killed Crapper but he doesn't really know what's going on because he doesn't have all the information I have.'

Hattmann looked at his watch and Baslow continued, 'As I see it, Crapper and his wife tipped off a firm of blaggers, pros by the sound of it. Probably agreed a cut. But there was a fall-out before the blag and this firm have made it look like Crapper was one of the robbers. They didn't expect Crapper to get nicked on the night of the blag though. If it had gone to plan you would probably have killed him. It's obvious that Crapper and his wife are involved somehow. Personally I suspect his wife but you can't go near her. I can though, and you need my help. So what I'm suggesting is we share information and split the money when we find it.'

'Fuck off. Why should I share it with you?'

Baslow stared at him coldly. 'Because I think Kanavan is dead that's why. He never got to Spain. You and Reg killed him and took his share.'

'Bollocks.'

'I can steer the investigation in any direction I want, so smarten up, co-operate—'

Several vehicles suddenly drove into the yard and pulled up outside the cabin. Doors slammed and Maidencoombe and another officer burst in the door. 'Dennis Hattmann I'm arresting you—'

He stopped in mid sentence astonished to see Baslow. 'What are you doing here?'

'I might ask you the same question ... Inspector.'

'Shirley Smallwood has been abducted and I'm arresting this ape in connection with it. His sister's being picked up as well.'

'Abducted? How? When?'

'Probably Tuesday. Neighbours reported something suspicious. I'll fill you in later if you don't mind.'

Hattmann stood up and shouted at Baslow. 'What's your fuckin' game ya cunt?'

Several uniformed officers had now entered the cabin. Baslow stood back and let Maidencoombe proceed. 'Cuff this man and search the whole place. Check the yard, everything.'

Baslow flicked his thumb towards the door. 'Come outside Ralph, now.'

The two detectives left the cabin and stood together beside an excavator.

'This had better be good.'

'Can we do this back at the station? It's text book. Someone's taken Shirley Smallwood and the Hattmann pair are all over it.'

***

Maidencoombe stood outside the interview room and

waited for Sandwell to emerge.

'How's it going with Miss Hattmann?'

'As you'd expect, no comment.'

'Have we found Jarrett?'

'Not yet. Don't really know where to start. He's been living with her since he was released as far as we can make out and his car's still here. He wasn't on parole so we don't have any other address or contact information. I've got John looking for relatives and so on.'

'I'm beginning to think we've been a pair of chumps. It's been staring us in the face all along. This whole plumber thing has come from Christine Hattmann. The other witnesses only believe it because she told them. She's cooked this whole thing up with Jarrett. I can't believe we missed it. The robbers were pros, Jarrett's a pro and Christine knew about the money.'

'But why kill Smallwood?'

'Blaggers are never as smart as they think they are. Christine thinks *"let's fit up Crapper Jim, let him take the blame"*. Then by sheer bad luck Crapper gets himself arrested on the night of the robbery. So Dennis knows it can't have been Crapper on the blag but still thinks he's involved. Our love-birds panic, kill Crapper and try and make it look as if he's sailed off to France with the money. I don't think it was planned.'

'OK, so lets mix it up a bit. We have a go at Dennis and tell him his sister's behind the whole robbery. Then we tell Christine that Jarrett's legged it with the money leaving her in the frame for Shirley's disappearance. See how they react to that.'

They sat down in the interview room. A young PC pushed Hattmann into the room and Sandwell made him sit down.

'I'm not fuckin' talking to you so you're wastin' your time and I want my lawyer.'

'He's on his way but he's been held up. Won't be here for another half hour, so I thought we could have an informal chat until then.'

Sandwell stood up. 'We're not taking notes, we're not recording this, it's off the record.'

Hattmann sneered.

'Angry bloke aren't you? And you don't like dogs?'

Hattmann's expression changed. He looked surprised and shifted in his chair.

'Get tried for robbing a bank and the jury will give you a fair hearing. They'll want to make sure there's good evidence. But kick a dog to death?' Sandwell blew out. 'They won't believe anything you say, they'll hate you.'

'Fuck off.'

'Shirley Smallwood has been taken, probably dead—'

'Nothin' to do with me.'

'You've been chasing your tail. We don't know if Jim was involved in the blag but think about it. He wasn't there, but who was? ... Christine. Who knew all about the money? ... Christine. Who told you it was Crapper? ... Christine. Who's taken up with Russell Jarrett, a known blagger? ... Christine. Who would know other blaggers? ... Jarrett. Who's ruthless enough to kill someone if they got in the way or threatened to grass them? ... Jarrett.'

Maidencoombe took over. 'You were supposed to believe it was Jim. They calculated you would go after him maybe even kill him and you'd get banged up leaving them free with the money.'

'Rubbish.'

'So where's Jarrett then?'

'How would I know?'

'He's vanished and here's the interesting bit. Shirley Smallwood made only one call when she returned home from the nick on Tuesday. Can you guess who? ... Christine.'

Hattmann looked up.

'You look surprised Dennis, didn't she mention it? When we went to Shirley's house, a meal for two had been prepared but it's still lying there uncooked going rotten. Signs of a struggle in the hall and no sign of Shirley but her keys and her purse are still there.'

Hattmann glanced at both detectives.

'Christine didn't tell you she was going to Shirley's for a nice meal and a catch-up? No of course she didn't because you weren't supposed to know.'

'This is bollocks.'

'Why do *you* think they were meeting up?'

'Don't believe you.'

'Maybe Shirley knows that Christine and Jarrett robbed you and she's blackmailing them but I think that's unlikely. It all looked a bit too cosy, nice meal, bottle of wine. Suggests to me that they're pals. Suggests to me that Christine is putting on an act and fooling her hot-headed big brother.'

Sandwell pointed at Hattmann. 'Christine was spotted at Shirley's, banging on the door, but you'd already been there and abducted her.'

'Nah.'

'Where is she then?'

'Dunno,' he shook his head, 'no comment.'

'Dennis, both Smallwoods have vanished and you've been threatening to kill them. You can't control your temper. You've just kicked a dog to death and you've served time for violence before.'

Maidencoombe leaned back in his chair. 'Face it Dennis, Christine's robbed you and fitted up Crapper with Shirley's help. She wanted you to go after him. Where were you on Tuesday evening?'

'No comment.'

Sandwell walked behind Hattmann. 'Your sister's in the frame already and if you can't prove where you were that night you'll be joining her.'

Hattmann leaned back on his chair and looked at the ceiling.

'Think about it and we'll speak later.'

***

Sandwell and Maidencoombe entered the other interview room and noticed that Christine was still handcuffed. Sandwell looked at the uniformed sergeant and tilted his head towards her. The sergeant came up close and spoke quietly. 'You wanna keep her cuffed. I know her, she'll lash out.' He handed Sandwell the key and left the room.

Maidencoombe stared aggressively at the prisoner. 'So Christine ... to start with I'm not going to ask you any questions or at least none that I expect any answers to. I'm going to tell you some stories, paint you some pictures. We think you've abducted Shirley Smallwood. You were seen at her house on Tuesday evening. Your car was spotted by two separate neighbours.'

'Piss off.'

'Your little get together not quite go to plan? Fall out over the money? Hit her? You've got history. That girl in Peckham you jumped on, still has trouble breathing. Not a bad idea though, robbing your dimwit brother. Who came up with it? You or Russell? I'm asking you, because of course I can't ask Russell … he's disappeared. Keeps happening in this case, people just vanish. Left his car at the workshop but with eighty grand in his pocket he won't have much trouble picking up another one.'

She looked up.

'Yeah that's right, he's taken the money. You've been played like a fish. Not only has he taken the cash, he's left you to take the blame for Shirley and Jim. What happened, did *you* kill them or was it Russell?'

Christine tried to fold her arms but couldn't. She moved her gaze to a spot on the opposite wall and said nothing.

'Now when it comes to court, you can of course say it was Russell who robbed your brother, killed Jim and killed Shirley. He's conveniently not around. But both you and Dennis have a proven track record of assaulting them and threatening to kill them. Loads of witnesses and the two most credible ones are standing in front of you.' Maidencoombe leaned against the wall and folded his arms. 'There's overwhelming evidence that you were at Shirley's on Tuesday evening and she hasn't been seen since. You're not going to wriggle out of this. You will have to talk because staying silent is only going to make things worse.'

Sandwell sat down in front of her. 'Seriously, are you going to go down for this to protect Russell Jarrett? We know Shirley phoned you at your workshop that day. So why did you go to her's that evening?'

She glared at each officer then turned away. 'Cos she asked me to.'

'She asked you? You were threatening to kill her a few days before.'

'Said she knew where the money was. Said we could do a deal.'

'But you didn't tell Dennis?'

She looked down and didn't reply.

'You didn't tell Dennis because ... you were gonna cut him out?' He paused but she didn't reply. 'You've just admitted you went to her place. What happened?'

'Went there and knocked at the door. Lights were on but she didn't open up. Shouted through the letter box but she didn't come, thumped on the door a bit then I gave up and went 'ome.'

'What time was this?'

'About half seven.'

That's it?'

'Yeah that's it.'

'Did you see anything through the letter box?'

'No.'

'Didn't notice a smell?'

'A smell? No.'

'Where did you go when you left?'

'Just went 'ome, told you already.'

'Was Russell there?'

'Yeah, said he was just back from the pub.'

'Did you try phoning Shirley when you got home?'

'No.'

Sandwell looked at Maidencoombe and nodded towards the door. 'A quick word?'

They went outside and stood in the corridor but said nothing until two uniformed officers had passed.

'Maybe she's killed Jarrett as well as the Smallwoods?'

'The Smallwoods maybe, but Jarrett would be tough.'

'She's got it in her. Did three years for GBH. According to that joiner Figgs she was at the yard threatening the men with a hammer and a pair of scissors.'

'Scissors?'

'Yeah. Threatened to cut their tongues out apparently.'

'Christ.'

DC Akerman suddenly ran along the corridor towards them. 'A body's been found in Hither Green railway yard.'

'Smallwood?'

'Doesn't look like it. Old bones and some clothes. They reckon ancient, five years or more.'

'Just when we need a body the wrong one turns up. Who found it?'

'Some workmen clearing ground. They phoned it in to Lewisham.'

'Any ID?'

'Not yet but it looks suspicious—'

'OK John, tell me later. Vic? Canteen?'

'What about the lovely Christine?'

'Let her stew for a while then we'll put it to her that she's killed Jarrett as well ... a body's been found.'

'That might not work,' said Sandwell, nodding towards the stairwell, that's her lawyer.'

'Damn ... go and get John back, tell him to meet us in the canteen.'

The three officers sat around a large table in the corner of the canteen. Akerman opened a folder and Maidencoombe started. 'Got any more on the body? Not just some old tramp?'

'Looks like a bullet hole to the forehead and it wasn't buried, just hidden underneath a pile of old wood. Whole area is completely overgrown.'

'When exactly was it found?'

'Yesterday around midday.'

'And Jarrett's disappeared not long after?'

'What're you thinking?'

'Maybe Jarrett's responsible for that body and has made himself scarce.'

'Who would've told him?'

'This place leaks. That pair over there are known for it,' he said, nodding his head towards two officers sitting at the other side of the canteen.

'It's a bit of a stretch.'

'Well nothing about this case is straightforward is it? Three disappearances, possible links to an old robbery, the whole fake plumber thing?'

'It's more likely he disappeared because of Shirley

Smallwood than because of this new body.'

'Hmm, I don't know.'

'That nose of yours again?'

Maidencoombe turned to Akerman. 'How's the search going?'

'Nothing so far.'

'What about the building sites?'

'We're leaving that until we've wrapped up the house and the yard. They've just finished at Christine's house and nothing significant there. They're at her premises now but apart from Jarrett's car with a wing off there's nothing. Her men said it was just a bump with a bus and the forensic boys aren't contradicting them.'

'We'll end up having to bail them again though we could hold Dennis on the dog murder.'

'Any bets on who's next to disappear?'

'One of *us*, the way things are going.'

14

The Real Thing

Moose said goodbye to Maureen and left the showroom. It was getting dark outside but he walked around the cars in the forecourt to inspect the line-up. He noticed an MG was missing it's radio, and wires hung out over the dashboard. He made a mental note to get it fixed and walked over to the reserved parking spaces. He was surprised to find the door of his Mercedes unlocked and told himself to be more careful. As he got into the driver's seat he noticed an unfamiliar smell, a soapy aftershave mix that he didn't like. 'What the hell is that?' He started the car, left the forecourt and had been driving in the direction of Beckenham for about a mile when he heard movement in the back seat and saw a face appear in the mirror. *Jesus Christ.* He swerved slightly as Jarrett cocked his gun and held it at Moose's neck. 'Keep driving.'

'Who the hell are you?'

'You know who I am.'

'I really don't. What d'you want?'

'I want you to drive to that nice pub near Sevenoaks we met in before.'

'I don't know you.'

'Have another look.'

Moose peered into the mirror. The man had a shaven head, glasses and what looked like a stuck-on moustache. The voice seemed familiar.

'I used to have hair. Keep driving. We were gonna do some jobs together but I got nicked. Was never sure who'd grassed me.'

'Russ?'

'Yeah, Russ.'

'I didn't grass you. I didn't know anything about it.'

'Don't suppose you did. Anyway, here I am. My brother still limps by the way.'

'Russ I'm sorry abou—'

'Don't be. It was the stupid cunt's own fault. That's not why I'm here. Pull over somewhere and let me in the front.'

Moose stopped the car and Jarrett covered the gun with his jacket but kept it pointed at Moose. 'I'm coming in beside you. Don't even think about trying anything, this is loaded.'

Moose looked around, concerned they'd be seen. 'Russ what's this about?'

'Just wait till we get there. Go down the A20 to Farningham and then the back road.'

Moose drove carefully into the Kent countryside and eventually passed through Kemsing to arrive at the Railwayman Inn. The large car park was surrounded by mature trees and although the building was illuminated the parking area had several dark secluded areas.

'Over there, right in the corner. Reverse in so I can see what's going on.'

Moose parked the car. 'Will you stop pointing that gun at me I'm not gonna try anything.'

'I'll stop pointin' it at you when you hand over the money you robbed from Den Hattmann.'

'What are you talking about?'

'Come off it. Den's an idiot but I figured it out soon as I realised Ron Gooch was married to your sister. It was fuckin' obvious, Den's too stupid to see it though. It's my money, sixty of it anyway but I'm having the lot, I'm owed interest.'

'Russ—'

'Don't fuck me about, I know it was you and Ron and don't bother with alibis I'm not messin' about here. Get me the money and I wont kill him.'

Moose looked at him and exhaled. 'OK we robbed Den but we only found eighteen and a half. We—'

'Piss off. Den's looking for eighty cos he lost eighty.'

'We only found eighteen so we split it.'

'You must think I'm fuckin' stupid. There was at least eighty there.'

'Look, we found eighteen and some passports, that was it. We split it and then Ron was turned over by some bent coppers. They took his nine. Then they came to me demanding the rest. *They* were looking for eighty as well.'

'Moose I want all of that money and—'

'Ron was expecting eighty. He wouldn't have done it

for eighteen. We reckoned if there was eighty someone else had got to it first.'

'What? Crapper? That's bollocks. Only an idiot would believe it was him.'

'We finally figured out Christine had probably cleared most of it before we got there. She knew about it, she practically lives there.'

'Fuck off.'

'You hooked up with Christine to get at it but she's cut you out. How'd you know about it anyway? And how come it's yours?'

'It's mine that's all you need to know and—'

'Would you put that gun away for Christ's sake. I'm not gonna have a go.'

Jarrett lowered the gun to his lap but kept hold of it. 'It can't have been Christine.'

'Why not?' Who else could have got it without Den noticing?'

'If she'd taken it she'd 'ave legged it. Anyway she's been nicked again.'

'What'd she do?'

'Crapper's wife has disappeared.'

'What?' Is that why you're in disguise? ... Christ, you're on the run. Did you kill Crapper?'

'It wasn't me. I don't know what happened.'

'So why're you in disguise then?'

'I had something else that had to be done. Nothin' to do with Crapper. I need that money.'

'So does Ron but we haven't got it. It has to be Christine.'

'Can't be.'

'You mean you can't believe you've been had? You were using her but she was using you and she got in first. Where were you on the night?'

'At her place watchin' telly.'

'Just like me and Ron then,' Moose laughed, 'but we're backed up by our wives. Who have you got?'

Jarrett said nothing but continued fingering the safety catch on the gun.

'Why didn't you get in touch when you got out? I've got a couple of jobs at the planning stage.'

'I just wanted to get my money from Den. If I'd got it I was off to Spain. How did *you* know about Den having the money?'

'Ron told me about Den having a load of cash in the house. Ron's stoney at the moment and really needs it. We both thought it would be easy and it was ... until Crapper got arrested then disappeared. Ron was gutted that we only found eighteen but I wasn't surprised at the time. I didn't think Den would have that much but I thought it would help out Ron and see how he performed. I thought he could earn some more working with me.'

'So you think Christine nicked most of it before you got there?'

'Yeah exactly. No-one else had the opportunity.'

'But you've made your blag look like Crapper?'

'Seemed like a clever idea at the time and it might've worked only Crapper got himself nicked that night. What's happened to his wife?'

'I honestly don't know.'

'Could it have been Christine?'

'Fuck knows.'

'Well either Crapper and his missus have run off or they've been done in.'

'They must have known somethin'. I can't see Christine involvin' Crapper by choice, nobody would.'

'Maybe they've robbed Christine and she's caught up with them?'

'I doubt that ... who're the bent coppers anyway?'

'Baslow and M—'

'*Baslow, fuckin' Baslow*. I should've guessed.'

'You know him then?'

'We go back years. He's a fuckin' snake. He turned up at Den's yard offerin' to help find the money for a cut.'

'What did Den say?'

'I dunno, I told Den not to trust him and I left.'

'Was it Baslow arrested him?'

'Don't know.'

Jarrett put the gun away and they relaxed into the friendly discourse they'd been used to in the past.

'What are you gonna do?'

'I need somewhere to stay.'

'You can't stay in South London, too risky. You got wheels?'

'No, had to leave them at Christine's, a wing's off.'

'We could ask Matt. He might be able to put you up for a couple of days. Wait here and I'll go to the pub and phone him.' Moose took the keys from the ignition and opened the door.

'I wouldn't nick anythin' this flash.' said Jarrett.

Moose returned a few minutes later. 'Matt's OK. He's got empty rooms so you can stay for a while. You're booked in as Mr Davidson, Eric. Just go to reception like a normal punter. I'll get a car to you in a day or two. Not a bad disguise by the way, apart from the moustache. You need to grow a real one.'

'It was all I could get. Who was the other copper?'

'Murris, DI Phil Murris ... know'im?'

'Don't think so. How'd they get on to you anyway?'

Moose hesitated. 'It was my own fault. I got a car same as Crappers so if we were seen they'd assume it was him but the bloke that got it for me turned out be be one of Baslow's informers, so he and Murris knew about the plan all along. Just after we did the job they blagged Ron at his yard and then came to the showroom and demanded the rest. Threatened to tell their mates unless I paid up. A higher up owed me a favour so I was able to scare them off but I had to give them four grand as part of the deal. Cost me the other five to pay off my car guy.'

'Will he keep quiet?'

'I think so. He's going back up north.'

'You didn't want to do somethin' a bit more permanent?'

'I did but it was way too risky.'

'Sorry about the gun and so on.'

''It's OK but this whole thing is a mess. You might be better off gettin' to Spain anyway.'

'Can't, I'm skint. Got a few grand hidden at my ex's place but I can't go near it at the moment.'

It doesn't look good you disappearing when Crapper's wife vanishes.'

'It's nothing to do with that.'

'They'll assume it is. Are you gonna tell me how the money is yours?'

Jarrett looked down and exhaled loudly. 'It's from the Rotherhithe wages job, a hundred and twenty grand. I planned it, everything. Worked it all out and brought in Kevin Kanavan, but I got nicked for that Southwark job so Kevin teamed up with Reg Wilson's firm and it went ahead without me. Cake was supposed—'

'Cake?'

'Kevin's nickname. K K, Cake ... get it? Cake was supposed to get half and keep my share for me but he disappeared. I heard he'd gone to Spain.'

'So how did Hattmann get hold of the rest?'

'I think Den was just looking after it until Reg got out.'

'Why him?'

'Den is Reg's half brother but they keep quiet about it.'

'So Hattmann knows about your involvement in the Rotherhithe job?'

'Nah, he hasn't a clue. I think Cake went to Reg without tellin' him it was my plan in the first place.'

'So it looks like Cake just went off with your share?'

'The story about him going to Spain is all from Reg and his firm but I've spoken to everyone in the game and no-one's seen Cake in Spain or London since the job. I think Reg did the dirty on him—'

'But Reg's firm were all collared?'

'Yeah, but they didn't tell the bill about Cake. The regular police don't know he was involved, or me.'

'Any idea who grassed you for the Southwark job?'

'No idea, could have been Cake for all I know. I think there was a bent copper working with 'im.'

'Baslow?'

'He was around but I don't think so. Might have been this other bloke Pilling, Inspector—'

'Pilling, Jesus.'

'You know him?'

'Could Pilling really have been working with Kanavan or Reg Wilson's firm?'

'I don't know what happened. All I do know is someone grassed me up for the Southwark bank job and the only people who knew about it were Cake and some of his mates. How come you know Pilling?'

'He got Baslow off my back, he's a Chief Super now.'

'I fuckin' hate bent coppers, they help you then they screw you.'

'If you still want the money you need to go after Christine when she's released ... if she's released.'

'I want the money, I need it but—'

'How'd you get together with her anyway?'

'Knew her from way back ... years ago. When I got out I made sure I bumped into her, she's not exactly fightin' blokes off.'

Moose grinned. 'As it stands, Den's been robbed and you were helping him threaten Crapper and his missus. They've disappeared and so have you. It doesn't look good.'

'Do you trust Ron?'

'No reason not too. I got the money from the hiding place while he was downstairs so he can't have taken it.'

'Somethin' doesn't add up.'

'According to Ron, Crapper found the money by accident when he was working at Den's house. So he knew about and if Christine got it then most likely she's got rid of him. Anyway … look, I'll take you to Matt's now and we can meet up in a day or two.'

'OK.'

'Hang on, if Den only got sixty from Reg, and the rest of the firm got nothing, where's the other sixty.'

'No idea.'

***

Vince left the Croydon site early and drove home. After checking every room to make absolutely sure his wife was out, he climbed into the attic and retrieved six thousand pounds from a briefcase hidden behind the water tank. He put it in a plastic carrier bag, climbed down and closed up. Then he left the house by the back door and walked cautiously to the front and looked all around. There was no-one in sight so he put the bag and a toolbox into his car and drove off.

He headed north up Bromley Road but after about a mile suddenly turned right into a side street. He stopped and watched. Satisfied that no-one was following, he turned around and continued up the main road turning right onto the South Circular. He drove for about half a mile then turned into the parking area behind a small block of flats and stopped beside a row of lock-up garages. He got out to open one of them, then moved the Maxi inside and closed the up and over door. Then he opened the adjacent door and got into a dark blue Morris Marina. He moved it outside, closed up, then drove out and turned onto the South Circular and continued until he reached Baring Road. From there, he turned right and drove through Bromley towards Westerham. About a mile from the village he pulled into a lay-by and stopped to see what cars passed him. He didn't recognise any of them but he did a u-turn and headed back about a mile before suddenly turning left onto a single track road. He followed the meandering route for about a mile and stopped just short of the main road.

He sat for a few minutes but a tractor approached him from behind and sounded it's horn so he moved onto the main road and drove into the rear car park of The Four Way House. He saw a man's face at an upstairs window and raised his hand. After a few seconds the man returned the gesture. Vince waited in the car until Matt appeared at a doorway and signalled him to come over. He collected the carrier bag from the boot, walked over and noticed the hotelier was wearing gloves.

'I didn't recognise the car.'

'I've still got the old one. I don't want it to be seen going anywhere unusual.'

Matt raised his hands in mock surrender. 'You don't need to explain, I understand. It's through here,' he said, leading Vince down a long narrow corridor with a very low ceiling. At the end he took Vince through an old oak panelled door into a tiny office with a small window overlooking the car park and woodland at the side of the hotel. Matt seated himself behind his desk and pointed to the other chair. Vince sat down. Matt unlocked a drawer on his desk and handed him a large brown envelope. 'Have a look I think you'll be impressed.'

Vince opened the envelope and took out the

passports. 'Blimey,' he held them up to the light, 'well they fool me.'

'That's the point, they don't need to fool anyone because they're real.'

'What do you mean?'

'The names are real. They're actual people who've never had a passport. So although we've used *your* photos, they *are* the real thing. I told you quality costs but as you can see they're worth it. There's more in the envelope.'

'More?'

'Empty it out.'

Vince shook the envelope and two driving licenses fell out.

'They're a bonus, a freebie – no charge. They could be useful.' He reached into the drawer again and handed Vince a document wallet. That's background information about the people you're impersonating. You need to memorise it all.'

Vince flicked through the passports and studied the photographs and the text. 'These are perfect.'

'I aim to please.'

Vince reached into the carrier bag and handed over the money. 'Another six, as agreed.'

'When're you off?'

'Not soon, it's all about timing. I need to wait a while. A few things haven't gone quite to plan.'

'They rarely do Vince. Anyway, I've got a funeral reception upstairs needing to be fed and watered, so I need to get back to work.'

They shook hands and Vince returned to his car. He

got in and looked again at the passports. 'Unbelievable. She looks different in black and white.'

On the way back home he stopped in Orpington at a telephone box. He started to dial Julie Hattmann's number but looked at his watch and changed his mind. He got back into the car and drove towards the lock-ups. As before, he made a couple of last minute turns to see if anyone was following but nobody was. He swapped cars again and drove home in the Maxi.

***

The phone rang at Maidencoombe's desk and he picked it up.

'Ralph, you and Vic come to my office in ten minutes and update me on the Hattmanns and the Smallwood pair.'

Sandwell stopped to talk with Maidencoombe in the corridor before going in. 'What are we gonna tell him?'

'As little as possible without being obvious.'

'He'll sniff us out.'

'Maybe, but he's hiding stuff himself. Maybe *we'll* sniff *him* out.'

They walked in. Baslow was standing at the window looking out and turned round as they entered. 'Sit down. So, tell me what's happened ... or have you just been sitting on your hands?'

'We've—'

'Before you start DI Phil Murris here has been seconded from the Regional Crime Squad. He'll be working under me.'

Astonished, Maidencoombe and Sandwell turned round to see Murris standing almost hidden behind the door.

'Ralph, Vic.'

Sandwell put his hand out to shake but Murris ignored the offer and sat down.

Maidencoombe started to talk. 'Both Smallwoods have disappeared. We don't know the circumstances surrounding mister but it's likely missus has been taken against her will. The Hattmann siblings have been threatening to kill them and with Christine being spotted at the house on the night we think missus vanished, it looks pretty straightforward.'

Murris stood up. 'Well I don't think anything about this is straightforward. You two have been chasing shadows from the start. Where's the money? The eighty thousand.'

'Well either Christine or Jarrett has it.'

'Jarrett?'

'Jarrett's been living with Christine Hattmann since he got out but she was obviously surprised when I told her he'd disappeared. We think Christine is the inside man. She's setup the whole thing and got Jarrett and others to do the robbery. She's acted her part on the night and she's told Dennis that Smallwood did it. Unless we find the money at Christine's it's likely Jarrett's gone off with it.'

'So why have both Smallwoods disappeared?'

'They were trying to make it look like the Smallwoods have run off with the cash to divert attention from themselves.'

'And you think they're dead?'

'It's possible.'

'They've actually planned two murders as well as the blag?'

'Well—'

'Two murders doesn't sound planned to me. More like improvisation as things didn't work out. I take it they're both no comment?'

'Pretty much. We've told Dennis we think his sister's robbed him but so far he doesn't seem to believe us.'

'And we've told Christine we think Jarrett's gone off with the money,' said Sandwell.

'So what's your plan moving forward?'

'We'll keep working them in the hope that one of them cracks and we're searching high and low for Jarrett, but if he has taken the money I doubt we'll find it.'

'What you don't have is any hard evidence that either of the Hattmanns have abducted or killed the Smallwoods.'

'But—'

'You only have Julie Hattmann's word that eighty thousand was stolen.'

'Why would she lie? She could have said nothing, denied there was a robbery.'

Baslow sat down and pointed at Maidencoombe. 'Keep up with the searches but if nothing turns up soon, bail Christine Hattmann.'

'Guv—'

'Bail her and watch her. In fact you bail her and we'll watch her. Phil will look for Christine and Jarrett. You two keep looking for the Smallwoods.'

'Where? The only leads we have are the Hattmanns.'

'Well you haven't got much from them so far—'

'Guv—'

Baslow raised his hand 'You heard what I said.'

Maidencoombe and Sandwell left the room and walked towards the canteen.

'Why the hell is Murris involved?'

'Something dodgy with Baslow.'

'Does he know something we don't?'

'Probably, though I thought he'd muscle in at some point. They're after the money and they must reckon Christine has it. Notice he didn't ask much about Jarrett?'

'I did. Could they be in contact?'

'No, I think they're hoping Christine will lead them to Jarrett or the money.'

They entered the canteen and walked over to Akerman at the corner table.

'We'll join you. I wanted to ask you about the searches.'

'Nothing so far, anywhere. We've been to all the building sites we can identify. They're all just mud and bricks and scaffolding. We've searched all the structures on site and questioned the men again, but they couldn't tell us anything useful. If you wanted to hide something on a site it wouldn't be difficult, there could be anything under the ground.'

'What about family?'

'The Hattmanns don't have much and what they *do* have, won't talk.'

'And the Smallwoods?'

'Jim has a brother, they haven't spoken for years, that's it on his side. But on Shirley's side there's a mum and two sisters and various others. That's the funny thing. You'd think they'd be frantic with worry but they all seem a bit too relaxed. They don't care about Jim, think Shirley should have left him years ago.'

'Their close relative has been abducted and they're not too bothered?'

'Usually they're shocked, sometimes they feint. Especially the mums, but this one talked to me as if it was *my* daughter that had disappeared.'

'Well this time my nose really is twitching. Get some more men together and turn those rellys upside down. Houses, sheds, attics, workplaces, the lot.'

'You think we're being played?'

'Maybe.'

'Why?'

'Fear of the Hattmanns, meeting up with her husband, running off with the money, who knows.

'If she staged the whole thing surely she'd have left the anorak as well as the handbag?'

'If she'd walked out of her house in something unfamiliar then the locals might have noticed but in her old coat maybe not.'

'And the call to Christine?'

'That's the most suspicious thing. Tells Christine she knows where the money is and suggests a deal. Christine, with an eye to the main chance, falls for it and comes round without telling her brother and walks right into a trap.'

'Bloody well organised. We've contacted everyone in her address book and no-one's admitting to seeing her.'

'Get some photos printed and show them around the area. Shops, banks, buses, trains etcetera. And do another search of her house, see if anything's missing, a suitcase for example.'

'What about her husband, Crapper Jim?'

'She could have have met up with him.'

'Hard to believe that plumber could organise anything.'

'The husband probably not but I'm beginning to think Shirley's a lot smarter than we thought.'

15

Biggin Hill

'What d'ya think?'

Murris sat down and turned to Baslow. 'They're gonna find the cash before we do, if we're not careful.'

'Well we don't know what's happened to Jarrett so until he turns up we'll just have to squeeze Christine Hattmann. She's a tough old bird so we'll need to go in heavy, she won't spill easily.'

'Where d'you want to do it?'

'Arelton woods, that place near Edenbridge?'

'Hmm, there's usually walkers about. What about those old Nissen Huts near Biggin Hill, the ones with the big oil tanks. It's closer and it's a dump. Nobody goes there.'

'If they're still standing. Let's check it out now and get prepared.'

'Blowtorches?'

'Yeah, and some petrol.'

***

Moose sat at his desk and answered a call. He listened for a couple of minutes but said nothing then he replaced the handset and immediately phoned his brother-in-law. 'Ron, I just heard, Hattmann's sister's being bailed.'

'Who told you?'

'Never mind. Any chance you could follow her?'

'Wot? Now?'

'Well she might go home, more likely she'll go to her workshop.'

'I'm tied up at the moment but I'll go as soon as I can. What d'ya think's gonna happen?'

'Dunno but something's up. She was under arrest for Crapper's wife and all of a sudden she's out. Don't go in the Jag, use something that won't be noticed. Have you got a camera?'

'Yeah, it's rubbish though.'

'Just take it anyway, and a pen and paper. Make notes of anything or anyone you see.'

Ron parked his van about a hundred yards from Christine's premises and watched cars going in and out. At four-thirty, men started leaving the building as the roller shutter lowered and the lights went out. A man came out of a side door and locked up. Ron watched for another twenty minutes and was just about to leave when an old Morris Marina parked beside the entrance. Two men got out, looked around and went to the side door. The younger thinner one inserted a key and seemed to have some trouble unlocking it but eventually it opened and the older man went back to the car. Ron took several photographs. Two minutes later the roller shutter opened and as soon as there was enough clearance the Marina reversed inside and the shutter came down again. Ron sat still and watched. After another ten minutes, a taxi appeared and he watched Christine Hattmann get out and enter the premises by the side door. Lights came on but nothing else happened so he got out of the van and walked the short distance to a telephone kiosk.

'Moose, I'm watching Christine's workshop. About half an hour ago, her men went home then two blokes in a Marina opened it up and reversed inside. Ten minutes later Christine arrived in a taxi and went in the side door.'

'Describe the men.'

'Raincoats. Looked like coppers. One in his fifties maybe, heavy. The other one younger and skinnier.'

'Sounds like Baslow and Murris to me. The ones that robbed you and came after me.'

'What d'ya think I should do?'

'Just watch. If Christine leaves, follow her ... I dunno, play it by ear, something's going on.'

Ron returned to the van. After about twenty minutes the shutter opened and the Marina moved out and stopped. The shutter lowered again and the lights went off. The older man came out of the side door, pulled it shut and locked it, then he went to the Marina and got in the passenger side. The car turned left driving in the direction of Beckenham and Ron ducked as it passed him. He watched in his mirror for a few seconds then quickly turned the van around and followed it, staying about a hundred yards behind.

The Marina passed through West Wickham and used the minor road towards Biggin Hill but turned off suddenly up a narrow lane before reaching the town. Ron decided it was too risky to follow them up the lane so he drove past and managed to park at the entrance to a field. He got out and crossed the road. In the distance he could see the outline of old Nissen Huts and large storage tanks. 'I know this place.' He walked back to the lane and walked carefully towards the huts keeping close to the hedge and stopped when he reached the old perimeter fence.

The gates at the entrance were open and in very poor condition but the fence although rusty was largely intact. There was no obvious other way in except through the gateway, so he moved forward slowly, ducking down so as not to be any higher than the stacks of pallets and oil drums scattered around the site. He reached the smaller hut and saw the Marina parked outside the larger one. He could see movement inside the car but couldn't make out what was happening.

After about ten minutes the two men got out of the car, took off their coats and placed them carefully on the back seat. Murris pulled out a holdall and picked out two boiler suits and two pairs of boots. He handed one set to Baslow, then they opened the rear doors and each man sat down to pull a boiler suit over existing clothing and change footwear.

'Will we bother with masks?'

'Well she didn't see us at the shop but ... she'll figure out we're coppers.'

'We don't know how this is going to end. Let's be safe.'

They put on balaclavas and gloves then Murris went in the small side door of the hut and opened the main doors. Baslow moved the car inside the hut and Murris closed the doors behind him. They shone their torches around and Murris checked the office room at the rear and looked at the inspection pit that ran the length of the building on the left. Two inches of oily water lay on the bottom and pieces of stained and dented wood lay at intervals along one side. Baslow checked the other side doors and asked Murris to help him move some corrugated roofing sheets to block the windows, but they only had enough to cover the windows at the front.

Both men went back out the main door and looked outside. Satisfied there was no one around they went to the car and Baslow opened a rear door and lifted out another holdall. He pulled out a gas lantern, lit it and hung it on a nail. Then he went back to the car and lifted out a jerry-can from the rear footwell placing it down on the floor a few yards away.

Back at the car, Murris pointed his revolver as Baslow opened the boot. Inside, Christine Hattmann lay on her side, hands behind her, tied with rope. She moved frantically and moaned.

'We're gonna pull you out of the boot. Don't struggle, there's a gun at your face.'

They grabbed her legs and lifted them over the rim. Then they pulled her upright by her shoulders.

'I'm gonna take the hood off, don't try anything.'

Baslow untied the the canvas sack and pulled it from her head. Her face was smeared with blood and her right eye was badly swollen. Murris pulled the tape from her mouth in a sudden rapid jerk. She yelped. He prodded her with the gun. Scream if you want, we're miles from anything.'

'All you had to do was hand over the cash and we'd have left you alone.'

'I ain't got the money, I told you already, Russ got it ... the coppers told me.'

'Well that's what they think but we know Russ is still looking for it. Not surprising, it is sort of his money in a sense ... It's from the Rotherhithe wages snatch ... Yeah, that's right, we know about Reg being Den's brother. Just out of interest what did you do with Crapper and his wife?'

'I didn't do nothing', didn't touch 'em.'

'But you went to her house the day she disappeared?'

'Wasn't in, I just went home.'

'Well we don't really care, we just want the money.'

'I fuckin' told you I ain't got—'

Murris slammed the butt of his revolver across her face. She shouted out and more blood poured down her face.

'Walk over there.'

She turned and walked slowly in the dim light to the edge of the inspection pit.

'Lie down.'

She hesitated.'

'I said lie down.'

'Wot? In there?'

'At the edge.'

She lowered herself slowly to her knees and then fell on to her front and Murris tied her legs together with a length of chain and a padlock.

'If you don't talk you know where this is going Christine.' Murris cocked his gun.

She started shaking.

'Don't pee yourself, I really hate that.'

'I ain't got the money ... honest.'

'Honest? ... huh ... we won't kill you right away, we're gonna warm you up a bit first.'

Murris went to the holdall and took out a blowtorch. He tried to light it with matches but the gas kept blowing out the flame. Baslow gave him his lighter and after several attempts it fired up. Christine turned her head to look at them. 'You cunts, I ain't got it.' Tears formed in her eyes.

'Never thought I'd see a bruiser like you getting tearful. It's usually *you* doing this sort of thing to other people. Not so tough now eh?'

'Please don't, please, plea—'

'Bet that's what that girl in Peckham was saying when you were kicking her half to death.'

She wriggled and writhed and managed to turn herself on to her back to look up at the men. 'Please don't, please I'll do anything.'

'Anything? ... Not with *you* love.'

'Just tell us where the money is and we'll let you go.' Murris knelt down, pulled up one of her trouser legs and briefly held the blowtorch at her ankle. She screamed. 'It was robbed, it's gone. I don't know who took it.'

'You told your brother's wife it was Smallwood.'

'Thought it was.'

'You came up with that story to divert everyone away from yourself and Russ. But the thing is, Crapper Jim couldn't get himself out of a paper bag, never mind carry out a robbery.'

Murris put down the blowtorch and picked up the jerry-can. He flipped open the cover and sprinkled a capfull on her chest. She wriggled furiously and managed to sit up. He pulled out matches and started lighting them and throwing them at her. The third one ignited the petrol but she fell onto her front and managed to extinguish the flames.

'Well done. But it won't be so easy when I've poured a gallon over you.'

She tried to move away from the side of the pit but Baslow hit her on the arms with a small crowbar.

Outside, Ron watched the larger hut but couldn't see or hear anything so he crept around the side where he spotted a feint glow from the windows. He stopped and listened. He could hear talking but couldn't make out what was being said. He moved closer to the Marina and tried to memorise the registration number but he was looking at an angle and couldn't be certain. 'BNC 34L?'

Inside, Murris splashed some petrol on Christine's face and started flicking the lighter. 'There's only a little on you, it won't kill you but it will scar you a bit.'

'Are you gonna tell us or do you actually want to fry?'

'Ya stupid cunts, don't know where it is, I'd tell you.'

Murris picked up the jerry-can and emptied half the contents over her. She tried to roll away but Baslow hit her on the legs. 'Stay still, we're not messing around any long—'

Outside, as Ron moved forward intending to look in the window, he dislodged a piece of wood causing a stack of empty oil drums to wobble and one of them to fall over making a loud clattering noise as it tumbled over the other drums. He ran quickly back towards the gate and hid behind a stack of pallets.

Inside, both men looked towards the entrance.

'There's someone out there.'

Baslow put the crowbar down quietly and held his gun at Christine's face. Murris ran to the side window but couldn't see anything. He went to the side door, opened it slightly and listened. Hearing nothing, he left the hut and went outside. There was just enough light to walk about without a torch. He moved slowly alongside the hut to the front and stopped. Everything looked the same except that one drum had rolled across the path, and several others stacked precariously on top of each other looked as if they might do the same. He couldn't see or hear anything else, so he walked quietly around the two huts before returning to Baslow. 'Can't see anything. A lot of wobbly oil drums out there, looks as if one of them fell over.'

'Sure?'

'There's no car or anything but it might have been a fox. I'm gonna walk around the fuel tanks, kill that light.'

As Baslow went over to the lantern, Christine started to wriggle and shout so he went back to her and held the crowbar to her face. 'Fucking shut up.' He pulled her up by the shoulder and rolled her into the inspection pit. She landed in the shallow water with a heavy thump, hitting her head on an empty tool box. 'Stay quiet or I'll shoot you.' As he stepped back he knocked over the jerry-can and the rest of the petrol started to pour out, so he kicked it into the pit beside Christine.

Outside, Murris switched on his torch and slowly swept the beam across the yard. He went over to the two large oil tanks and walked around them while Ron stayed frozen to the spot and watched him.

Inside the hut, Baslow went over to the lantern and lifted it off the nail but as he turned around he didn't notice a loose piece of metal pipe lying across his path. He stood on it and found himself falling forward as his legs went out from under him. The lantern flew out of his hand and into the inspection pit, igniting the petrol that now floated on the water. The flames engulfed the prisoner and she thrashed about furiously and screamed for help. Baslow picked himself up and ran to the side of the pit but couldn't get near her because of the heat.

Coughing as the smoke increased, he had to stand back watching the outline of Christine flailing about in the flames. He turned away and managed to recover enough to get to one of the windows where he grabbed a corrugated sheet. He tried to throw it over her, but it struck her on the side of the head and clattered down on the other side of the pit.

Murris came back into the hut. '*Jesus*, what's going on?'

'Open the big doors quickly.'

Murris wrenched the heavy doors open and Baslow went to the car and quickly reversed outside. They both stood at the entrance and watched.

'Is there anyone out there?'

'No. What happened?'

'I pushed her into the pit and I tripped with the gas lamp, it set her on fire.'

'*Christ*, is she still alive?'

'Don't know, couldn't get near her.'

They waited until the flames had died down and the smoke had almost cleared, then covered their mouths with bits of rag and went back in. As they moved closer to the inspection pit they were almost overwhelmed by the smell of burning flesh and smouldering clothing. They cautiously looked over the side and saw Christine lying motionless in a fetal position. They stood looking at her for a few minutes, almost paralysed.

'She's fucking dead.'

'What now?'

'Christ, I don't know.'

'We have to clear up our gear and get everything into the car. We need to get out of here.'

'What about her?'

'There's nothing we can do.'

'We could take her to the allotment, bury her there.'

'Too risky. We don't want that in the car. If we leave

her it could be months before she's found and everyone will assume it was Jarrett. That's if she can even be identified, this is Bromley's patch, they might not link it.'

'Someone's bound to report her miss—'

Suddenly Christine moaned and her legs jerked violently. The men jumped back and looked at each other.

'Jesus.'

They moved back to the pit and peered in. Murris shone his torch at her head. Christine moaned again and moved slightly.

Murris exhaled. 'What are we gonna do?'

'Can't do anything, we can't take her to a hospital.'

'Finish her off?'

'I'm not doing it. Do you want to?'

Murris said nothing.

'She's never gonna survive. Let's just clear up and get out. Could be ages before she's found.'

What if she does survive and talks?'

'She hasn't seen us.'

'She could describe us, she's seen the car.'

'I don't know, I don't know what to do.'

The shock sinking in, the two bent detectives stood together awkwardly for a minute then went back to the car and sat inside.

'Christ what a mess. If she's hidden the money we're not gonna find it now. We didn't want to kill her.'

'We knew it might happen. She won't live long and she'd have done the same to us, so don't feel sorry for her.'

'I don't, but she could still get us collared.'

'Let's just clear up and go.'

They both scanned the hut with torches and removed everything incriminating.

'Leave the suits and boots until we're back in the car.'

They left the building. Murris closed the main doors and they both got in the car.

'What about the gas lamp and the chain and padlock?' said Baslow.

'I'll go back inside and get the lamp but I'm not touching her.'

'Are you sure the chain can't be traced to you?'

'I didn't buy it, I found it. Could be anyone's.' He went back inside and spotted the smashed lantern inside the pit. He lay down at the side but couldn't reach so he looked around and found a metal pole. He managed to insert it under the hoop on the lamp and lifted it up. It slid towards him. The outer glass shield had smashed and the element was charred and damaged. It was still warm.

After closing the doors he returned to the car and put the lamp into a holdall and got in. Baslow started the engine and headed out of the gateway using only sidelights. 'What about tyre treads? They'll spot them.'

'I've got a spare set of wheels, I'll swap them over and get rid of this lot.'

Baslow stopped the car just outside the gates and they both removed their boiler suits and put ordinary shoes back on.

Outside, Ron watched and kept repeating the registration

number as the car went out of sight. BNC34L, BNC 34L. He waited a few more minutes before moving. Continuing to look around, he made his way cautiously to the hut. He used his torch and walked around the building trying to look in the windows. He couldn't see anything but became aware of a burning smell. He thought about going inside but hesitated, reluctant to find something he'd rather not. He looked around and picked up a piece of rusty iron bar that was lying beside the oil drums. Then he went to the side door and pulled at it carefully. It scraped across the threshold noisily and he only opened it just enough to look inside. He shone his torch around but still couldn't see anything.

The acrid burning smell was much stronger. 'As if someone's put a carpet on a bonfire' he thought. He ignored the inspection pit and went instead to the office room at the rear but found it empty apart from an old desk. He came back out and shone his torch up at the roof. He expected to see pigeons but only saw rusty light fittings and a few small holes where bolts were missing. He looked behind the sheets of corrugated iron that had been propped up at the windows but finding nothing he was just about to leave when he was startled by a moaning sound to his left.

He spun round with the iron bar raised. Waving the torch around he still couldn't see anything so he moved slowly towards the inspection pit and peered in. He only saw water at first but as he moved his gaze to the other end he saw what looked like a bundle of blankets. The bundle groaned and moved slightly as he walked slowly towards it.

Inching closer, he saw the charred clothes and burned flesh but it took him some time to recognise the shape. 'Jesus Christ, Jesus fucking Christ.'

It wasn't obviously female but he realised it had to be Christine Hattmann. He jumped over the pit to the other side and shone his torch at the blackened head. He could see her scalp where the hair had been burned off and some bone was visible in amongst red exposed flesh. He started to feel sick. Her tongue was hanging out and he could hear quiet laboured breathing. Her head lay on it's side partially submerged in the shallow water and instead of an eye there was only a charred and gooey socket. Her clothes were still smouldering but not alight and one leg was exposed and inflamed. She moved slightly, coughed and inhaled some of the water. Then she convulsed and coughed again and went still. 'What am I gonna do?' He kept looking and thought she had stopped breathing but couldn't be sure. He walked over to the main doors then went back to the side door and walked out. He looked around but couldn't see or hear anything so he went back to the inspection pit. He watched closely, shining his torch at her mouth, then he crossed over to the other side and looked again. She didn't move. He got down on his knees and listened. Nothing. He stood up and watched for a few more minutes.

Certain now, that she was dead, he shook his head and left the building by the side entrance. He closed up and moved the fallen barrel to the side of the path. Then he walked out of the gateway back to his van and drove straight back to his yard. He parked inside one of his sheds and threw a tarpaulin over the van, then he went into his office to phone Moustrianos' showroom. It was nearly eight o'clock and he didn't really expect anyone to be there so he was surprised when Moose answered after a couple of rings.

'Moose it's me. I followed them. We need to talk now, urgent.'

'Can't, I'm with someone. Where are you?'

'At the yard.'

'I'll come over, half an hour.'

16

Disappearance

Moose skidded to a halt and left the car quickly, slamming the door behind him. He burst into the office and Gooch stood up. 'Want a drink?'

'Do I need one?'

'You will once I've told you what's happened ... whisky?'

Moose nodded and sat down. Ron handed him the drink.

'So tell me.'

'Christine Hattmann is dead.'

'Those coppers?'

'Yeah.'

'What'd they do.'

Moose sat with his elbows on the table and his hands clasped together at his chin as Ron described what he'd seen.

'You're absolutely certain she's dead?'

'She looked like a barbecue. She was still alive when I

got there but her face was in the water and she inhaled some of it. Then she coughed and went still. Watched her for quite a while but she didn't move. I'm pretty sure she'd stopped breathing.'

'So we don't know what she told them, if anything.'

'They must've thought she had the money.'

'And Den is still inside.'

'What about Jarrett? Has he turned up?'

'He was waiting for me in my car.'

'Wot?!'

'He knows we robbed Den.'

'How?'

'He realised you're my brother-in-law that's how.'

'So wha—'

'The money, the eighty grand. It's his from the Rotherhithe wages blag. He set it all up but he was nabbed for another job before the raid. Russ never got his share. He reckons Reg Wilson gave the money to Den, they're half brothers.'

'I didn't know that.'

'Me neither 'til Russ told me.'

'So what's he gonna do?'

'He's lying low at the moment.'

'Could he be working with the bent coppers?'

'No.'

'D'ya think they planned to kill her?'

'Unlikely. If it was planned they wouldn't have left the body there. Sounds like they slipped up and went too far. Probably panicked when you disturbed them. It does mean we've got something on them, could be useful. Did you get any pictures?'

'A few at her premises. What do we do now?'

'Well first off, were you wearing those shoes at the depot?'

'Yeah.'

'Well get them off now and burn them. Your footprints are all over that place ... blokes have been convicted on that sort of evidence. Also your van, how far away were you parked?'

'About four hundred yards beside a field entrance. But it was on the main road, not up the lane to the depot.'

'Where is it now?'

'Under a tarp in one of my sheds.' He pointed outside. 'They might not know it's Christine even if they find her.'

'They'll figure it out eventually. I can see you're shaking a bit. Sure you're OK?'

'Wish I hadn't followed them.'

'Well you did. You couldn't know what was gonna happen. I didn't expect that but it makes me wonder if they've done the same to Crapper and his wife.'

A car pulled into the yard.

'You expecting someone.'

'Definitely not.'

They both stood up. Moose grabbed a shovel and Ron picked up a wrench. They stood waiting, one on each side of the entrance. The door flew open and Ron's wife Eleni breezed in. 'Thought I might find you two here. Up to more schemes?'

'What're you doin' here?'

'What are *you two* doing here and don't come all innocent. I'm fed up with all this and if you want me to alibi you, you'd better tell me exactly what's going on. I know you robbed Den Hattmann so what are you up to now? Come on, out with it.'

'El—'

She glared at her brother and he went quiet. Ron hung his head.

'What's happened now? Something else? Is it something to do with Den?'

Moose put his hand up. 'It's better that you don't know.'

'So you robbed him, you never told me how much, what happened?'

'There wasn't as much as we expected, only eighteen so we split it fifty fifty but I was robbed here a few days later by two bent coppers.'

'Were you robbed as well?'

'They came to the showroom and tried to blackmail me. I had to pay them off.'

'How much were you expecting?'

'Eighty at least.'

'From Den Hattmann? That's ridiculous and what's happened to Crapper?'

Moose answered. 'We can't figure it out, we don't know.'

'Really?' She looked at Ron. 'Funny that he vanished the same day you and Vince were out running in the middle of the night.'

Moose looked at Ron.

'That's right. He came in at four in the morning wearing a track suit, said he'd been drinking here with Vince but he was sober. Vince told Steph the same story

... yeah, we do speak occasion—'

Moose stood up. 'What day was this?'

'It was a Saturday and I knew he was lying, up to something.'

'What were you doing with Vince?'

Ron avoided his gaze and said nothing. He poured himself another drink then he looked at each in turn and put his hand over his mouth. He couldn't speak.

'Ron, what happened? What was Vince doing here?'

Ron's hand started to shake and he lowered his head almost touching the desk. He mumbled 'Crapper's dead.'

'What? We can't hear you.'

'Crapper's dead.'

'How d'ya know? What happened?'

'He died here. It was an accident.'

Eleni sat back in her chair. 'An accident?'

'He came here. Me and Vince were looking at some new work, some plans. Crapper thought me and Vince had robbed Den and he wanted a share. Said Den was after him but he knew it was us. We pushed him out the door but he locked us in and tried to set fire to the place. We broke the door down. There was a struggle outside and I pushed him and he hit his head on the digger. He just died in front of us. I'm sorry, didn't want you to know 'bout this.'

Eleni stood up and started hitting her brother. 'You stupid, stupid ... you and your blags. We're all gonna end up inside.'

Moose grabbed her arms and forced her back to her chair. She sobbed and tried to wipe away tears with her scarf.

'I don't believe this, why didn't you tell me? And what did Vince do?'

'We didn't know what to do. Wasn't as if we had a plan.'

'Wait a minute, does Vince know it was us that robbed Den?'

'Yeah, he figured it out.'

'How?'

'He was with Den that night and he knew Crapper was in the nick so he just knew.'

'Could have been anyone. How could he possibly know it was us?'

'We'd talked about it a while ago, robbin' Den.'

'For fuck's sake, you fucking idiot. What happened to Crapper? The body?'

'We buried it behind Bell Green gasworks on Den's piece of ground.'

'And the car, you drove it to Newhaven?'

'Yeah.'

Eleni lifted her head. 'You could have gone to the police if Jim had tried to kill you.'

'I'd just been robbed by the police. I didn't know what to do. Newhaven was Vince's idea.'

Nobody spoke for a couple of minutes.

Moose sat down again. 'Will you tell her or will I?'

Ron looked up and shook his head.

'She's gonna find out eventually and we need alibis.'

'What now? What is it?'

'Christine Hattmann's dead.'

'Christine's dead? Did you two kill her?'

'What? No, it was those bent coppers, the ones that robbed Ron and tried to blackmail me.'

'They took her from the workshop an—'

'It's better you don't know the details.'

'What about Shirley? Is she dead too?'

'We don't know what's happened to her.'

'Why'd they kill Christine?'

'Probably trying to get the rest of the money.'

'But you got it.'

'There was probably eighty at the start but we think Christine got to it first and cleared out most of it before we got there.'

'She's robbed her own brother?'

'Looks like it.'

'Where did Den Hattmann get eighty grand?'

'From a blag years ago, a wages snatch in Rotherhithe. His half brother was on the job but got nicked. We think he gave his share to Den to look after.'

'Will the bent coppers come back for you two?'

'I don't think so but if they do, we know about them killing Christine so that should give us a bit of protection.'

'Why'd you involve Ron? He's a builder not a robber.'

'Ron came to me with the plan cos he's desperate for cash. I went along with it to help him out. He needed the money.'

She looked at Ron. 'Why? We're OK.'

'Ron sat up and stiffened. 'We're not OK at all. I'm up to my ears in loans and the bank's after me.'

'But why?'

'The business makes money but you spend too much. Way too much.'

She started to sob. 'You should've said.'

Ron stood up, his voice rising. 'I've been saying for years. You don't fuckin' listen. I did this for you.'

Moose pointed at him, 'Ron, Ron, sit down. You lied to me about Crapper. How do I know you aren't lying about his wife? How do I know you aren't lying about Christine?

'I don't know anything about Shirley, I ain't been near her and she ain't been here.'

Moose raised his eyebrows.

'I'm serious. I ain't got a clue what happened to her. Maybe she just legged it.'

'With the money?'

'I dunno.'

'What did she know?'

Ron shrugged and Eleni wiped her eyes. 'Maybe those coppers killed her as well.'

'It was Crapper told me about the cash so he probably told Shirley. Maybe Christine killed Shirley, she was arrested for it.'

'But they let her go. It would have been Baslow's call.'

'Den is still being held for Crapper and Shirley. With a bit of luck that'll stick and we won't get dragged in.'

'If those coppers didn't get the money they'll keep looking. We're gonna have to keep our heads down, get our alibis straight and you especially need one for the last few hours.'

***

'We've got a result on that body at Hither Green.'

Maidencoombe looked up.

'Dental records say that it's Kevin Kanavan known as "Cake" to his associates. Career villain who disappeared in seventy four. His girlfriend made a fuss at the time.'

'So there is a missing person report?'

'Yes. A lot of checks were made and his dental records were looked at when a body was found a few weeks later but it wasn't him ... completely unrelated. Then intelligence reports said that he'd simply gone off to Spain so nothing else was done after that.'

'Did Baslow or Murris do any of the reports?'

'No but Chief Superintendent Pilling was responsible for some of them. He was Chief Inspector Pilling then.'

'Anything on the gun?'

'They've got the bullet but no matches so far.'

'No obvious connection to our current problem then?'

'Not really.'

The phone rang and Maidencoombe answered. 'What? ... I don't believe this. OK, make him wait, I'm sending Vic down.' He shook his head. 'You're never gonna believe this. Christine Hattmann's foreman has just turned up at the front desk and reported her missing. Get down there and help John.'

'So what's the story?'

'Her foreman, Wilf, got a phone call from her to say she'd been released and would be in after closing on

Thursday, to do the wages. Nothing unusual about that, she leaves them in the safe for Wilf and the men are paid on Friday. When Wilf came in the next day the safe was locked but no wages inside so he phoned her at home several times but no answer. He tried her brother's house but Julie Hattmann hadn't seen her, thought she was still in the nick. Anyway, Wilf went round to Christine's house and no one in but he could see unopened mail on the floor through the glass door. Also said that a desk had been moved and a wall clock smashed in her office ... and the roller shutter at the workshop hadn't been closed properly. It has to be pushed or pulled somehow from the inside to lock up properly. Says he didn't leave it like that and he's certain Christine wouldn't either. *He* thinks something bad's happened.'

'So we've got a tussle of some sort and another missing person, Christ.'

'Do we tell upstairs?'

'We'll have to, but sit down for a few minutes. Baslow said he and Murris were going to arrange obs on Christine. Do you know if that happened?'

'Don't know. You don't want to ask him?'

'I don't know how to play it ... shut the door. Is this just a co-incidence? Baslow orders me to release her and almost at once she goes missing?'

'If she's got her brother's money maybe she's just run off with it, she could be in Spain by now with all the other villains.'

'Then why the mess, the shutter and so on?'

'In a hurry, clearing stuff before she went?'

'Come on Vic, it stinks. If she'd planned it she'd have done the wages and maybe left a note for her foreman. Could have been another week before anyone reported her missing, giving her plenty of time to make a good escape.'

'Maybe she knew Baslow was going to watch her so she's been in a rush to get in and out.'

'And the smashed clock? No. Something's happened at that workshop. The foreman's right.'

'Maybe Jarrett's been waiting for her?'

'That's a strong possibility, he'd know how to get in.'

'So, we've got four people missing. Jim Smallwood and Jarrett have just vanished without a trace but with the two women there's evidence suggesting a fight or a struggle. Eighty thousand has been taken although the owner of the money won't say anything.'

'To simplify, Hattmann has a lot of cash, probably from the Rotherhithe wages snatch and his sister Christine knows about it and gets Jarrett to rob him. The Smallwoods get mixed up in it somehow—'

'And Jarrett and Christine fall out.'

'Something doesn't quite fit. I think if Jarrett wanted to get rid of Christine he'd have dealt with her before he vanished.'

'Hmm.'

'He would have been taking a much bigger risk coming back.'

'I assumed he vanished in the first place because of the Smallwoods.'

'*I* thought it might have been because of that body at Hither Green.'

'Could just be a co-incidence?'

'Looks suspicious to me'

'I don't think there's anything suspicious about the body being found, just a load of workmen clearing some ground.'

'Jarrett's car is still at the bodyshop with a wing off.'

'He'll be in something else by now.'

'OK, I'll present it to Baslow as Jarrett connected to body at Hither Green and also most likely connected to Christine Hattmann's disappearance.'

'But you're not really sure?'

'No I'm not, but we have to give him something and I want to see how he reacts, what he tells us to do.'

'You really think he's bent? Involved in this whole thing?'

'I'm not sure about involved at the start but he and Murris are opportunists. They're after that cash.'

'You think they'd go as far as abduction, even murder?'

'Maybe not, but I think they might help someone else, or cover up for them for a cut.'

'If you're wrong and this gets out your career is over, mine too by association.'

'I've only got nine months to go and no-one's going to promote me now.'

'I've got ten years ahead of me. I'm not sur—'

'We keep it to ourselves, put nothing in the official paperwork here at the nick. Keep all the information at home.'

Sandwell stood up.

'Let's go upstairs now, See if we can catch him on the

hop, unprepared.'

Baslow looked up from his desk. 'I hope you two have got something good?'

'Christine Hattmann's vanished. Her men were expecting her to do the wages but she didn't turn up at the workshop and there's evidence of a struggle.'

'Well it can't have been her brother so who else?'

'Jarrett. We think he might be responsible for that body up at Hither Green as well ... Kevin Kanavan.'

'He's disappeared and then come back to abduct Christine? Why?'

'Well it's highly likely he robbed Hattmann in the first place with her assistance and he's come back for the cash or he already has it but needs to shut her up.'

Baslow sat back in his chair, swivelled it from side to side and sighed. 'He's certainly got the right history, it's the sort of thing he would do. What makes you think he's connected to Kanavan?'

'Both from the same area, same profession. They will have known each other.'

'That doesn't prove Jarrett killed him. Any one of two hundred villains might have done it in a dispute about money or if they thought he'd grassed them. Is he on our books?'

'No record of it but Jarrett went down because someone grassed him for the Southwark bank job. If that was—'

'Jarrett couldn't have killed Kanavan, he was inside at the time. Do we know anyone else might have had a clear motive for killing Kanavan?'

'No, but we could ask Chief Superintendent Pilling. He was a chief inspector up at the river when the Rotherhithe job happened.'

Sandwell opened a folder. 'Someone has murdered Kanavan so we're wondering if he was actually involved in the Rotherhithe job but was never identified.'

'Nothing on the file?'

'Only four were caught and convicted but if there was a fifth and even a sixth man involved, how about Kanavan and Jarrett?'

'Well it would be quite neat but as you haven't found Jarrett yet how do you propose to link him to Kanavan?'

'If I could have some more men then I could speed up the search for Jarrett and dig a bit deeper into the Rotherhithe job. Could you speak to Pilling?'

'Maybe, but he likes things neat and tidy. He won't appreciate you opening up old history that he regards as "*closed and nicely wrapped up thank you*". All right, you can have two more DCs. I'll get Phil Murris to move them over and I'll gently broach the subject with Pilling. In the meantime, Phil will concentrate on the hunt for Miss Hattmann. I have to say though, I think she's probably just run off with Jarrett.'

Sandwell and Maidencoombe left Baslow's office and went to the canteen.

'What d'ya make of his reaction?'

'Distracted. Not so self-assured.'

'Looked very tired to me, worried.'

'He didn't seem too surprised that the prime suspect in a disappearance has herself disappeared and he didn't really dispute my flimsy hypothesis about Jarrett and Kanavan being connected to the Rotherhithe job.'

'And he kept the search for Christine with Murris.'

'He did, and I'll bet Murris makes a very good job of not finding her, or at least not reporting that he's found her.'

17

Common Denominator

Akerman left the front desk and ran up the stairs pushing past a WPC. He burst in the double doors of the main office and went straight to Sandwell's desk. 'That foreman has just come back in and said that a shop owner opposite saw a dark coloured Marina reversing into Christine Hattmann's premises after the men had all left. Possibly dark blue or dark green but not black.'

Sandwell looked up. 'Interesting.'

'Says there's no Marina booked in and none of the men have one.'

'Jarrett?'

'A man in a raincoat, forties maybe, that's all he could tell us. He's convinced it's connected to Christine's disappearance.'

'OK, you need to talk directly to that shop owner. We're not supposed to be looking for Christine though, only the Smallwoods.'

'Will I tell Murris?'

'Not yet. Let me speak to Ralph.'

'There's another thing that looks connected to this.'

'Yeah?'

'When I looked into Hattmann's sparkie friend, Vince Allarth, I confirmed it was his Maxi regularly parked outside Hattmann's house. But it's a very uncommon name and I noticed there was another Allarth, Anthony, who is the registered keeper of a blue Marina.'

Murris pursed his lips. 'Relative? Brother maybe? Common car. Allarth seemed clean enough when we looked at him.'

'Maybe not. Anthony Allarth died two years ago, he was Vince Allarth's dad.'

'Really? Where's this car registered?'

'To a flat in a side street off the South Circular. I asked uniform to have a look at the time and a neighbour told them that Vince kept the flat on and rents it out. Also said that Vince owns another flat in the block and each flat has an associated lock-up garage but Vince doesn't let the tenants use them. Didn't think it was significant at the time but as a Marina was seen going into Christine Hattmann's premises around the time she disappeared it now looks suspicious.'

'I can almost feel Ralph's nose twitching.'

'Neighbour said he'd seen Vince in the Marina but couldn't remember exactly when.'

'Why would he keep another car away from home and why would he need two lock-ups? He's got a garage at his house and he didn't mention any of this when we talked to him.'

'To be fair we didn't ask him about anything else.'

'He was with Hattmann the night of the robbery and drove him to Smallwood's house. Right, pick him up, voluntarily if you can. I'll get over to the lock-ups and open them up. We'll need a warrant to have a look at his flats.'

***

'Co-operative?'

'Very, happy to help.'

'Where was he?'

'Building site in Croydon, subbing for another builder, a Ronald Gooch.'

'That name's familiar, do we know him?'

'Suspected of receiving stolen materials a long time ago but not provable. Cautioned after a brawl around the same time ... along with James Smallwood, the missing Crapper Jim.'

'Really? OK. Talk to him once we've done Allarth.'

'Do you want to join in?

'Go over the night of the robbery with him, his car, see anything unusual, need to eliminate him and so on, friendly. Then I'll burst in after ten minutes and hit him with the Marina and the lock-ups.'

'Mr Allarth, Vince, please sit down. This is a voluntary interview. You're not under caution and you're free to leave at any time.'

'What d'ya want to know?'

'As you're aware, Jim and Shirley Smallwood have

been reported missing and we're concerned for their welfare. We'd like to clear up a few details about the night of the robbery at Dennis Hattmann's so we can eliminate you, and we think you might be able to help us with some other questions. Last time we talked, you said you picked up Dennis Hattmann in your Maxi?'

'Yeah.'

'Neighbours say you're quite a regular visitor?'

'I've been doing a lot of work there recently.'

'On that evening do you remember seeing any other cars near Dennis Hattmann's house? Any that looked suspicious or out of place.'

'Don't remember anything.'

'I'm specifically looking for a large silver Mercedes. Did you see one that evening? In fact did you see one in the area in the days and weeks before the robbery?'

'Don't think so, don't really remember but I don't think I've ever seen one in Falmer Close.'

'How about the surrounding streets?'

'Don't think so ... is that the robber's car then?'

'We really don't know. Just something we need to check on. Going back to your own car, how long have you had it?'

'About three years.'

You didn't buy it new then?'

'No, it was two years old, got a good deal,'

'Where do you keep it?'

'At home.'

'In the garage?'

'No, on the drive. I use the garage for work stuff.'

'So you don't have business premises then?'

'No, work from home.'

'You saw Shirley Smallwood that evening when you went to her house with Dennis Hattmann.'

'Yeah.'

'Prior to that when did you last see her?'

'Don't really remember. Used to see her in the pub with Crapper sometimes but not for a while.'

'I was coming to that. Did you see Jim Smallwood that evening?'

'No. He wasn't at his house. Shirley said he'd been arrested.'

'Did you see him earlier that day before you picked up Dennis?'

'No.'

So prior to that day when did you last see him?'

'At Den's house a week or two earlier. He was fixing a boiler. I helped him and I fixed the shower.'

'Was Jim sober at the time?'

'Smelt of booze as usual but wasn't fallin' about or anything ... did his work OK as far as I could—'

The door flew open and Sandwell burst in. 'Your Marina was seen at Christine Hattmann's premises around the time she disappeared.'

'Wot? What is this?' Blood drained from his face.

'Handy pair of lock-ups you've got. You hide the Marina in one. What's the other one for? We've had a look inside.'

'You can't do that.'

'We can, reasonable grounds. Neighbours have seen you arrive in your Maxi and leave in the Marina. Where do you go?'

Vince's hands started to shake and his left heel rhythmically tapped the floor as his thigh moved up and down. 'Just drive about, turn it over now and again. It was my dad's.'

'Why did you go to Christine Hattmann's premises and how did you get in?'

'I haven't been in, I've never been to her premises.'

'Christine Hattmann has been reported missing and your car was seen reversing into her workshop and coming back out again around five thirty on Thursday. A man in his forties looking like you was seen going in the side door. Raincoat was a nice touch.'

'Haven't got a raincoat.'

'Who was with you, who else was in the car?'

'No-one. I wasn't there.'

'Thing is Vince, you've been seen. You and your car at Christine's. You were with Dennis Hattmann at Shirley Smallwood's and she's also missing so you're gonna be sleeping here for a while. I've got a warrant to search your flats and your house.'

Akerman arrested him and took him down to the custody Sergeant.

***

Maidencoombe opened the door to find Sandwell and Akerman already in the interview room. 'Why are we meeting in here?'

Sandwell got up and closed the door. 'We need to keep this quiet.'

'So is Vince Allarth our man?'

'I'm afraid not. At least not for Christine. We searched the flats. Tenant in the first one not too happy. The other flat is a bit odd. A few sticks of furniture, a bed, a kettle but no clothes or food. No-one's living there although the bed has been slept in.'

'Love nest?'

Perhaps, but you'd expect more signs, more stuff. Maybe he just kips there when he falls out with his wife.'

'Wonder if she knows about the flats?'

'She must know about his dad's.'

'Ask her. Now what about the lock-ups?'

'First one is empty, some oil stains on the floor. The other one had the Marina in it and some car stuff but otherwise empty. No visible blood anywhere. The car's back at the lab but it doesn't look promising.'

'Maybe he's been careful, put covers down.'

'He's got a solid alibi for that time, the whole day in fact.'

'How solid?'

'He was at an optician appointment in Croydon at the same time the Marina was seen at Christine Hattmann's workshop

'And before that?'

'Croydon, on a building site. Met with an architect and a council bloke. After that he went to a garden centre in Purley. He's got a receipt and the checkout girl remembers him as he needed help to get a huge planter into his Maxi. It's about as solid as it gets.'

'What about his house?'

'Nothing apart from the planter and a pissed off missus. She confirms he arrived home about six.'

'So why's he so nervous then?'

'Well he's been up to something but he's in the clear for Christine Hattmann ... on that day anyway.'

'He could have let someone else use the Marina.'

'He could've but there is something else, something possibly more interesting.'

'Akerman looked at Sandwell, 'Will you tell him?'

'No you do it, you deserve the credit.'

A frown passed over Maidencoombe's face.'

'I went to Allarth's customer Ron Gooch at his yard, to ask him about Allarth and Smallwood. In the middle of it Gooch's wife appeared so I took her details. I thought I recognised her but couldn't place her so I asked for her maiden name as well. Not keen to tell me.'

'Come on, come on.'

'Moustrianos.'

'What?'

'She's Eleni Gooch now but she was Eleni Moustrianos. Kostas Moustrianos' sister.'

'Jesus, Moose.'

'There's more.'

'Go on.'

'I spotted a big silver Merc in Moustrianos' forecourt last week. I assumed it was just a car for sale but I took a note anyway. After I met his sister I looked it up. It's a 450 S class registered to his wife Karen Moustrianos at his home address in Sevenoaks.'

'Sandwell slapped Akerman on the back. 'Well done mate.'

Maidencoombe grinned. 'You've been using a disturbing amount of initiative. It'll damage your promotion prospects.'

'I can't help it.'

'So ... what do we think?'

'Gooch, Allarth and Hattmann all know each other. They also work with Crapper Jim, go to the pub with him sometimes—'

'And Hattmann used to go with Smallwood to the dogs.'

'How did we miss Gooch earlier?'

Sandwell shrugged.

'I can understand Christine Hattmann's involvement in the robbery but I still don't understand the Smallwood's involvement or why they've gone missing.'

The door opened slightly after two faint knocks and WPC Meacher put her head around the door. 'Sir, Sirs, I've got some information about Shirley Smallwood.'

'Come in.'

'We've been showing her photo around the town centre. The lady in the stationers recognised her and said she sold her an address book and saw her walk into the butchers. Several other shop-owners recognised her as a regular.'

'When was she at the stationers?'

'Same day she was bailed.'

'An address book?' Maidencoombe looked at Sandwell. 'The one we found at the house? Clever little bitch isn't she.'

'What about trains and buses, taxis?'

'One taxi driver thought he'd seen her before but couldn't remember when, probably an old fare.'

'Anything else?'

'That's it sir.'

'Well done Meacher, keep us informed.'

'My head's spinning.'

'So's mine.'

'John, you're starting to look like the smartest bloke in the room, what do you think?'

'Well, as Shirley Smallwood's disappearance has probably been staged then maybe her husband's has been as well. Maybe they did get the money.'

'And Christine Hattmann?'

'I don't think that's been faked, something's happened to her.'

'I agree. Right, get a warrant to search all Gooch's properties and building sites. Bring him in and let's see what he says. We'll focus on the Smallwoods. He might slip up about Christine Hattmann if he thinks we've missed the connection.'

'So how are we gonna tackle Moose?'

'With difficulty. I talked to him a couple of times years back. It's like a fencing match and he really enjoys the game.'

'I heard he sometimes give us tit-bits?'

'He has standards. Armed robbery is a perfectly legitimate business to him but he really hates other car dealers selling dodgy motors. Damages the trade in his view, so he shops them now and again.'

'And robberies?'

'Used to feed us stuff in the past but I'm not aware of anything recently.'

'Not on the books then?'

'No.'

'What do you think? Could he have been working with Jarrett and Hattmann's sister?'

'Possibly, likely even.'

'So Christine's on the inside, Moose and Jarrett do the robbery.'

'And maybe Gooch is the driver.'

'It would fit.'

'Doesn't help us with the Smallwoods though.'

'What about Vincent Allarth, the sparkie?'

'I don't see *Moose* involving him, why would he?'

'And what do we do about the missing Christine Hattmann?'

'Well first off we should tell her brother. Quiz him about Allarth and Gooch as well. Probably won't talk but you never know. He's lost all his cash. If he thinks they're involved he might open up.'

'As for Gooch and Moose, we want Gooch's alibis for the times Christine and the Smallwoods disappeared.'

'Will we go to Moose at the same time?'

'Not really sure what's best. We're not gonna catch him out easily, he's too smart and we don't really have enough men. No, do Gooch only and when we visit Moose we'll be asking for his help about the Mercedes and so on. Then we'll talk about Hattmann and ask him for alibis, softly though.'

Maidencoombe returned to his desk and made two separate sets of notes. One set for official records, and another more extensive set that went straight into his briefcase for storage at home. Irritated at constant interruptions, he looked up impatiently when Sandwell popped his head around the door. 'What is it?'

'Gooch's yard is huge but there was nothing of interest. No disturbed ground.

'And alibis?'

'Says he was at Moustrianos' showroom and nowhere near Christine Hattmann's workshop. I expect Moose will back him up. We can ask him when we visit. For Jim Smallwood, a lot less convincing.'

'Explain.'

'Both he and Allarth have good alibis for Saturday morning and for Sunday onwards, multiple witnesses. But he and Allarth alibi each other for the Saturday afternoon and evening. They claim to have been at Gooch's yard all afternoon discussing some new building plans and stayed there into the evening, drinking and playing cards ... went home about eleven. We talked to their wives and their stories are identical, the same script, so I'll twitch my nose on your behalf.'

'Thanks, mine needs a rest.'

'John's been to the building sites. There's several, but as we've already seen they're a mess. All the ground is disturbed. A body could be anywhere.'

'It looks like Shirley Smallwood has tried to fit up Christine for her disappearance so has anyone been made to look responsible for her husband's vanishing act?'

'Dennis Hattmann made himself look like a suspect without any help. I think we can rule out Crapper Jim staging his own show.'

'Agreed.'

'We've got no clear evidence linking Hattmann to it apart from making threats and he has fairly good alibis. It's family members mostly so not the best quality, but a lot of them and some removal men also back him up. We're going to have to let him go.'

'For Smallwood mister, my money is on his wife Shirley along with Allarth and Gooch.'

'Mine too. Motive?'

'Divert attention?'

'Maybe.'

'It was Christine said that Crapper Jim was one of the robbers.'

'Only according to Hattmann's wife.'

'So we've got two competing theories. Moustrianos and Jarrett raid the house with Christine as the inside man and maybe Gooch driving.'

'Or Allarth and Gooch organise someone else to do it and the Smallwoods get involved somehow.'

'Common denominator?'

'Ron Gooch.'

18

Alibis

Jarrett looked out of the hotel window cautiously. For the twentieth time that morning he scanned the car park and made a note of car types and numbers. A black Vauxhall Viva hadn't moved since eight o'clock. It faced towards the building and there was no-one in the driver's seat but he thought there was someone in the back. He was just about to head downstairs to the lounge for a better look when the phone rang.

'It's Matt, Moose has delivered a car, it's round the front. Come to my office and I'll give you the keys.'

He went downstairs and made his way through the lounge. Pausing to look at the Viva through the main window, he couldn't see inside it because of reflections from the windscreen. He went through the door marked "Private", walked down the narrow corridor and entered Melshott's office. 'That Viva out there, I think someone's watching me.'

Matt stood up and turned round to look out of the

tiny window and shook his head. 'It's the chef's, no-one watching you, trust me.' He handed Jarrett an envelope. 'Want's you to meet him at the Railwayman in Kems—'

'I know it.'

'Tonight at seven.'

Jarrett opened the envelope and picked out the British Leyland key. 'What is it?'

'It's a Princess, nice maroon colour.'

Jarrett raised his eyebrows.

'Safe, respectable, won't stand out. You'll blend in perfectly in rural Kent.'

***

Moose parked his car at the rear of the Railwayman and waited. At exactly seven o'clock a maroon Princess drove in tentatively. Spotting Moose in the corner, Jarrett parked under some trees four cars away from the Mercedes. Moose got out and walked over, looking around before getting in the passenger side. 'I've got you another three hundred,' he handed the bundle to Jarrett, 'but there's bad news, very bad news.'

Jarrett looked at him but didn't speak.

'Christine's dead. It was Baslow and his sidekick, Murris. They waited at her workshop and took her to an old depot near Biggin Hill.'

'Fuck.'

'Yeah, fuck. It doesn't look good for you at all.'

'Did they get the money?'

'We don't know.'

'We?'

'Me and Ron. He got photos of them outside her workshop then he followed them. He was outside the building when they killed her.'

'Shot?'

'No. Look's like they burned her alive, trying to get her to talk probably.'

'Jesus.'

'Look. If they can do that they're capable of anything. The best thing is for you to get to Spain.'

'That would suit Baslow just fine. Have the regular coppers found the body?'

'Don't think so. As far as I can make out they're assuming you and Christine robbed Den Hattmann. They also think you may be connected to Crapper and his wife. With you disappearing it's a reasonable assumption. If you re-appear now, they'll collar you but you shoul—'

'Can't. I was up to something.'

'You gonna tell me what exactly?'

Jarrett opened his window. 'I can't.'

'Look, I can help you but you need to tell me what's going on.'

'I'm stuffed either way. If I re-appear I'll get collared for Christine. If I go to Spain that'll look as if I'm running away, makes me look guilty and I can't come back.'

'What about this other stuff?'

'If I use it as an alibi I'll get ten years ... I need a lot more money to go to Spain, I need the sixty, all of it.'

'Well we haven't got a clue where it is and I don't think we're gonna find it. It's too risky to keep looking. The most important thing is, we all stay out of prison. Sod the money.'

'Are you sure you can trust Ron?'

'We've been through this before, he's married to Eleni. He couldn't have taken the money, I was there.'

'It's only Ron tellin' you about Baslow and the car, Christine dying in some depot. Maybe *he* killed her?'

'What? No, that's impossible.'

'You weren't there.'

'Neither were you. Why would he kill her?'

'To shut 'er up? Maybe he did a deal with 'er and they fell out. So he's tried to squeeze her and she's died, so he's blaming Baslow.'

Moose leaned his head back and exhaled loudly.

'He started this whole thing, got you involved, it was his idea. He said Crapper told him about the cash. So why's Crapper vanished? Him and his missus.'

'I don't know.'

'For all you know Christine isn't dead at all. Ron's just helped her to escape.'

'What? This is bollocks. You just said Ron might've killed her.'

'Moose, one way or another Ron's at the centre of this and he's gonna drag you down.'

'I've known him for twenty years.'

'Maybe you don't really know'im at all.'

'I don't exactly know you well, do I?

'I think we should speak to Ron, lean on him.'

'It's family, I'll deal with him myself.'

'It's my fuckin' money.'

'I'll phone him. Get him to meet us at his yard. Moose left the car and went into the pub.

He returned ten minutes later. 'Ron's been nicked along with Vince the electrician.'

'For what?'

'Looks like they've got them for Crapper. Go back to Matt's and keep your head down. I'll call you.'

***

The next day, Moose swung his Mercedes into the forecourt and parked in front of the main showroom in one of his reserved places. He glanced in his mirror and noticed two men sitting in an old Volvo parked in the visitors space. One of them looked familiar. 'Police.' He got out of the car and avoided looking at them. As he shut the door both detectives got out of the Volvo and approached him.

'Mr Moustrianos, I'm Detective Inspector Maidencoombe.'

'And I'm Detective Sergeant Sandwell.'

'Can we have a few minutes of your time please?'

'Of course gentlemen, always happy to help.'

They followed him into the showroom, past Maureen's desk and into his office.

'Have a seat please. I assume this is about Ron?'

'Yes, but we have a few other things we need to ask you. A bit of a list actually.'

Sandwell opened his pocket-book. 'Can you confirm that Ronald Gooch, your brother-in-law, was with you on Thursday?'

'Yes he was ... Drink?'

Both detectives shook their heads.

'What time did he arrive?'

'Four thirty.'

'Exactly?'

'Sure of it. He always arrives about that time.'

'Why was he here?'

'If he's working at his office he often knocks off early and drops in. We have a drink. Usually here but sometimes we go round to the pub.'

'The Gilded Cat?'

'Yeah.'

'When did he leave?'

'About six, half past maybe.'

'Can anyone else confirm that Ron was here?'

'I dunno, you'd have to ask the staff but they're usually gone by half five,' he smiled, 'earlier if I'm not around.'

Sandwell made notes and Maidencoombe opened a folder and flicked through some papers before pulling out a typed list. 'A dark coloured Marina was seen going into Christine Hattmann's premises around the time she disappeared?'

'Not really the type of car I deal in.'

'We also want to ask you about the robbery at Dennis Hattmann's house.'

Moose snorted.

'Can you confirm your whereabouts that evening, the seventeenth?'

'At home with my wife Karen. Actually I went to the golf club first on the way home for a quick one, then I was at home all evening.'

'We noticed you arriving in a very nice Mercedes. We're interested because a car similar to your's was seen in the area on several occasions in the weeks preceding the robbery.'

'Hang on a minute, your colleagues have already asked me all about his.'

Maidencoombe looked at Sandwell and back at Moose. 'Which colleagues?'

Moose opened a large desk diary. 'Tuesday the twenty-second. DCI Baslow and DI Murris. I assume you know them.'

'Ah ... I see ... of course.' Maidencoombe floundered and Sandwell took over.

'The Mercedes, how long have you owned it?'

'About six months. It was bought to sell on, but Karen liked it so I decided to keep it.'

'Have you ever driven in or around Falmer Close?'

'Where exactly is Falmer Close?'

'Catford. Dennis Hattmann lives there.'

'Oh I see. No, never.'

'Verdant Lane and neighbouring streets?'

'Unlikely, but I know where you mean.'

'A large silver Mercedes was seen in the area,'

'Well it wasn't mine but there's a lot of them around. I've sold dozens over the years.'

'Of that model?'

'Yeah a few and other big ones. Silver's a common colour. Anyway I've been through all this with Baslow and the other one ... Murris.'

'We're just trying to eliminate you and your car.'

'And Ron I hope? This robbery seems to have grown

legs. Have you got any proof that it really happened?'

'Witnesses and a lot of circumstantial. Also four people we believe are connected to the robbery have disappeared which brings me to my next question. 'Do you know Christine Hattmann?'

'No.'

'But you know her brother Dennis?'

'A bit. I thought he'd been nicked?'

'He has, in connection with something else. Christine Hattmann disappeared in suspicious circumstances last Thursday. James Smallwood and his wife Shirley have also van—'

'I've never met them, Christine or Crapper Jim and his wife. I don't move in those circles.'

'Circles?' Sandwell smiled, 'where were you on the Saturday that Jim Smallwood disappeared?'

'What Saturday?'

'The nineteenth.'

Moose opened his diary again. 'I was at Lingfield Races all day with friends. Went home with them to Forest Row and stayed over.'

'And the next day?'

'Went for Sunday lunch with them to the Cantelupe Hotel in East Grinstead. Got back to Sevenoaks about five.' He started writing on a sheet of paper. 'These are the details.'

Sandwell took the piece of paper from him.

'Check with them. Look, if money's been nicked and people have vanished then either *they've* nicked it or someone has shut them up. I can't believe Ron had anything to do with Hattmann's sister disappearing or

Smallwood. I think you should be looking closer to home.'

'Whose home?'

'Think about it, that's all I'm saying.'

The two detectives left the showroom and got into Maidencoombe's car.

'Closer to home? Did he mean Hattmann's wife?'

'I think he meant closer to our home, the station.'

'Hmm ... Baslow was here three days after the robbery, and with Murris, *before* he was officially seconded to him.'

'Why would he come straight here? We only picked up the connection to Moose a couple of days ago.'

'He must have assumed or suspected that Moose was involved.'

'Or he *knew* that Moose was involved.'

'If that's the case he's had a fortnight to get rid of anything incriminating.'

'Including Christine Hattmann and Jim Smallwood.'

'Well it nails one thing for me. Baslow is bent and so is Murris.'

'Right, back to the station and say nothing to anyone.'

'We need to talk to Hattmann again, then do Gooch and Allarth. But unless they slip up we're gonna have to bail them.'

Sandwell drove back to the station and as they walked in they overheard a man at the desk asking about Ron Gooch.

'That looks like a solicitor.'

'OK we'll do Gooch first, get it out of the way.'

They used the stairs to get to the third floor as the lift was broken. Akerman appeared at the landing. 'Guv.'

'John. Go and get Gooch. Bring him and his solicitor up to room two. Take Meacher with you.'

They all sat down in the interview room and Sandwell placed a pad on the table to take notes. 'Ron, we just have a few more questions.'

The solicitor spoke into Ron's ear. 'You don't have to say anything.'

'No he's quite correct, you don't have to speak, but you'd be helping yourself and us by co-operating.' He looked down at his notes. 'You've known Dennis Hattmann a long time, since school in fact?'

'Yeah. So what?'

'You're friends but also competitors in the building trade?'

'Every builder in South London's a competitor. Don't think I've ever been up against Den for a contract.'

'But you see each other socially?'

'Sometimes. Used to see him a lot more but not now.'

'Why's that then?'

Gooch paused. 'Don't really like him any more. Can't be bothered with 'im.'

'Were you surprised he was robbed of eighty thousand?'

'Well someone was bound to rob him but he never had that much.'

'How do you know that?'

'When he's sober he keeps quiet but after a few drinks he brags about all this money he has from cash-in-hand jobs. I never believed it was eighty, a tenth of that maybe, but if he really has been robbed it'll have been his sister.'

'Well as you know she's disappeared. Very conveniently for many of the parties under suspicion.'

'This has to stop, detectives. My client has a robust alibi for the date and times in question and you have no other evidence linking him to Christine Hattmann's disappearance.'

'Yes, your brother-in-law Kostas has confirmed your alibi so you're free to go. You look a bit surprised? Did you not expect him to back you up?'

Ron stood up and left the room with his solicitor.

'So onto Vince Allarth?'

'Let's talk to Hattmann first and chuck him out. Then we'll sweat Vincent a little.'

***

They both entered interview room number three to find Hattmann standing on the other side facing the wall.

'I'm not speakin' to you so you can fuck off.'

'Christine has been abducted from her workshop, or at least it's been made to look like she's been abducted. We're not sure.'

'Fuck off again.'

'She was supposed to do the wages on Thursday night but none were made up.'

'Nothin' to do with me.'

'Look, would you turn round? Come on sit down.'

'Fuck off.'

Maidencoombe sat down and they both talked at Hattmann.

'Dennis. As you know, we think that Christine set up the robbery with Jarrett and possibly some others. But something's happened to her. It looks like she's been taken from her premises on Thursday.'

'Before she got there, someone drove a car into the bay and waited for her. When she arrived to do the wages we think she was overpowered and taken somewhere else. So either she's fallen out with her accomplice Jarrett, or someone else has taken her to try and get the cash. She hasn't been seen since Thursday and we need your help to find her.'

'Any of your associates own a dark coloured Marina?'

Hattmann hesitated. 'Eh ... no.'

'Sure about that, you seem uncertain?'

'What colour?'

'Dark. Could've been blue, green maybe, but not black.'

'No.'

'I think you do Dennis. I think you know exactly who owns a Marina.'

'Unless of course she's faked her disappearance but why would she do that? And who's been working with her? Someone waited for her in the premises so either they're helping her or harming her.'

'Dennis?'

'No comment.'

'For Christ's sake Dennis, the only chance you have

to get your money back is to tell us what you know.'

'Let's suppose she's got the money, where would she hide it?'

Hattmann shook his head.

'Where would she go if she needed to lie low?'

'Spain.'

'Good, we're getting somewhere. Has she got a place there?'

'Yeah.'

'Address?'

'Dunno, never been. She only just bought it, somewhere near Nerja.'

'Has Jarrett got a place in Spain?'

'Dunno, maybe.'

'Do you know anyone with a dark blue Escort van?'

'No.'

'Because along with the Marina, another witness saw an Escort van parked further up the road. A man in his forties got out to use the phone box. The van was facing the workshop but did a U-turn turn and went off in the same direction as the Marina.'

Hattmann shrugged.

'Probably nothing. Tell us about your mates Ron Gooch and Vince Allarth.'

'No comment.'

'We've released Ron as his brother-in-law gave him an alibi but Vince is still helping us with our enquiries.'

Hattmann stayed silent.

'Nothing to say? OK. Dennis we'll continue our enquiries and you remain a suspect for various crimes but we're bailing you for seven days. You know the routine. DS Sandwell will show you out.'

Hattmann turned around smiling. 'You've got nothin' on me ya cunts.'

'Don't look so smug. You're the one that lost eighty thousand.'

Maidencoombe waited in the canteen and Sandwell appeared a few minutes later, stopping to pick up a coffee before coming to the table.

'I didn't know about the van.'

'John gave me a note just before I went in.'

'There's one under a tarp at Gooch's yard.'

'I know, I've sent John to have another look. It's probably circumstantial and Gooch is alibied for the times in question but we've sown some seeds in Hattmann.'

'What do you think he'll do?'

'Go after Gooch and Allarth probably.'

'So what about Allarth?'

'I don't think we're going to get any more from him but we could talk to his wife, ask her about the flats and the car.'

'OK. Bail him and we'll take him home.'

19

Move It

The taxi stopped outside Hattmann's yard. He paid the driver and pulled keys from his pocket but didn't need them as the padlock was missing from the gate. He pushed it open and walked to his Portacabin, unlocked it and went inside. A pile of opened mail was neatly stacked on the left of his desk and the whole cabin looked cleaner and tidier than usual. 'She's been at it again.' He checked the safe but inside there was nothing missing and nothing new. On his desk the answering machine was flashing but he didn't listen to the messages. He picked up a notebook and walked out of the cabin, locked the door and left the yard, pulling the gate shut behind him.

Quickly walking the short distance to his home, he squeezed past his Triumph and into the back garden, entering the house through the back door as quietly as he could. As he walked through the kitchen Julie came out of the living room and jumped back, startled.

'Dennis, the police phone—'

'What happened at the yard? The padlock?'

'It—'

'You fuckin' left it open. Where's the padlock?'

'It jammed. Alf had to cut it off.'

He punched her hard in the stomach and she fell backwards sitting down on the floor, gasping for breath and sobbing.

'Who did you see that night we was robbed? Fuckin' out with it.'

'No-one, I couldn't see them.'

'Christine said one of 'em was a plumber.'

'I don't know.'

'Was the other one Russ?'

'I don't know Den.'

She moved to the front door like a crab and stood up hunched over, holding her stomach. 'Christine's disappeared.'

'I fuckin' know that ya stupid cow. Ron and Vince were collared. You've all been up to something.'

She moved slowly towards the staircase keeping her eyes firmly fixed on Dennis. He went back into the kitchen and put the kettle on as Julie made her way upstairs to the bathroom. After flicking through a notebook and circling names he went back out to the hall and made a phone call. Upstairs in the bathroom, Julie heard him speaking but couldn't make out who he was talking to. After a couple of minutes she heard the front door slam followed by the familiar rumble of the Triumph exhaust as her husband reversed out of the driveway. She ran to the bedroom window and looked out to see the car pulling away.

Back downstairs, she looked out of the living room window for several minutes. Certain now, that he'd gone, she went back to the hall and dialled a familiar number on the phone.

'Steph? It's Julie, is Vince back? Our shower's on the blink again.'

'He's just back from the nick. Is Den still locked up?'

'No he's been bailed. He came home but he's gone out again.'

'You don't sound too good, you OK?'

Julie didn't reply.

'Jules, you there?'

'Yeah. I'm not feeling great with everything that's happened.'

'Vince is in the bath. I'll tell 'im about the shower but he's really tired, didn't sleep at the nick.'

Half an hour later Julie's phone rang.

'Jules, it's Vince. I hear your shower's not working again?'

'He punched me. I can't take it any more. You need to get me out of here, he's goin' to kill me.'

'Look, Den needs to fork out for a new one. I can't keep fixin' that old thing, it's knackered.'

'He's just gone out, he knows I've done something. I'm frightened Vince.'

'What? The powers off completely? Right, when you switch the shower on? Don't use it ... What? ... It still won't come on?'

'Please Vince, please come round.'

'I can't do it tonight, the wholesaler's are shut. I'll

come round tomorrow. I'll phone you when I've got a new one.'

'Please Vince.'

'Best I can do is get your power back on, that's all I can do tonight. I'll be there in about twenty minutes.'

Vince put the receiver down and turned to Steph. 'I think she's in a bit of a state. I'll go round and get her power on.'

'Is Den there?'

'Don't think so, hope not. She doesn't sound good.'

'He knocks her about doesn't he?'

'She's hinted a couple of times. I don't say anything.'

'Den's a cunt, a total animal.'

Vince put on his bomber jacket and picked up his car keys from the table. 'Won't be long.' As he turned the door handle he was pushed backwards and struck on the face with a baseball bat. Hattmann and Norman Hickmett barged in. Steph turned to run for the kitchen but Hickmett rushed forward and forced her onto the floor and stood with his foot on her back. Hattmann grabbed Vince's collar. 'Wot were you doin' at Christine's? And where the fuck is she?'

'Honest Den, I don—'

'I'll do you a fuckin' kneecap, where's Russ?'

Vince recovered enough to snatch a coat from the rack and throw it over Hattmann. Hickmett tried to get hold of Vince but he wrenched himself free. Hattmann swung again with the bat, but missed, hitting Hickmett on the shoulder. 'I know you robbed me ya cunt, you and Ron.'   As Hickmett stumbled backwards, Stephanie scrabbled towards the kitchen and ran out the back door while Vince ducked and managed to push past Hattmann and run out the front door pulling it shut behind him. He got into the Maxi and started the engine just as the huge builder reached the car. Hattmann grabbed at the door handle and it opened but he had to let go as the car accelerated, clipping his Triumph as it sped off. Hickmett hobbled out of the house.

'Get in the fuckin' car.'

Further down the road Vince spotted Stephanie running towards the main road and stopped to pick her up.

'What the fuck have you done?'

'Me? Nothing, it was Ron. He robbed all of Den's cash.'

'So why's he after you?'

'Thinks I helped him.'

In the Triumph, Hickmett rubbed at his shoulder. 'I think you've broken something.'

'They're goin' right, bet they're goin' to 'is flat.' He tried to turn at the junction but had to brake hard as a passing bus swerved to avoid him.

In the Maxi, Steph glared at Vince as he jumped a red light.

'I think we've lost them. We'll go to your mum's.'

'What about the house?'

'We can't go back.'

'Wot? Where're we gonna go?'

'You stay at your mum's for a bit, I've got to see Ron.'

'I'm goin' to the police. If It—'

'You can't, just don't.'

'He's gonna kill you. Why can't we go?'

'We just can't tell them.'

'You're involved aren't you? You were helpin' Ron.' She started hitting him about the face and head and he struggled to keep the car steady. 'You fuckin' idiot, an' what about Julie? Think I'm stupid? No wonder Den's after you.'

'Just leave it, wasn't me it was Moose.'

'Wot?'

'It was Ron and Moose. I was at the dogs with Den when it happened but he thinks I'm involved, Christine as well.'

'Christine? You make me sick.'

'Not like that, the robbery.' He stopped the car outside her mother's house. 'I've gone down to a friend's in Margate if anyone asks.'

'Who's gonna believe that?'

'I'll phone you.'

'Don't bother,' and she slammed the door.

***

Moose drove his Mercedes through Ron's gateway closely followed by Jarrett in the Princess. Gooch's Jaguar was parked just to the side of the office as usual but neither man noticed the Maxi parked on the far side of the yard under some trees. Moose went to the office door and walked in. Jarrett followed and Ron looked up from his desk, surprised to see him with Moose.

'You and I need a serious talk.'

Jarrett joined him at the desk. 'Yeah, tell us exactly what happened with Christine cos I don't believe a fuckin' word of it.'

Ron looked at Moose. 'I told you already.'

'Well you lied about other stuff so I'm not so sure any more.'

Jarrett sat down. Ron looked at him and back at Moose and shook his head.

'What's going on? said Jarrett, 'what did he lie about?'

'We're all in the—'

A toilet flushed.

'Who the fuck is that? Who's here?'

A door at the back of the room opened and Vince walked in. A bandage had been crudely attached to his head partially covering his face.

'What's *he* doin' here?'

'Den came to his house with another bloke and hit'im with a bat.'

Vince sat down. 'I got away. He thinks me and Ron set up the robbery. Thinks we've done something with Christine.' He turned to Jarrett. 'He's after you as well.'

Jarrett looked round to Moose. 'What the fuck is goin' on here? I ain't done a thing to Christine and we've only got his word she's dead? He looked at Ron. 'Well maybe you fuckin' killed her or helped her get away.'

Vince stood up abruptly. 'Why're *you* here anyway?'

'It was my money.'

'How?'

'That money was from the Rotherhithe snatch. I set it up but Den got my share. That's how it's mine,' he pointed at Vince, 'you fuckin' sit down.' He turned to Moose, 'I don't fuckin' trust him.'

'Well you're gonna have to, we're all in this together.'

'How d'ya know he didn't kill Christine himself? And Crapper.'

'If … when they find Christine's body we're all gonna be suspected.'

'It was you two robbed Den in the first place, you pair started this.'

'Russ, we only got eighteen. Someone else got the rest. We thought it must've been you and Christine.'

'If I had it I wouldn't be here.' He turned to Ron. 'Go through it, tell me what happened to Christine.'

Ron re-told the story sticking closely to the facts.

'Russ, If what Ron says is true then we've all got problems. They're gonna link all of us to it.'

'And how are they gonna link this sparkie to it?'

'They're after Ron and Vince for Crapper.'

'What happened to *him*? He in the depot with Christine?'

Moose leaned back against the wall. 'He's gonna have to know.'

'Why?'

'What do I have to know? What the fuck is goin' on here?' He pulled a pistol from inside his jacket and swung it around at everyone. 'All of you up against that wall. Fuckin' NOW.'

'Russ, for Christ's sake—'

'Up against the wall.'

They all moved slowly to the wall and faced Jarrett. He

put the gun at Ron's face. 'What were you lyin' about? ... exactly.'

Moose started to speak.

'Don't Moose—'

'Don't what you cunt? Tell me what you lied about.'

'Crapper's dead,' said Moose.

'Well I fuckin' guessed that much, was it you?'

Ron slumped against the wall and looked down. 'He tried to burn us alive. It was an accident.'

'Us?'

'Me and Vince.'

'Wot?'

'Thought me and Vince had robbed Den. Wanted a share. There was a fight and he hit his 'ead on the digger. Just died in front of us.'

'You believe 'im Moose?'

'I do actually. Look, calm down—'

'I'll calm down when I get the money.'

'Forget the money.'

'So where's the body?'

'We buried it on Den's land behind the gasworks at Bell Green.'

'Jesus.'

'So if it's found they'll blame Den. He was threatenin' to kill Crapper before he disappeared.'

'Russ for Christ's sake put that gun away. By disappearing you've made yourself look responsible for Christine and you can't use your alibi. You were with Den when he was threatening Crapper. You were at Crapper's house ... the only way out of this for all of us, is to co-operate.'

Jarrett put the gun back inside his jacket and everyone relaxed. Ron sat down. 'I can't see any way out of this.'

'Me and Ron alibied each other for that Saturday but they don't believe us and Ron's van was seen near Christine's workshop.'

'And my Merc was seen in Falmer Close. Baslow knows it was me and Ron that robbed Den and he'll dump us in it with the straight police.'

'I don't believe you lot. What a fuckin' mess.'

'Well now we all know each other's secrets can we co-operate and do something?'

'Like what?'

Nobody spoke for a while.

'It's the bodies. No bodies, no real problem.'

'Well Crapper's four feet under the ground. It's Den's problem if he's found.'

'Baslow's the real problem.'

'Well we're a problem for him. We know him and the other one killed Christine.'

'So if we don't get arrested we might be killed to shut us up?'

'We've got to do something to take the heat off, divert the regular coppers elsewhere.'

'They might've moved the body by now.'

'Why would they move it?'

'I don't think they planned to kill her. Maybe they'll move it once they've got a hole dug.'

'How about we grass the bent coppers to the straight ones, tell 'em about the body and Baslow and so on. We've got photos.'

'How exactly? Walk in to the nick?'

'Anonymous letter, with the pictures.'

Jarrett pointed at Moose. 'Or you could speak to your mate Pilling?'

'No, he's helped me out but I don't want him to know about Christine. At the end of the day you can't really trust any of them. I'm not gonna involve him but we could lean on Baslow and his monkey. I've had a mate checking up on them, a bit of spying. They used an old Marina to take Christine to that depot. Well my spy told me they keep it in a unit in Tulse Hill. We could tell the regular coppers about it, give them times and places etcetera.'

'Assuming the straight cops really are straight. Even if they are, it's gonna be hard to go against their own boss, their own team.'

'We have to do something that can't be ignored or covered up.'

'If Christine's body hasn't been found, we could move it to that lock-up and put it in the Marina. Then send a note to the station.'

'Move it? Are you kidding?' I'm not goin' anywhere near it. I'll help as much as I can but movin' the body is crazy.'

'Is it? Would divert attention from all of us and put Baslow on the spot.'

'Russ, are you off your head? We could get caught moving it. We might not even get in the unit. Car might already be gone.'

'We could just dump it in the unit anyway. Look, one way or another that body's gonna be found and I'm the main suspect for—'

'But I'm not.'

'Course you are. You and Ron did the blag in the first place. When that body's found they'll turn everyone upside down. They're bound to link you and Ron to it ... but if we dump the body on Baslow then everything points to him.'

'It doesn't point to him for Crapper.'

'It could do.'

Everyone turned to Ron.

'I've got Crapper's wallet.'

'What?'

'Took it off the body. Thought about planting it on Den. We could plant it in Baslow's unit or in the car.'

Vince leaned forward. 'This could work. I know that depot. We don't need to go in by the main gates and risk being seen. There's a railway line at the back behind the fuel tanks.'

'How come you know it?'

'Did my national service there, some of it. The rail tankers used to come in at the back of the depot. The track swings round to the road and crosses over, there used to be a level crossing but it's closed now. We could park there instead of going in the gate then we could follow the line to the depot. It's in a bit of a cutting, less likely to be seen.'

'How long is the track?'

'About three or four hundred yards.'

'We'd have to carry a body all that way? In the dark?'

'Is the line clear? Is it even walkable?'

'There's only one way to find out, we go there and try

it. If not we'll just have to use the gate.'

'We'll need a big car or a van'

'And a tarp to wrap it up.'

'She's big, heavy.'

'Wheelbarrow would help or a trolley of some kind.'

'Torches.'

'Chances of pulling this off are slim.'

'If that body's found our chances are nothing.'

'I don't like the railway option. Leaving a vehicle parked on the main road, we could be there for an hour, bound to get spotted. Trust me on this, I work out a lot of plans and the railway's a bad one.'

'Moose is right. We drive past the lane a few times, make sure no-one's around, no cars on the road then we just shoot up the lane, straight to the hut. In and out in five minutes.'

'OK, so that might be the easy bit. What about this unit in Tulse Hill?'

Jarrett opened up Ron's tool cupboard. 'Get into anything with this lot. Probably be a roller shutter with a padlock, so bolt croppers'll do, but we'll take everythin' just in case.'

'The real risk is the car if we're stopped.'

'Four mates out for a drink?'

'As long as they don't check the boot.'

'Your car's big enough, we could go now.'

'The Merc? No, it's the sort of car that gets noticed. If that's seen we're stuffed. I've got an old Granada estate at the showroom, dark blue, it's ideal and I can get rid of it afterwards.'

'Tonight, now?'

Everyone nodded.

'Yeah. Let's do it now.'

'Will we take our cars to your place?'

'No leave them here. My car goin' into the forecourt won't look too suspicious but three other cars would.'

'Any overalls?'

'There's a pile in that locker, gloves and stuff. Take some boots.'

Jarrett and Vince started loading everything into the Mercedes.

'We need rope and torches.'

'Take this one, I've got some more here. There's rope outside in the hut. Bring the lot.'

Jarrett, Moose and Vince got into the Mercedes and Ron walked to the gate locking up behind them.

Moose drove carefully to the showroom and paused outside for a while to look around before driving across the forecourt to the "Bomber" yard at the rear. He unlocked the large wooden shed that served as the yard office and retrieved the Granada key leaving a note for the manager. They all helped to move the tarpaulin and tools from the Mercedes to the Ford.

'Will we put the overalls on now?'

'No, we might get stopped. Leave it till we get there.'

Moose drove out of the showroom towards Biggin Hill and Ron directed him to the back road leading past the depot. 'You can't see it in the dark, that's the lane there.'

'There's someone behind me, I'll drive past.' He reached the outskirts of the town and pulled over before doing a U-turn and heading back.

'See anything?'

'Can't see a thing, can't see any lights.'

'I'll go past and turn again. If there's no cars around I'm goin' up the lane.'

He drove past the lane twice more before suddenly turning into the lane at high speed.

'Jesus, slow down.'

He drove through the gateway and Ron directed him to the larger Nissen hut. They all got out.

'OK. Everyone quiet, get used to the dark.'

They shone their torches around but couldn't see or hear anything.

'Have a careful look inside the bigger hut. Vince, you check the other one.'

They came back a couple of minutes later.

'Nothing.'

'No-one.'

'It's in there.' said Ron pointing his torch at the door of the larger hut.'

Everyone changed into overalls and put on gloves and boots. Moose pointed to the gateway. 'Vince, you wait down there. Flash if you see anything. I'll stay at the door. Russ, you and Ron get the body.'

'Me?'

'She's your girlfriend and this was your idea.'

They went in the side door of the hut and Ron led the way to the inspection pit. Both men stood still for a few seconds looking over the edge at Christine's body. Ron noticed the shock in Jarrett's voice.

'Jesus.'

'They set fire to her.'

'Fuckin'ell.'

'We need to get on with it.'

Jarrett looked around and shook his head. 'What a place to die.'

Ron climbed down into the pit and stood in the shallow water. 'You need to come in and take an end.'

They tried to lift the body but it slumped in the middle and they couldn't get it up to the edge of the pit.

'There's steps at the end. Put the tarp there and we'll try and drag her onto it.'

Ron grabbed the body by the ankles and Jarrett tried to hold it under the armpits. 'She's tied up, can't get a grip on her.'

'Use the rope.'

They managed to get the rope under her arms and both men pulled at it, bumping it up the steps and onto the tarpaulin. The steps had scraped of a large piece of burnt flesh from Christine's leg so Jarrett went back into the pit and scooped it up with a piece of rusty scrap metal that had been lying on the floor.

'She's sodden.'

'There's a bit of a smell but I thought it'd be worse.'

'It's cold in here.'

They moved the body onto the middle of the tarpaulin and folded it over several times, securing it with rope. Moose appeared at the door. 'What's the hold up? Get a move on.'

'It's too heavy, come and help us.'

He made his way carefully towards them clearing debris as he went. They all took hold of the ropes but struggled as they half carried, half dragged the heavy parcel across the floor. Moose went outside and flashed his torch at Vince.

'What is it?'

'We need help to lift it, come on.'

With all four men now lifting they carried it outside and dropped it at the back of the Granada. Moose opened the boot but as they lifted one end onto the lip, water started to run out the other end of the tarpaulin.

'Let it drain out.'

They waited a couple of minutes until the water stopped, then folding the body over, they managed to get it into the car. Ron covered it with a plastic sheet and loaded the tools on top. Then they all changed out of their overalls and boots and put them in the holdall. Moose shut the boot lid. 'Everyone quiet for a minute.'

'What's up?'

'Nothing, just want to make sure.'

'There's no-one around.'

They could hear a car passing on the main road.

'Vince, you go down to the road and be look-out. We'll bring the car down part way. Flash us when it's safe.'

Moose drove carefully, following the same route back to Sydenham then on to Tulse Hill.

'What do we do with the body if we can't get in the unit?'

'Just leave it outside?'

'Christ no. We have to dump this on Baslow.'

'Ron's right though, we need a plan if we can't get

in.'

'Well the other thing my spy told me is that Baslow and Murris meet up at Camberwell Old Cemetery and they go to an allotment nearby. There's two sheds on their plot.'

'Surprised they didn't take the body there at the time.'

'I've had a look at it. It'll be difficult in the dark but we could do it, dump it in one of them.'

'There could be money in the unit, stuff they nicked from us.'

'Maybe, they won't keep it at home.'

'If they haven't spent it.'

'Why're you slowing down?'

'There's a police car behind us, about a hundred yards back.'

'Fuck.'

'Stay calm, they're not gettin' any closer ... it's OK, they're turning off. I'm gonna stop round the corner from the unit and we'll walk to it and have a look.' He parked beside some railway arches, and leaving Vince in the car, the other men walked under a bridge to Murris' unit.

'Gloves everyone.'

'We're well out of sight here, it's dark, there's no other way in'

'That padlock's a beast but we'll do it.'

Moose went back to the Granada, drove it around to the unit and reversed up to the entrance. Vince stood look-out under the bridge and Moose waited at the corner. Ron and Jarrett took both pairs of bolt croppers from the car and started to work on the padlock.

'Try the small one first, make a dent in it.'

'Could do with a grinder.'

'No power. Too noisy anyway.'

'Hacksaw?'

'Use about twenty blades, be here all night.'

They squeezed the cropper tightly on the shackle several times, denting it deeply but not getting through.

'Turn it round a bit, go to the side'

They gradually managed to dent the shackle all round.

'We're gettin' there, gimme the big ones.'

Jarrett handed the larger croppers to Ron.

'Both together.'

They squeezed in tandem and the arms of the cropper started to bend but the blades suddenly cut through and Ron fell against the shutter causing a loud metallic clatter.

'They went still and waited, listening.

'For fuck's sake be careful.'

Ron bent down and unhooked the padlock from the staple and Jarrett slowly pulled up the shutter. It moved smoothly and quietly. 'It's been well greased.'

Moose came to the door and looked in. 'Don't switch on the light, use the torches. Have a look around first and get the car open. I'll wait outside and keep an eye out.'

Ron checked the car. The driver's door was locked but the front passenger door was open so he leaned in and unlocked the other doors.'

'What about the boot?'

'We'll have to force it.'

'Do we really need to put it in the car?'

'Dunno ... Moose?'

'We want the regular coppers to find it in the car but if Baslow and Murris get here first we want them to panic. If we put it in the boot they might not even realise they've got it, so it has to be visible.'

Ron smiled. 'Get a bit of a shock.'

'We need to take it out of the tarp.'

'It's a mess.'

'Easier to dump it on the floor.'

Moose pointed at the Granada. 'Suit up before we handle that corpse, boots as well.' He went outside and opened the tailgate then signalled to Vince.

Jarrett shone his torch around the unit. At the back wall a door was fitted into the brickwork. 'Could be in there.'

'What?'

'The money.'

'Bit obvious.'

'Open it anyway.'

Ron cut off the small padlock without difficulty and Jarrett pulled the door open. Inside, a rusty steel box sat on a shelf along with a socket set and some other tools. He opened the box but there was no cash only a bunch of keys. 'I think that one'll fit the Marina, try it.' He handed the bunch to Moose.

'Yeah it does, we'll take it so they can't move it.'

'Might as well but they'll have a spare.'

'Open the bonnet and take the ignition leads.'

'They'll spot that ... just take the rotor arm.'

Jarrett pulled the bonnet catch. Ron opened it and

propped it up, then flipped off the distributor cap and pulled out the rotor arm. Then he clipped the cap back on. 'It'll be the last thing they check.'

'What about the other keys?'

'I bet they're for the sheds at the allotment.'

'We have to stop them moving the body into the boot so find something to jam the lock.'

'Best thing is a key, hammer it in and cut it off.'

'Just use the key we've got. We're not gonna need it.'

Ron took the bunch from Moose, removed the Marina key and opened the boot. Inside there were overalls and boots, some gloves and tools but no cash. He closed it and put the key in the lock. Jarrett cut off the top with croppers and hammered it further in. 'That'll slow them down a bit. If they want in, they'll have to force it.'

They all went out to the Granada and stared at the tarpaulin and rope bundle for a few seconds then hauled it out and carried it into the unit past the Marina and laid it out on the floor.

'Close the boot and get that shutter down.'

They stood around looking at each other, reluctant to start.

'Get the ropes off.'

Ron tried to untie them but gave up and used a knife to cut them. They unwrapped the tarpaulin and a meaty faecal smell mixed with fuel and burnt hair wafted upwards. Vince stepped back and covered his mouth but managed not to throw up. Most of her hair was missing and flesh had peeled from her face exposing bone. One leg had lost most of it's skin and her bound hands were swollen and red. Bits of scorched and wet clothing clung to burnt areas on her torso.

Moose and Vince took the wet body by the shoulders. Jarrett and Ron lifted it by the thighs. 'Fold her over, get her bum on the seat.'

Moose pushed and the others lifted the legs. Jarrett went round to the other side and pulled it across. The body stayed upright for a few seconds then slumped against the front seat.

'That'll do for fuck's sake. Let's get out of here.'

'I've got the wallet.'

'Wot?'

'Crappers wallet.'

'Put it in the glove box.'

'Better in the boot .'

'Too late.'

'Ron opened the passenger side door and put it at the back of the glove compartment. 'They won't notice it.'

They shut all the doors but Jarrett crouched down and shone his torch under the car. 'I knew it, there's a pit under there. That's where the money'll be.'

'We can't hang about, we've got to get away from here.'

'Come on Russ, just leave it.'

Jarrett reluctantly left the unit and Moose pulled the shutter down.

'Someone else could get in now.'

'They'll be straight out when they see that body.'

They all removed their extra clothing and threw everything into the Granada boot. Everyone got in and Moose drove back to Ron's yard.

'Put all the gloves and overalls, everything, in that big drum over there. Ron'll burn it tomorrow.'

'What about the note to the coppers?'

'Leave it with me, I'll get it done.'

20

Discovery

'Not over the phone, usual place twelve o'clock.' Baslow put the phone down and walked out of his office. He used the lift instead of the stairs and left the building by the rear exit. The raincoat he'd been wearing when he and Murris abducted Christine Hattmann, lay on the back seat of his Rover. He turned and looked at it, then rubbed his forehead. He tried to put his key in the ignition but fumbled and dropped the bunch on the floor. He picked them up and tried again. The engine started and he drove out of the car park and turned onto the South Circular. Arriving at the cemetery ten minutes later and stopping the car near the entrance, he didn't notice an old Bedford van parking a hundred yards behind him. He waited and tapped the steering wheel repeatedly while looking around for his colleague. Further down the road he could see an elderly couple walking towards the cemetery with a bunch of flowers and a carrier bag.

Murris drew up alongside him and nodded before

moving off, parking about fifty yards further along the road. Baslow got out and went to his car. 'Someone spotted us at the workshop, good descriptions, raincoats, the lot.'

'And the car?'

'They pulled in that electrician Vince Allarth because it turns out he owns a dark blue Marina but he's got a good alibi so he's been released. Maidencoombe's gonna get to us when that body's found. We won't be able to shut it down.'

'We need to move it, take it to the shed or bury it somewhere else.'

'Helluva risk.'

'Well we need to get rid of the car at least, and the raincoats.'

'Fairweather's?'

'Not sure. I think Moustrianos gets rid of motors there too.'

'We know him and it's the closest. Can you do it today? I can't, got a meeting with Pilling.'

'We should move it after dark.'

'Call Fairweather, make it worth his while to open late.'

Murris noticed Baslow's hand shaking. 'Sure you're OK?'

'It's the body, it's fucked up everything. Why did we leave it? ... Look I've got to go, ring me.'

Murris drove off and Baslow went back to his car. He started the engine and moved off without looking. A passing purple Capri swerved to avoid him and bumped up on the pavement opposite. A young man got out, stormed over to Baslow's car and hammered at the window. Baslow mouthed 'Fuck off' but the young man kicked the door and continued hammering. Baslow reached into his jacket for his warrant card and flashed it at the kicker who stopped hammering and glared at him before walking back towards his car. When he got there, he knelt down to examine the front wheels of his Capri, but unable to spot any obvious damage, he got in and drove off. Baslow, now more alert, finished his U-turn and headed back to the station.

He had only been at his desk for twenty minutes when the phone rang.

'It's me, we've got a problem. Serious we—'

'What is it?'

'Not on the phone, Jesus. Meet back at the usual place.'

'I can't I'm—'

'You have to, we're in trouble. I mean it, we're really stuffed.'

Baslow could hear the panic in Murris' voice.

'All right, quick as I can, just wait.' He put the receiver down and spun round on his chair. There was a knock at the door and it opened slightly. WPC Mcachcr put her head round. 'Sir?'

'I'm just going.'

'Sir, I've got that report for your meeting with the Chief Super.'

'I'm not well, I have to go home.'

Sir?'

He stood up. 'Just leave it on my desk.'

'Sir.'

He left her standing in his office and walked briskly down the corridor to the stairs. DC Akerman followed him. 'Sir, Sir, can I have a word?'

Baslow ignored him and moved quickly downstairs taking two steps at a time. Akerman gave up and went back upstairs to the window overlooking the car park. He watched Baslow march past two other officers. The two men stopped and turned to watch him get into his Rover, then they looked at each other and shrugged. Baslow sped off and drove to the cemetery. After parking behind Murris' empty car, he got out and looked around, spotting him just inside the gateway. He was signalling Baslow to follow him.

'You're shaking even more than me. What's happened?'

'I've been looking for a place to bury her ... I've been all ... we have to ... I don't hav—'

'Bury her here? What's going on?'

Murris was barely coherent. 'It's the body. I went to the unit, it's in the car. Someone's been there.'

'The body?'

'Christine Hattmann.'

'What are you talking about?'

'I went, I went ... I don't know, I went—'

'Slow down for Christ's sake. You went to the unit?'

'Someone's broken in, the padlock's gone.'

'Sit down on that bench.'

'I opened it up and the car was there. I didn't notice it at first. She was in the back seat.'

'Christine Hattmann?'

'Yeah.'

'That's impossible.'

'It's definitely her.'

'How can she possibly be in the car?'

'She must've survived. She must've got out.'

'What? And gone to the unit?'

'Well she's in there.'

'Actually in the car?'

'Yeah, but dead, it's horrible.'

Baslow leaned back and looked up at the sky. 'Is this your idea of a joke cos I'm really not in the mood?'

'George, this is no joke. She's in the back of the Marina.'

'She couldn't have got there on her own. Someone must've moved her. Someone's been watching us. That noise we heard at the depot, someone was there.'

'So who?'

Baslow looked around the cemetery before replying. 'Moustrianos is the only bloke that could organise this, the only one with the balls. We're being played.'

'We used to be in control.'

'Not any more. We've got to get that body out of there and get rid of the car.'

'Fairweather's expecting us tonight.'

'We can't wait until then. Is the car in your name?'

'No, it's in a villain's name. Put him away a couple of years ago. I pay the insurance and the tax. He doesn't know I've got it.'

'Where's the paperwork.'

'Comes to the unit but I take it home.'

'It'll have to be the allotment for the body right now, no choice, but we'll need to move it again.'

'You wanna do it now? In daylight?'

'We have to.'

'You haven't seen it. It's a mess.'

Baslow drove the Rover to Tulse hill and parked around the corner in exactly the same place as Moustrianos had parked the night before. They got out and looked around. Neither man noticed the same old Bedford van that had been near the cemetery parking further down the road. They walked cautiously under the bridge to the small industrial estate. Used to coming and going quietly at night, they were surprised to see most of the other units open with owners busy loading and unloading, using machinery and chatting to each other.

'We can't do it, they'll remember the car, we need another one.'

'Fairweather?'

'Have to be.'

They drove to Fairweather's yard and parked some distance from his office.

'Fot you wasn't comin' till tonight?'

'This is something else.'

'You want me to crush that Rover?'

'No, we need another motor, something with a decent boot, a van preferably.'

Fairweather sat back in his chair. 'In a hurry?'

'Yeah, we need it now. We'll bring it back later.'

'Don't do car hire. This is a one way operation. Cars come in, I crush 'em, that's it.'

'It won't be long, back in a couple hours.'

'Yeah? And when it comes back here I'm linked to whatever you're up to.'

'Five hundred.'

Fairweather rasped his lips and smiled. 'Are you kiddin'? You can do better'n that.'

'A grand then?'

'I can see you two are sweatin', you're desperate. There's a lot of rumours swirlin' around about you pair and that Hattmann robbery so I'm guessing it's somefing to do wiv that.'

'Guess what you like, we just need some wheels.'

'Five grand.'

'We could buy a new one for that.'

'Buy a new one then.'

'Two.'

'Hattmann lost eighty so you can afford it.'

Both detectives stood still, glaring at Fairweather.

'Gimme the evil eye all you want. Take the deal now or it goes up to ten.'

'Five and you crush it when we come back, along with the Marina we talked about earlier.'

Fairweather nodded. 'OK.'

'We'll be back in an hour.'

They left Fairweather's office and returned to the Rover.

'We've got no choice.'

'We could dump the body on Fairweather and arrest

him for it.'

'He knows too much.'

Baslow drove to the allotment and they retrieved all their cash and equipment from the hidden compartment under the floor and drove back to the breakers yard. Parked outside the office stood a grey Escort estate with roof bars.

'It's a good runner, you'll be fine.'

Baslow walked around the car and nodded to Murris who handed a carrier bag to Fairweather. The scrap dealer looked inside and smiled while the two men got in the car and drove off, leaving the Rover at the yard.

They arrived back at Tulse Hill half an hour later and parked outside the unit. They had secured a small pair of ladders to the Escort roof bars and dressed in boiler suits, workman's boots and wearing caps they didn't stand out against the other men working at adjacent units. Murris pulled the roller shutter up just enough to let them duck under then he closed it behind them and switched the lights on. 'There.'

Baslow looked in the car. 'Jesus ... we need to move this back so we can get the Escort in.' He looked to the back wall and saw the open door of the cupboard with the cut padlock hanging loose. 'They've taken the keys.'

'I've got the other set on me.' Murris tried the ignition but although the starter motor turned normally the engine wouldn't catch. 'For fuck's sake.' He turned the key several times.

'Let me try.'

Murris ignored him and tried again. 'The bonnet's

not shut properly, they've done something.' Baslow lifted it up and looked in the engine compartment but there was nothing obviously damaged. He pulled off an ignition lead and signalled Murris to turn it over. 'No spark.'

'Damn ... what is it?'

'Dunno, coil maybe.'

'Try another lead.'

They repeated the exercise with the same result.

'Check the distributor.'

Baslow undid the clips and moved the cap to one side. 'They've taken the rotor arm.'

'Well they slipped up. They dropped it outside, I saw it in the gutter. Cover up that mess with something before we open the shutter.'

Baslow grabbed a large piece of sacking from a pile in the corner and put it over the body. 'We'll just have to push it back.'

Murris released the handbrake and moved the gear lever to neutral then they both pushed the car to the back wall leaving enough space for the Escort. Baslow opened the shutter and went outside to pick up the rotor arm, then he got in the Escort and reversed it into the unit. Murris closed the shutter behind him.

'This is it.' Baslow lifted the Marina bonnet and fitted the rotor arm. He got inside and turned the ignition key. It started immediately and he switched it off. 'Open the boot,' he said, handing Murris the keys.'

'Can't, it's been sabotaged.'

'What?'

'There's a bit of metal in the lock.'

Baslow came round to look. Are the overalls and stuff still in there?'

'They were, the last time I was here.'

'They could've seen them or taken them.'

'Fat lot of use to them.'

Murris pointed to the body. 'So do we leave it in here or use the Escort.'

'We want the Marina destroyed as soon as possible so we need to move the body to the Escort then go back to the scrap yard in both cars and drop off the Marina, get that crushed. Then onto the allotment, hide the body there and go back to Fairweather's and make sure he crushes the Escort as well.'

'And if we get pulled by traffic or uniform?'

'Flash the warrant cards and say we're undercover. Look, if that happens we're stuffed anyway.'

'If we can't pull this off we're gonna have to run. I've got nothing here, flat's rented, not much family. What about your house?'

'Was hoping to retire quietly then sell up and split the money with the wife. If we'd got all of Hattmann's cash it would've worked out fine. Anyway we're wasting time, get the seats down on the Escort.'

Murris walked round to the Ford, opened the tailgate and folded the seats flat. Then he and Baslow moved one to each side of the Marina and opened the rear doors.

'The smell's gettin' worse.'

Both men stood back and looked at each other.

'Gloves.'

Baslow removed the sacking sheet and placed it on the floor on the driver's side of the car. Then he gripped the corpse by the shoulders and pulled it towards him. Murris came round and helped him. They let go and it thudded onto the sacking. They took hold of a corner each and dragged the body away from the car. Murris turned away and struggled not to vomit. Baslow tried to wipe at a damp stain on his overalls but gave up and started to fold the sacking over the body.

They managed to get ropes under the sacking and tied up the corpse into a package.

'It'll look like a carpet from a distance.'

'Looks like a body to me.'

They dragged the heavy bundle to the Escort and sat it up against the bumper. Murris got into the boot and tried to lift the body using the ropes and Baslow lifted from the outside.'

'She's a heavy cow.'

After several unsuccessful attempts to lift the body, Murris got hold of a scaffold board that had been lying at the back of the unit and propped it up on the edge of the boot to create a ramp. Pulling and pushing they slowly managed to slide the corpse up the plank and into the car. Baslow folded the legs up against the chest. Then trying not to touch the wet and bloody slime that had leaked through the sacking, he carefully took hold of the plank and threw it towards the back wall.

'Have we got anything else to cover it?'

Murris looked around and found some large plastic sacks. 'I'll cut these up.' He put them over the body and Baslow put some empty cardboard boxes and pieces of wood on top.

'Just looks like a pile of junk. It'll have to do.'

Baslow threw the keys to Murris. 'You take the Escort and I'll close up here, meet you at Fairweather's.'

***

Sandwell walked in to Maidencoombe's office and closed the door.

'What's up?'

He sat down and handed his boss an opened envelope.

Maidencoombe looked at it. "Inspector Maidencoombe?"

'Arrived about ten minutes ago, left at the front desk by a bloke in a motorcycle helmet. I opened it as per procedure.'

Maidencoombe took out the enclosed note and started reading aloud. 'Christine Hattmann is dead. She was abducted from her premises by Chief Inspector Baslow and Inspector Murris. They took her to a disused army depot near Biggin Hill. They tortured and killed her trying to get the money stolen from Dennis Hattmann. Her badly burned body is in a Morris Marina, registration number BNC 34L, hidden inside Unit H at Tulse Hill Industrial Estate. They also killed James Smallwood.'

Maidencoombe looked up at Sandwell but hesitated before speaking. 'Who else has seen this?'

'Only John Akerman.'

'It adds up but who sent it?'

'Typewritten, coherent, suggests educated.'

'Someone who knows what's going on.'

'Or someone trying to shift attention from

themselves?'

'Villains usually point the finger at other villains, not policemen.'

'I believe it.'

'So do I and I'm guessing the author is Moustrianos though we'll never prove it. Get John in here.'

DC Akerman entered the room.

'Pull up a chair ... you understand what's going on here?'

'I do.'

'If this is a hoax it'll go very badly for all of us.'

'I believe the note guv, every word.'

'So do we.'

'I've checked the number on that Marina and it's registered to a Martin Benson, currently a guest at HMP Brixton.'

'Go on.'

'Career criminal. Got five for a big list of burglaries and thefts. Used to do a bit of safe-cracking but no record of violence or guns.'

'And who put him away?'

'DI Murris or rather DS Murris as he was then.'

'If the body's still there it won't be for long. We've got to get there before they move it.'

'I'll need to go higher up before we do anything. Cottrell's on sick leave so it'll have to be Pilling.'

They all stood up and Akerman spoke. 'Sir, I've gathered all the relevant stuff that points to Baslow and Murris, it's all ready.'

Maidencoombe raised his eyebrows. 'When did you

start suspecting Baslow?'

'About two weeks ago. Since then everything has just fallen into place.'

'Who do you think did the robbery?'

'Moustrianos most likely, probably with inside help.'

'Christine Hattmann then?'

'Perhaps, not sure.'

'The note doesn't say what happened to the money.'

'Wouldn't surprise me if Moustrianos has it and now he's just wrapping things up.'

'And Baslow?'

'I think he knew all about the robbery and has been trying to extort the money from everyone he thinks is involved.'

'OK. Wait here, I'm going upstairs.'

Maidencoombe ran up the staircase to the top floor and approached the desk outside Pilling's office. 'I'd like to see Chief Superintendent Pilling, immediately.'

'You have to phone for an appointment.'

He moved right up to the desk and put his hands on the edge. 'Speak to him *NOW* please.'

Intimidated, the secretary buzzed through and spoke to Pilling then looked up. 'Go in.'

'Ralph, what's so urgent?'

'We have a problem, a massive problem.' He brought him up to date with the case and handed over the note. 'Confirms what we've been starting to suspect and explains some gaps in our understanding. We're certain it's true.'

'What about Smallwood? In fact, what about the wife?'

'We simply don't know what's happened to *him* but the wife has faked her own disappearance, certain of it.'

'Because?'

'She might be involved in the robbery or she may just be scared, Hattmann was threatening to kill her. We're sure she's still alive.'

Pilling stood up and went over to the window. 'And the money?'

'We don't know who got it. Could be any of half a dozen individuals connected to the case.'

'We need to keep this as quiet as possible for as long as possible. If this information is correct there's going to be a hell of a scandal so we need to get it right. Do you think Baslow knows you're onto him?'

'Possibly. He's been acting strangely recently. Very stressed and tired. He disappeared earlier today, no-one knows where.'

'Sick, according to the message I received, along with Murris.'

'Sir we need to act quickly before that body is moved and I'll need to go to their houses and so on, I'll need more men and warrants.'

'Commandeer as many as you need on my authority but only plainclothes to their houses and only tell the uniforms that we're looking for a body and a car, nothing about Baslow and Murris. I'll organise warrants. Remind everyone of the need to keep this quiet. There's a few in this building feeding stuff to the press and the last thing we need at this stage is reporters interfering.'

'Thank you sir.'

Maidencoombe left the room and as soon as the door closed Pilling phoned his golf club. 'I'd like to leave a message for a member please.'

***

Murris drove the Escort straight to the scrap yard and parked just inside the gate. Baslow arrived two minutes later and parked the Marina outside the office. Fairweather came out and Baslow handed him the keys. Fairweather grinned. 'You suit those overalls, there's a job here for ya if fings don't go to plan.'

'It needs to be crushed now, right now.'

'Don't worry.' He signalled to one of the yard men to come over and pointed at the Marina. 'Get on to it.'

The yardman got in and drove around a corner towards the crusher. Baslow walked back to the Escort and as he got in the smell hit him again. 'Christ, open the window.'

They drove to the allotments and parked outside the gates to their plot.

'We should wait until it's a bit darker, there's still people around.'

'We're gonna have to risk it, we've got to get rid of this car and get home.'

'We can't leave the body here for long, we'll have to move it again.'

Baslow got out and opened the gates and Murris reversed in as far as possible then he got out and went to help Baslow at the shed. They quietly removed all the tools and gardening paraphernalia from the bigger shed, lifted the false floor and removed the cover from the hidden compartment. Then they returned to the car, opened the tailgate and threw the plastic bags and other rubbish onto the front seats.

'Have you got a wheelbarrow?'

'It's round the other side I'll get it.' He came back round and positioned it at the rear of the car. They both pulled at the ropes and slid the bundle onto the ancient barrow but it collapsed under the weight and fell over to the side. Both men swore quietly. They took an end each but struggled to get a proper grip.

'Any more rope?'

'Some in the small shed.' Baslow returned quickly and they both tied more rope onto the bundle and tied two ends together to make a loop.

'Ready?'

They dragged the heavy bundle bumping it along the uneven ground until they reached the shed. They pulled it inside and rolled it into the coffin-sized hole. Then they replaced the cover, lowered the false floor into position and threw all the gardening equipment back inside. As Baslow closed the door and clicked the padlock shut, an elderly man suddenly spoke at their backs. 'Could I borrow some water?

'Both men jumped and turned around.

'My barrel's empty and it's a long way to the standpipe, only need a couple of gallons.'

'You gave us a start.'

'Sorry, I'm Bill by the way. I'm just the other side of that plot with the Rhododendrons.'

'Water?'

'Just a canful.'

'It's round here,' said Baslow leading the old man to the water barrel at the back of the shed. He filled the can for him and handed it back.

'Thanks, if you need any compost I've got plenty spare. What're you planning for here?'

'Haven't decided, gonna turn it all over and start again, flowers probably. Maybe a little bit of veg, not sure.'

'Didn't catch your name.'

'It's ... eh ... Reg, Reg Wilson.'

'Bill Hardy. Thanks for this,' and he walked off.

'Why'd you say Reg Wilson?'

'First thing that came into my head.'

They returned to the car and put the seats back up. Murris took the rubbish from the front and threw it in the back then they changed out of their workman's outfits and drove back to the breakers yard.

They parked outside Fairweather's office and walked in to find him sitting behind his desk reading a copy of the Racing Post. 'What happened to Jim Smallwood then?'

'No idea. Why?'

'Well one of your mates at the nick just phoned and asked me about a brown Cortina. Jim had one.'

'So what?'

'Thought you might know somefing.'

'Just forget about that and crush the Escort.'

'Perfectly good motor, why should I?'

'We paid you, don't piss about.'

'Well I don't fink you paid enough considerin' the

risk, considerin' you two are up to your necks in two disappearances. I want another five.'

Murris went up to the desk. 'Not a fucking chance.' He reached into his jacket and pulled out his revolver. Fairweather brought his right arm up and pointed a sawn-off shotgun at Murris and swung it in an arc to Baslow. 'Ya wanna get heavy?' He cocked the weapon. 'Shoot Crapper did ya? And Hattmann's sister?'

'The deal was five and you crush it.'

'Well my new deal is another five or I don't.'

Murris pointed the gun at Fairweather's head.'

'Go on then ... shoot ... nah ... didn't fink so.'

Baslow tugged at Murris' arm. 'Leave it.'

'That's right, fuckin' leave it.'

The two detectives turned and left the office and got into Baslow's Rover.

'We need to run.'

'Yeah, I know.'

'I'm going to Spain but I'll go to Portugal first and cross the border.'

'Got a passport?'

'Yeah, used Benson's details. What about you?'

'Ferry to Ireland, then fly to Spain. I've got a fake, never really expected to need it.

'How much have we got, altogether?'

'About seventy.'

'We should split it now in case we have to separate.'

'We need more, the rest of Hattmann's money.'

'It's hopeless, anyone could have it.'

'Gooch's wife, one last try?'

'Moose's sister?'

'She might have cash. She might even know what's really happened to the rest of the eighty.'

'Bit of a long shot.'

'Got a better idea?'

***

Maidencoombe returned to his office and shut the door behind him. 'Right. We're on.'

'How did Pilling react?'

'Wants to keep it out of the press but that's never going to work. Gave me authority for all the men I need, warrants, the lot. So set up teams to go to Baslow and Murris' houses. You co-ordinate everything from here. I'll take John and some uniforms to Tulse Hill.'

'What about the car? If it's gone they'll have torched it.'

'Hmm … more likely get it crushed, and we all know who sorts out cars for villains in this area.'

'Fairweather.'

Akerman interrupted. 'I spoke to Fairweather this morning about Smallwood's Cortina.'

'Why? It's in the compound here.'

'It just occurred to me, if someone wanted to impersonate Smallwood a brown Cortina would help … pick one up from a scrap yard.'

Sandwell smiled broadly. 'You're becoming a regular Poirot.'

'What did he say?'

'Said he couldn't remember, deals with so many cars

etcetera.'

'Predictable answer. Vic, get a team over to Fairweather's immediately. Search the yard, check all his paperwork and grill him about the Marina. Don't remind him about Smallwood's Cortina at this stage.'

Maidencoombe and Akerman arrived at Tulse Hill Industrial estate and four uniformed constables arrived minutes later in a van.

'It's Unit H, get it open.'

A young PC grabbed the handle and pulled up the shutter to reveal a space, empty but for a set of wheels and some rubbish.

'Damn, it's gone.'

'What are we looking for sir?'

'A dark green Marina reg number BNC 34L and a body.'

They all walked inside and looked around. Maidencoombe pointed to the floor. 'Get that pit opened up.'

Two of the PCs removed the planks from the floor to reveal an inspection pit filled only with rubbish and some polythene bags.

'What's in those carriers?'

'Just rubbish.'

'This one's got a boiler suit.'

'And this one's got rope and a balaclava, gloves as well.'

Akerman walked over to the back wall of the unit. 'Someone's cut a padlock on this cupboard, nothing inside.'

'Right, you lot, ask around the other units about the Marina and any other cars or people seen going into this one.'

The four constables went off and Maidencoombe pointed to Akerman's radio. 'Is that thing working?'

'It is, yes.'

'Speak to Vic and update him. Ask him about the scrap yard.'

A few minutes later one of the uniformed PCs came running back to Maidencoombe. 'Sir, the Marina was moved earlier, two men, one fortyish, one fiftyish, overalls. They also had a grey Ford Escort estate which went into the unit and came out again. Both cars then left at the same time.'

Another PC butted in. 'Man in the furniture unit says he's seen a bloke in a raincoat moving the Marina in the evening on a couple of occasions. Doesn't talk to anyone, keeps to himself.'

'Sir, the radio, DS Sandwell.'

Maidencoombe grabbed the handset. 'Vic?'

'Ralph, we just got another note to say the body's been moved to an allotment near Camberwell Old Cemetery. A dilapidated plot near the entrance with two green sheds. The body's in one of them apparently.'

'Anything else?'

'We didn't manage to catch the messenger but the team at the scrap yard have found the Marina.'

'Brilliant, anything in it?'

'A bad smell from the rear seat but otherwise empty.'

'What about the houses?'

'Only the wife at Baslow's, he's not there, she assumed he was at work. They took the door down at Murris' flat but he's not there either. They're searching it as I speak.'

'Right, get DS Hayward to take over. You get to the scrap yard and grill Fairweather. I'm going to the allotments.' He handed the radio back to Akerman. 'John we're going to Camberwell Old Cemetery. Round up the uniforms and get them to follow us.'

They raced to the old cemetery and Maidencoombe directed Akerman to the north side and down a lane to the allotments. They drove in the main gateway and quickly spotted the two wooden buildings.

'Open up those sheds.'

A young PC used cutters to remove the two padlocks and opened the doors. 'Tools and stuff, no body in this one and the other one's the same.'

The two detectives went inside the larger shed but could only see gardening equipment and bags of compost, plant pots and a bundle of canes.

'If it was in here it's been moved. Get on to Vic and find out what's happening at the scrap yard.'

A uniformed constable went over to speak to an old man who was just closing his shed. After a few words he brought him over to Maidencoombe. 'Tell him what you saw.'

'Just came over for some water, there was two of them. They were dragging a carpet or something into that shed, the big one.'

'Did they bring it out again?'

'No they just locked up and went off in their car.'

'Overalls?'

'Yes.'

'What kind of car?'

'Grey, shooting brake, didn't really look.'

'You're certain they didn't put the carpet back in the car?'

'Definitely, I saw the boot before they closed it, nothing in it.'

'Right, thank you. John, take this gentleman's details. Can you wait around for a bit?'

'Of course, happy to help. What's it all about?'

'I'm not able to tell you at this stage but we may need you as a witness.'

He turned to the other constables. 'Search the entire plot, look for disturbed earth, look in the water barrel, everything.'

The constables started scouring the ground.

'You said a carpet?'

'Well it was quite long, wrapped in sacking, tied up with ropes. Could've been something else but it was heavy whatever it was. They were struggling with it.'

Maidencoombe went back inside the large shed and Akerman followed with his torch.

'Mr Hardy, would you come in please?'

The old man came in and looked surprised. 'Where is it?'

Akerman asked him to wait outside then he shut the door.

'What're you doing?'

'Can't you smell it?'

'Can't smell anything.'

'I can.' Akerman got down on his knees. 'It's coming from the floor.'

Maidencoombe got down. 'Maybe a bit.'

Akerman tapped the floor. 'I wondered about that. There's quite a lip at the door.'

'A lip?'

'It's higher than the threshold. I think this is a false floor.' He tapped again at various points then stood up and walked around. As he moved to the corner the floor creaked. 'It's warped, it's not fixed down.'

Maidencoombe went out and gestured to two of the constables. 'Get all this stuff out of here.'

They emptied it quickly and Akerman grabbed a spade and inserted it into the crack between the floor and the sill. He pressed the spade handle down and levered the floor up a couple of inches.

'Let me get out of the way.' Maidencoombe stepped over the threshold and let Akerman raise up the floor enough to get a hand underneath then he helped him push it up against the side of the shed. 'I can smell it now.'

Akerman lifted up the cover to the hidden compartment and both men stood still for a minute looking at the wet bundle of sacking and rope.

'No prizes for guessing what that is. Have you got a knife?'

Akerman knelt down and cut away the ropes. Then he pulled the sacking back but there were several layers and he couldn't see the body. 'We need to lift it out.'

'Leave it. We need forensics and some more men. Radio the station and get this area cordoned off.'

21

The chase

Sandwell arrived at the scrap yard and flashed his warrant card at the constable standing beside the gate. He parked beside the old sub-station building that served as an office and spoke to Radcot, the uniformed sergeant standing outside. 'Pete, glad it's you. Where's the Marina?'

'Round that pile of cars at the corner.'

'And Fairweather?'

'In there and saying nothing.'

'OK. I'll look at the car first then talk to him.' He walked around the stack of damaged rusting vehicles, stepping carefully over puddles and pieces of scrap. Two junior detectives stood beside the Marina making notes.

'Sir.'

'Sir.'

Sandwell walked around the car and peered through the windows. Then he opened a door and looked at the stain on the rear seat. 'Anything in the boot?'

'Can't get in, it's jammed up with some metal.'

'Well go and get some tools, get it open.'

The young detective went off and returned with a crowbar, some other tools and gloves. The other one helped him prise the boot open. Inside were several carrier bags and a small holdall. The jack was lying at one side and the floor cover dipped in the middle as the spare wheel was missing. Sandwell looked inside the bags and found overalls and tools. 'More robbery kit.'

'Sir, looks as if the body might have been on the back seat.'

'Well I can see that. What about the Escort?'

'Empty apart from some rubbish but it's got the same smell, it may have been in there as well.'

'Or there may have been two bodies.' Sandwell turned and walked back to the office.

Fairweather was sitting at his desk while two detective constables looked through his paperwork.

'Have you got documents for the Marina and the Escort?'

'For the Escort yeah but not for the Marina.'

Sandwell gestured to the two constables. 'OK, leave that for now and wait outside.'

The puzzled constables left the room and Sandwell pulled up a chair to sit opposite the scrap dealer. 'You've got nothing to say?'

'Don't know anyfing.'

'Well I know you're in a lot of trouble, you're connected to two murders.'

'Don't fink so.'

'No? Well I'll tell you what I know, it'll save time. We've found Christine Hattmann's body and the cars used to move it are both in your yard, so why did you kill her?'

'I didn't—'

'And why did you kill Jim Smallwood?'

Fairweather stood up. 'Didn't kill anyone ya cunt.'

'Sit down and convince me then because if you can't you're going down for murder.'

A young constable entered the room. 'Sir?'

'Not now, stay outside.'

The door shut and Sandwell continued. 'Come on, convince me.'

'Two blokes asked me to crush the Marina.'

'Baslow and Murris?'

Fairweather hesitated ... 'Yeah.'

'And the Escort, the grey Escort?'

'They borrowed it.'

'For how long?'

'About an hour.'

'So Christine Hattmann was in one and Jim Smallwood in the other?'

'Nuffin' to do wiv me.'

'But you knew that's what they were doing?'

'Nah, course not.'

'You had a look in the cars and didn't notice the smell?'

'Look, these are old cars, most of 'em stink, I don't bovver about it.'

'Did you clean out the cars, remove anything?'

'Nah.'

Sandwell stood up and went to the door. 'You two in here, and *you*, get out from behind there and stand against the wall.' He pointed at the desk, 'search that.'

The two constables started looking but didn't find the shotgun taped on the underside of the desktop. There was nothing of interest in the drawers but when they emptied the waste basket they found a bunch of keys underneath the rubbish.

'Strange place to keep keys, Tony?'

'I don't—'

Sergeant Radcot appeared at the door. 'Vic, we've found a safe hidden behind some cars.'

'Interesting, come with us Tony.'

They all walked round the back of the building to a stack of cars that obscured a small corrugated iron hut. Sandwell looked inside at the substantial safe. 'You may as well open it, we'll get in one way or another.'

'Gimme the keys then.'

Sandwell handed him the bunch and Fairweather unlocked the safe swinging the door wide open. Inside were several cash boxes, some document folders and a polythene carrier bag on the lowest shelf. Sandwell picked it up and looked inside. 'Five bundles, looks like five grand to me. Open the cash boxes.'

Fairweather obeyed and showed the detective the contents.

'Another few grand and some change. Why didn't you put the five grand in one of the cash boxes, they're big enough?'

Fairweather remained silent.

'Nothing to say? He looked again inside the carrier bag and noticed something else under the money. He picked out the wallet. 'This yours?'

'No.'

Sandwell opened it and stopped smiling as he looked back at Fairweather and read out the name on the driving license, "*James Smallwood*". 'Christ, you're in trouble Tony ... bring him inside.'

They frogmarched him back to the office and made him sit down at his desk.

'Keep him there and watch him, don't let him touch anything.'

Sandwell left the office and walked over to one of the patrol cars. He tapped on the window startling the young PC sitting in the passenger seat. 'Any messages from the nick?'

'Inspector Maidencoombe's on his way here.'

A few minutes later Akerman's Fiesta drove through the gates and stopped beside him. Maidencoombe got out of the passenger side. 'So what've we got?'

Sandwell updated him while Akerman used his radio to talk to the team still at the allotment.

'What do you think?'

'He obviously wasn't expecting us and he's very nervous.'

'Think he's been working with Baslow?'

'He's been sourcing and disposing of cars for him but I don't know if it goes beyond that.'

'So why's he got Smallwood's wallet?'

'Beats me. Crazy to hold onto it and he's had weeks to get rid of it. Apart from that, there's nothing else to link him to Smallwood's disappearance.'

'No brown Cortinas kicking around?'

'Well there could be anything under this lot but if he did have have one, it'll be crushed by now.'

'Let's go inside.'

They both stood at the desk looking down at Fairweather and fired questions at him aggressively.

'Didn't think you went in for murder Tony.'

'You thought we'd look the other way because Baslow and Murris are coppers.'

'You thought you were safe?'

'We've got Christine Hattmann's body and I expect we'll find Jim Smallwood's under some cars in this yard.'

Fairweather started to open his mouth but stopped and said nothing.

'It's OK Tony, go no comment. We've got a body, two cars, loads of witnesses and best of all Jim Smallwood's wallet. Baslow and Murris will probably escape but you're going down for the lot. We don't really need anything else.'

'I don't know a fing about the body.'

'So explain to us how you have Jim Smallwood's wallet and a load of cash?'

'I checked the Marina after they left it, found the wallet in the glove compartment. Cash was from Baslow. Paid me to crush the cars.'

'*All* the cash was from Baslow?'

'The five large in the bag, the rest's mine from the business.'

'Why didn't you crush the cars?'

Was goin' to.'

'Weren't expecting us to turn up so soon, if at all?'

'And the wallet? Why hold onto it?'

Fairweather looked at each detective in turn but didn't reply.

'There's two possibilities here; either you killed Jim Smallwood or you're telling the truth and you found the wallet in the Marina. In which case I think you kept it to squeeze money out of Baslow, even more money.'

Fairweather shook his head.

'Either way, it suggests to me that that you know all about Jim Smallwood.'

'Don't know a fing about Crapper.'

'I think you know him quite well, got a common interest in racing.'

'Used to see him sometimes at Catford Dogs till he got barred, but he's not a mate.'

'No I suppose not. People don't usually kill their mates.'

'I didn't kill 'im.'

'If you're to have any chance of getting out of this you're gonna have to tell us everything about your relationship with Chief Inspector Baslow and Inspector Murris. Start at the beginning.'

Fairweather told them everything that had happened, more or less sticking to the truth but not mentioning the armed confrontation.

'You must've known what they'd done. Nobody pays five grand to get rid of a car. In fact you usually pay the owners twenty or thirty quid.'

'Knew they were up to somefing but not murder.'

'Don't think a jury's gonna believe that Tony. What were they wearing?'

'Overalls earlier, then the usual suits.'

'Raincoats?'

'Nah, car-coat fings, short, looked brand new.'

'Colour?'

'Dark, black maybe.'

'So they arrived the second time with the Escort. How did they leave?'

'In Baslow's Rover, a gold SDI.'

Maidencoombe went outside and talked to Sergeant Radcot. 'Keep him in here until you've finished the search then take him to the nick.'

'Will do.'

Akerman came over to join them. 'Dennis Hattmann was picked up on Thursday night. Reckless driving and had a baseball bat in the car.'

'Why on earth weren't we told?'

'Don't know. He was released quickly, along with a Norman Hickmett.'

'OK. Vic and I need to go back to the station and update Pilling. John, you stay here. He turned to Sandwell. 'You and I can talk in the car.'

'So we're assuming that Baslow and Murris are now on the run?'

'We'll need to alert other forces, airports etcetera.'

'Ferries?'

'Them as well, don't want them doing a Smallwood.'

'Think he might be be hidden in the yard?'

'Probably not but we'll have to check, and we'll need to dig up that entire allotment and find out about any other properties they may have access to. Any stuff missing from their houses?'

'Hard to tell. Murris lives alone. His passport's still there. Baslow's wife isn't sure. They don't speak much, just share a house.'

'Make sure everyone's looking out for the Rover. I expect they'll ditch it but we might get lucky.'

As they drove round the back of the station they saw Chief Superintendent Pilling loading golf clubs into the boot of his car. Sandwell parked up and they walked over to him.

'Sir?'

Pilling looked up. 'How bad is it? ... Wait, not here, come up to my office, ten minutes.'

'Sir.'

'Sir.'

The two detectives turned away and headed to the canteen.

'I'm not sure I want to tell him everything.'

'Why not? ... Oh I see, your nose again. Well I don't think we can hide very much and you're asking for trouble.'

They finished at the canteen and took the lift to the top floor offices. Pilling invited them to sit down.

'We think they're on the run. So far we've found a lot of robbery kit in different places, balaclavas, tape, coshes, rope, you name it. Enough for about six or eight men.'

'Are they part of a bigger firm? Have they been doing blags themselves?'

'Don't think so. We think they've been robbing villains. They keep intelligence secret, undermine investigations and so on. Then they muscle in and help themselves and of course the villains can't complain. They've probably been getting away with this for a while but the Hattmann job has blown up in their faces.'

'And it's Hattmann's sister at the allotment?'

'Almost certainly.'

'And the other one, the plumber?'

'No sign so far but I'd be very surprised to find him alive. We're searching the scrap yard and tearing up the allotment. The scrap dealer, Fairweather, says he found Smallwood's wallet in a car given to him by Baslow. Could be true ... Fairweather's got no obvious motive for killing him, but with so many connections to the Hattmann mess we just don't know what to believe.'

'Well the main priority is to collar Baslow and Murris. It's going to look terrible but if they escape it'll look worse. I just wish there was some way to put a lid on all of this.'

'I'm afraid that's impossible now sir.'

'And you think Moustrianos sent the notes?'

'Probably.'

'You've got my home number, keep me informed.'

***

Baslow turned the car around and headed towards

Beckenham. Murris removed the guns from the glove compartment and spun the chambers. 'We need to ditch this car.'

'Got another one?'

'Ex brother-in-law might lend me his, we're still friendly but it's over the river.'

'There was an Alpha at Gooch's place we could take that.'

'If it's there, if she's in.'

'If not, it's taxis, we've got to get rid of this.'

'Any dealers we could phone tonight?'

Baslow hesitated. 'Farniston, Grove Park?

'Stop at a phone box. It's late, he'll be closed but I've got his home number ... somewhere.' He flicked through a notebook. Baslow drove on past the gasworks and pulled over beside a call box. Murris looked around. 'No-one's around but that box is a mess.' He put on gloves.

Several windows had been smashed and the receiver was swinging loose. He got out of the Rover, and looked around again before opening the kiosk door. A torn directory lay on the floor covered in vomit. He carefully picked up the receiver and put it to his ear. The harsh unobtainable tone suggested it was working so he put it back on the hook, picked it up again and heard the dial tone. He called Farniston and spoke for couple of minutes then went back to Baslow. 'He wants five, he'll meet us at his yard.'

'For fuck's sake, is that the going rate now, five for everything?'

'It's out there, everyone knows about us, they're all gonna screw us. Says he'll be there in half an hour. He'll wait, I didn't give him a time.'

'Gooch's place first?'

'The Rover'll be spotted.'

'It's dark.'

'Too risky, Ralph's team might be watching. Let's get the new car then swing by Gooch's place, see who's around before we burst in.

They parked around the corner from Farniston Autos, switched the engine off and watched.

'Does he know we're in a Rover?'

'He's expecting it as part of the deal.'

'As well as the five?' Baslow shook his head.

Murris opened the glove compartment and pulled out a revolver. 'I think we can negotiate better terms.'

Baslow sucked in through his teeth. 'He's got mates in Spain, dangerous mates, could get messy over there.'

'Spain's a big place, we know where to avoid.'

Half an hour later a Porche 911 drove up to the premises and a man got out and opened the gates. Baslow recognised Farniston though he seemed fatter and shorter than he remembered. 'Think he might have a shooter?'

'Maybe ... let's assume he has, so be ready.'

Both men put their revolvers into their coat pockets.

'Get the five grand and let's see what happens.'

Baslow moved the Rover into the forecourt and they both got out. Farniston was standing smiling. 'You two on the run then ... with Hattmann's money?'

'Yeah, we're on the run but we didn't get Hattmann's money.'

'Not what I heard. Word on the street is you robbed Hattmann—'

'Never mind about that, what car are you giving us?'

'Got a choice. An Audi 100 or a BMW. They're both good runners and fast but the beamer is only a two door.'

Both detectives were surprised as they had been expecting something more ordinary.

'Where are they?'

'Show me the money first.'

Murris held the bag open and showed the cash to Farniston.

'Good, this way.' He led them through a door marked "Workshop" and as he switched on the lights they saw the two cars parked side by side. As they walked over, the door closed behind them and both men turned. They recognised Jeff Linby, a former colleague. He was pointing a shotgun at them.

'You cunt Farniston.'

'Don't be like that, you know the game, survival of the fittest. Gimme the five and the Rover keys.'

The door opened and another man came in carrying a crowbar and two holdalls. 'I've got the lot. Looks about seventy or eighty.'

'So you *did* get it.'

'It's not Hattmann's.'

'Well it's mine now, up against that wall.'

As they moved, Baslow fired a shot through his coat pocket at Linby. Expecting return fire he jumped to the side but the shotgun fell to the floor and Linby slumped backwards.

'Murris took out his gun and pointed it at Farniston.

'Give me the fucking keys to both cars ...*Now*.'

Farniston reached into his pocket and handed over a single key.

'I said both of them.'

'That's the Audi, the Beamer one is on the board over there.'

Murris grabbed the key and put it in his pocket. Baslow pointed his gun at the man with the holdalls who dropped them and put his hands up. Baslow went over to him. 'Turn around, up against the wall.' Then he went over to Linby who was bleeding but still conscious. He picked up the shotgun, broke the action and was amazed to find it unloaded. 'It's empty, just a bluff.'

Farniston smirked and Murris kicked him in the groin then smashed the butt of his revolver across the man's forehead. The car dealer fell to the floor and rolled onto his side, groaning. Baslow walked over to Murris and spoke quietly. 'We'll take both of these cars, use one for the trip to Gooch and hide the other one in case we need to switch cars again.'

'Where?'

'There's some back streets beside the railway yard and a lot of waste ground.'

'What about this lot?'

'Well Linby isn't going anywhere. We'll tie up the other two and get out of here.'

Murris found some rope at the back of the workshop and they dragged Farniston across the floor and tied him to a radiator pipe. Then they turned the other man around and Murris shattered his knee with the crowbar. The man screamed in pain as he fell backwards. Baslow pointed his gun at the man's head and Murris tied him to a workbench. Then he went to the main doors and opened up, while Baslow moved the cars out onto the forecourt. They transferred more bags from the Rover to the new cars and closed the doors.

'Think they'll grass?'

'Doubt it, though it'll be hard to get that bullet wound treated. Not our problem right now.'

'Gooch?'

'Let's go.'

Baslow drove the BMW to Hither Green and Murris followed in the Audi. As they drove down the secluded lane at the back of the railway yard an Austin 1100 with it's lights off passed them at speed. The gate to the site was open and Baslow drove the 3 Series through the opening and turned the car around. Murris stopped the Audi and got out.'

'What was he up to, the Austin?'

'Dumpin' rubbish probably, it's an unofficial tip.'

'The railway people could lock that gate any time. In fact this isn't safe at all. We can't leave a car round here, it'll get nicked or someone'll have the wheels.'

Baslow looked around. 'You're right.'

'Let's take it into Bellingham, park it up in a quiet road under a streetlamp, we're only gonna be an hour or two.'

'Best take the Audi to Gooch, in case we have to take someone with us.'

'Moose's sister?'

'May have to.'

They left Bellingham in the Audi and drove across Southend Lane heading for Beckenham before turning down Wickham Road to Park Langley. Murris drove the car slowly around the area, looking for police surveillance vehicles but couldn't see anything. 'There's hardly a car on the streets, and there's no-one about.'

They approached Gooch's house and passed slowly. A dim light was visible through the translucent curtains of the lounge. The Alpha Romeo was parked in the driveway but Gooch's Jaguar was missing and there wasn't a single vehicle parked on the roadside.

'Keep going, one more pass.'

Murris drove to the end of the road, turned the car and stopped. 'They'll have put all their resources into finding the Rover. Unless they've set up an obbo from a nearby house I think we're safe to go.'

'Let's do it, park up at that bend in the road just out of sight, then we walk to the house.'

'Mask up?

'Take them with us but not yet.'

They both got out, opened the boot and stuffed robbery kit into pockets.

'Duct tape as well?'

'Good idea.'

Murris closed the boot and they walked confidently to Gooch's house slipping on gloves as they went up the drive.

'Front or back?'

'Let's check the back door first, might be open.'

There were several windows at the back of the house

overlooking the garden but light was only coming from the kitchen door. Baslow peered inside, then checked the other ground floor windows. 'No-one, I think she's in there alone.'

'Check the door handle.'

'Locked.'

The kitchen light suddenly came on so they moved to each side of the door. Murris peered round carefully. 'It's just her.'

'We're not overlooked, better to go in the back.'

'Don't think we can force that door without making a racket, it'll have to be the front.'

They walked to the front of the house and stood outside the door with warrant cards in hand. Murris pressed the button and "Bells of St. Clement's" sounded loudly. The hall light came on and the door opened partially, limited by a chain.

'Who is it?'

'Police.'

'It's nearly midnight, what d'ya want?'

'We'd just like to ask a few—' Murris kicked the door and it flew open breaking the chain. Eleni Gooch jumped back and Baslow rushed in, put his hand over her mouth and forced her into the dining room at the rear of the house. Murris shut the door and carefully peered around the lounge door but didn't go in. Seeing nothing, he checked all the other rooms in the house before joining Baslow in the dining room. 'There's no-one else in the house.'

'Big place you've got here.'

They tied her hands behind her back and Baslow

pulled out a metal cosh from his coat. 'Co-operate and you'll be fine otherwise it's this.'

'Or this,' said Murris, pointing his gun at her.

'First things first, keys for the Alpha?'

'On the rack, out there.'

Murris went to the hall and pocketed the key. Baslow forced Eleni to sit on a chair.

'Where's Mr Gooch?'

'At Kosty's, could be back any time.'

'Cash, where is it?'

'Haven't got any ca—'

He slapped her. 'A builder with no cash in the house, come on.'

Murris walked back in and forced his revolver barrel into her mouth. 'Tell us where it is or we're gonna kick you to bits.'

'It's in the kitchen under the sink.'

Murris went through and pulled out a bucket and cleaning materials. The back panel looked permanently fixed so he felt behind the sink and found a package taped to the side. He pulled it off and came back through to the dining room, opened the package and put it on the table. 'There's only about a grand there. Where's the rest?'

'That's all there—'

Baslow slapped her again and Murris slammed the butt of his revolver down on her thigh. She screamed and started to sob. 'Starting to get the idea are you? Where's the rest?'

'There's more in the loft.'

Murris ran upstairs and looked out of a front

bedroom window before going into the main bedroom and finding a pole with a hook. He went back to the landing and pulled the hatch down. As he did so the attached ladder started to slide so he caught it with the hook and lowered it to the floor. As he went up he flicked the light switch beside the hatch opening. He stood up, amazed at how well the loft had been fitted out. It was completely lined and floored with cabinets and storage boxes in matching finishes and expensive handles. The water tank had been panelled over in the same way. He quickly searched the boxes and cabinets but couldn't find anything so he climbed back down the ladders and shouted to Baslow. 'I can't find it, bring her up, quickly.'

Baslow grabbed her by the hair and forced her up to the landing.

'It's in the floor, there's a safe under the rug beside the tank.'

Murris moved the rug and found the floor safe. 'It's fucking locked, where's the key?'

'Inside the panel on the water tank. Push it and it'll open.'

Murris opened the safe and found a small bundle of cash. He went back to the hatch. 'There's only three or four grand, I'm coming down.'

Baslow forced her into a back bedroom and threw her on the floor. 'You'd better start helping us, where's the rest of Hattmann's money? Yeah that's right, it was us robbed Ron and your brother.'

'So you've already got it you clowns.'

Murris kicked her in the side. 'Where's the rest of it?'

'They only got eighteen and you already took it.'

Murris pulled Baslow out to the landing and spoke quietly. 'There could be cash all over the house so what do we do? Keep hitting her and get it in dribs and drabs? We need to get moving.'

Baslow pursed his lips. 'Take her out of here and phone Moose, "A*nother fifty or we kill her"?*

Murris shook his head. 'Chances of a handover going smoothly are not good, Moose is a pro, he'll bring a crew.'

Baslow went to the landing window and looked out the front. 'Still no one about, nothing.'

They went back into the main bedroom. Eleni had managed to sit herself upright against a wardrobe door.

'We know Hattmann had at least sixty, probably a good bit more. So if hubby didn't get it, who did?'

'Kosty thinks someone else got there first, maybe Den's sister.'

'We don't think so and neither does Jarrett, he's still looking for it. Make another guess.

'I don't know.'

Baslow slapped her and Murris held up his revolver. 'Next time it'll be with this and your pretty little face won't ever recover, so try again.'

'Julie and Vince.'

'Who?'

'Den's wife.'

'And Vince Allarth, the electrician?'

'Yeah.'

'How d'ya know?'

'I don't know, I'm guessing, but they've been seeing each other. Den doesn't know.'

Murris signalled to Baslow to come out to the landing. 'She's just trying to get rid of us.'

'But it *would* make sense. Everyone chasing their tails and all the time the wife's got it, might still be there.'

'More likely with the electrician.'

'Go to Hattmann's now?'

'What? No, this is bollocks. If it was the wife she'll have given it to Allarth and he's gone.'

'Maybe not. The last place Hattmann's gonna look for the cash is his own house. We go there now, they'll probably be asleep, take them by surprise. There'll be no-one around.'

'I'd rather just get out of this right now. There's a flight tomorrow morning from Luton and another one from East Mids later, I'm gonna try and get one of them.'

'We really need that cash.'

'She's just pissing us about.'

'I'm not so sure, it would explain everything. Look, we drive over there do a recce.'

Murris said nothing and Baslow pulled him further along the landing. 'We take the Alpha and hide it somewhere so Moose and everyone else thinks we're using that. Come on, one last effort then we split up.'

Murris reluctantly agreed and they went back to the bedroom and looked in on Eleni. She was still sitting propped up against the wardrobe. Baslow closed the door and they both went downstairs and out the front door. As soon as Eleni heard the front door close she started wriggling furiously and managed to get her hands free. She got up and went to the window in time to see the Alpha driving away. Then she went to the bedside telephone and dialled.

'Julie, it's Eleni.'

She finished the call and put the receiver down then picked it up immediately to make another call. 'Kosty it's me.'

'Ron's here, what is it?'

'Those two detectives that robbed you have been here. They took our cash and the Alpha. I think they're going to Julie Hatt—'

'Slow down, they came to the house?'

'Kicked the front door open and forced me to give them our cash, about four thousand.'

'Are you hurt?'

'They were rough, hit me a bit but I'm OK. They tied me up.'

'And they've taken the Alpha?'

'They were after the rest of Den's cash. They don't believe Christine got the money. I told them it might have been Julie and Vince took most of it before you got there.'

'Why'd you tell them that?'

'Cos Julie and Vince have a thing going.'

'Are you kidding? Since when?'

'A year or two.'

'I don't believe this, why didn't you tell me before.'

'Ron knows, I thought he'd have told you.'

'Stay there, we're on our way.'

Moose put the phone down and went back into the billiard room. Ron looked up before taking his shot. 'What's up?'

'You didn't mention that your mate Vince is havin' it off with Hattmann's wife.'

'Wasn't a hundred percent sure, but so what?'

'Well Baslow and Murris have just been to your house and robbed your cash and taken the Alpha. Now they're going to Hattmann's house cos they think his wife has the rest of it, the sixty we didn't find.'

'That's crazy. Is Eleni OK?'

'A bit shaken up. Go and get the Merc out, I need to speak to Karen.'

Ron sat in the driver's seat with the engine running. Moose marched up to the car, opened the boot and threw in a large bag that landed with a heavy thump.

'What's that?'

'Tools.'

'Tools?'

'You know what I mean.'

'What? Are we gonna tackle them? Christ, if Eleni's OK leave them to it. I'm not risking anything to help Den.'

'It's just in case. We don't know how this is going to turn out. Drive through Kemsing and stop at the phone box beside the pub.'

***

The two fugitives left Ron Gooch's street in both cars but stopped in Beckenham, hid the Alpha behind a pile of old skips near the railway station and took the Audi to Catford. Murris drove past Falmer Close twice but couldn't see anything suspicious so he turned the car slowly into the quiet residential street. He switched off the car's lights and coasted, stopping just short of Hattmann's semi. 'I still think this is crazy.'

'The Triumph's not there, if it's only her it'll be easy.'

'I think we should turn round, we've got *some* cash and cars our workmates don't know about. It's just not worth—'

Baslow's window shattered and a hammer struck him on the cheek. The door flew open and another blow hit him on the ear.

'Ya fuckin' cunts'

Baslow raised his arm but Hattmann grabbed it and hauled him out of the car. Murris struggled to get the revolver out of his coat pocket as Hattmann hit Baslow about the head. He fumbled with his seat belt but eventually managed to unclip it, open his door and get out. Seeing the gun, Hattmann threw his hammer at Murris hitting him on the arm just as he fired. The shot hit Baslow in the chest and he slumped to the ground. Murris fired another shot at Hattmann hitting him in the stomach, but he seemed to absorb it without any effect so he fired again and the huge builder staggered backwards and fell over. Murris went over to Baslow. 'George, George for fuck's sake.'

A large pool of blood appeared on the pavement and started pouring into the gutter. He felt for a pulse but found nothing. He quickly went through Baslow's pockets and took his gun and several bunches of keys. As he looked up he saw lights coming on in neighbouring houses and curtains opening. Cursing to himself, he got back in the Audi, turned the car around and headed for Bellingham.

***

The Mercedes pulled into Ron's driveway and stopped abruptly. Ron and Moose got out and Eleni opened the front door as they approached.

'You all right?'

She said nothing, just stared at them and started to cry. Her brother barged past holding a pistol and searched the entire house. Ron took his wife into the lounge and they both sat down. Moose came into the room and Eleni looked up, 'This is all because of you pair, you started this.'

'They took the Alpha?'

'Yes.'

'What did they arrive in?'

'No idea, didn't see it.'

The phone rang and Ron went to the hall and answered. 'What? ... Jesus.'

Moose came out to the hall and mouthed at him, *'what's happened?'*

'They're there now? ... OK ... OK.' He put the receiver down and turned to Moose.

'Well?'

'That was Julie Hattmann, Den's been shot, Baslow's dead.'

'Dead?'

'Yeah, outside Den's house.'

They went back into the lounge.

'What about the other one? Murris?'

'Didn't mention him. Said other police were there now and ambulances. Den's still alive but shot twice, it looks bad.'

'Is Julie OK? What happened?'

'She's OK. She didn't see it, looked out after she heard the shots. She couldn't say any more, there's coppers in the house.'

'What about the money?'

'Didn't ask.'

'Did they get in the house. The bent coppers?'

'Don't think so, it all happened outside.'

Eleni wiped her eyes and interrupted, 'If she did take the money, she'll have given it to Vince. If Den had found it in the house, he'd have killed her.'

'So what's happened to Murris?'

'God knows. Anyway who cares? Baslow's dead and Den's heading that way so surely we're out of it.'

'As long as that money's out there people will be chasing it, it'll never end.'

'If it ever really existed.'

'Any idea where Vince might've gone?'

'I could phone Steph, but not tonight.'

Moose stood up. 'I need to see Russ, tell him what's happened. I've a couple of contacts at the station might be able to tell me a bit more. For now, don't say a word to anyone about any of this.'

22

Change of Plan

'It's OK. I wasn't asleep, go on.'

Maidencoombe briefly outlined the evenings events and Pilling told him to meet at the station as soon as possible.

'Sir.'

He replaced the receiver and turned to Julie Hattmann. 'Thank you. We'll need to ask you some questions tomorrow but in the meantime you should be with your husband at the hospital. I'll get a car to take you.' He turned to Sandwell. 'You take over here, I've got to go and meet up with Pilling at the nick.'

He drove the short distance to the station and let himself in the back door. He made his way to Pilling's office and even though it was the middle of the night he half expected to find his superior's obstructive secretary sitting at her desk.

'Come in.'

Pilling looked exhausted and slightly comical in his golfing trousers. Maidencoombe reported the evening's events as he understood them though he left out a few significant details.

'This is a disaster but it could be worse.'

'How could it be worse? ... Sir.'

'If we find Murris it'll be a lot worse. He could say anything and drag the whole station into it. As it stands though, we have a respected senior officer, shot dead trying to protect a civilian from a solitary bad apple who's now disappeared. So we can pin everything on Murris. Hattmann, his sister and maybe even that other body at Hither Green. George Baslow was the gallant hero trying to bring him to justice—'

'But sir—'

'Let me finish. I take it you didn't record your suspicions about George and Phil on any official paperwork?'

'Kept it at home.'

'Good, that simplifies matters. Destroy everything. Then we make a great show of looking for Murris without actually finding him.'

'What about the missing plumber, Smallwood?'

'I don't know what to do about Smallwood but it's not a priority. Downgrade it.'

'That won't fly. If it was only him that had disappeared we could put it down to his history of going on benders but his wife has faked her own abduction. It's in the system and we've found his wallet at the scrap yard. We can't close it down, we've linked both of them to the Hattmann robbery.'

Pilling stood up and started pacing the room. He was sweating heavily. 'Ralph surely it's obvious. Take the scrap dealer at his word. He found Smallwood's wallet in the Marina when Murris handed it over so Murris is responsible for Smallwood's disappearance.'

'And the wife?'

'It's coincidental and unrelated. In fact do we really want to find either of them?'

'Not especially but—'

'Put someone else on it, separate team with very limited resources. You concentrate on clearing up the mess around Baslow.'

'And Kanavan?'

'It would be nice to put that on Murris, wrap it up neatly.'

'Unless it turns out to be the same gun as tonight, we've got absolutely nothing to connect Murris to Kanavan. We won't get the ballistics report for a few days.'

'Hmm.'

'There's a risk that Murris is picked up anyway. He might even hand himself in.'

'No. He'll skip the country, use a false passport. Now what about the money?'

'Nothing at the scene or anywhere else.'

'Well someone's got it.'

'You want us to assume Murris? ... He and Baslow robbed Hattmann in the first place? But why did they go back?'

'I'm as puzzled as you are. Go home and get some rest and meet me back here at noon.'

Maidencoombe went down to his office and phoned the control room. He asked them to relay a message to DS Sandwell then he left the building and went home. He came back to the station at eleven thirty and met Sandwell in an interview room. 'Did you find any useful witnesses?'

'None ... a lot of neighbours heard the shots and they looked out but none of them witnessed the actual shootings, just saw the bodies on the ground. One did glimpse the back end of a car speeding off but no model or even colour. So we've really got no idea what actually happened. We don't know yet if both men were shot with the same gun though it's likely judging by the positions they ended up in.'

'Why on earth would they go to Hattmann's house?'

Sandwell shook his head. 'I haven't a clue.'

'I talked with Pilling last night and nothing about that meeting makes me comfortable. Have you notified airports and so on about Murris?'

'The major ones but still working through the list. Haven't done the ferries yet.'

'Well stop. Pilling doesn't want Murris found.'

'What?'

'The official line is going to be, "Baslow's the hero and Murris the villain". A lone bad copper who's going to get the blame for everything, Christine Hattmann, Dennis, the robbery and Smallwood. He even wants to blame Murris for that body at the railway yard, Kanavan.'

'What's going on?'

'Honestly? ... I can only assume that Murris has

something on Pilling.'

'It was Pilling that produced the intelligence reports that Kanavan had left the country and gone to Spain.'

'So it was.'

'You realise where we're going with this Ralph?'

Maidencoombe looked down at the floor. 'I'm not sure I've got the energy for this anymore and if *you* pursue it, you'll be damaged either way. No-one'll ever trust you again.'

'And John? ... You know what he's like. He may already have worked it out.'

'Don't tell him about this for now. I'm seeing Pilling again at twelve. Wait for me in the canteen.'

Maidencoombe left the room and went back to his office to collect some paperwork before going back upstairs to see Chief Superintendent Pilling.

'Anything else from the scene?'

'Nothing that helps.'

'What about the allotment?'

'There's nothing there apart from the body in the hole. We're digging up the rest of it but I think if there was any other incriminating stuff they'll have taken it with them.'

'Well an old informant has been in touch with me. His information suggests Murris is probably driving a dark blue Citroen CX.'

'How could this informant possibly know about it unless he's involved?'

'Murris bought the car from someone known to the informant. The point is, make sure everyone is on the lookout for a Citroen. Do you understand?'

Maidencoombe nodded his head in disgust. 'Perfectly.'

He left Pilling's office to meet up with Sandwell and Akerman in the canteen. He noticed the usual hubbub quietening down as he walked across the room and became very aware of officers at other tables staring at him. 'Information from upstairs, Murris is likely driving a dark blue Citroen CX.'

Sandwell looked at him sceptically and blew out through his lips. Akerman leaned forward. 'I saw one in Moustrianos' forecourt'

'I'm starting not to care.'

Akerman looked confused.

'Come upstairs.'

They left the canteen and went to Maidencoombe's tiny office. Sandwell and Akerman pulled up chairs close to the desk.

'John, we were going to try and keep you in the dark about some of this but as you'll probably work it out for yourself anyway, you may as well understand what's going on right now. Murris must not be found. We're guessing that apart from all the embarrassment he's already caused, he has compromising information about CS Pilling.'

'Embarrassment? He's killed two people. This is a cover up.'

'A partial cover-up.'

'Why're you doing this? It makes a mockery of everything.'

'John, I'm trying to protect you. Baslow's dead and can't be prosecuted. Pilling'll be gone in a year or two. It wouldn't make any difference to my career though I'd hate to leave under a cloud but for you and Vic, it'll ruin the rest of your lives if you pursue this.'

Akerman stood up, indignant.

'John, sit down. There may be another way of dealing with this.' Sandwell went on, 'we could gather all the information we have linking Pilling to Kanavan, perhaps dig up some more and then lean on him, try and nudge him out sooner.'

'Very risky Vic, we don't know who else is behind him higher up.'

Akerman stood up again 'Well I'm for it.'

'Both of you ... for the time being we've got enough to do with Baslow and Hattmann so leave it for now. I'm going to get my thoughts together and have a short snooze. Wake me in a couple of hours and update me.'

Sandwell nodded his head towards the door. 'Come on.'

They walked together silently, passing other officers who avoided looking at them. They arrived back at the main office and sat opposite each other. Referring to pocketbooks, they filled in forms and made phone calls. After half an hour, Sandwell leaned back on this chair and put his hands behind his head to look at the ceiling. 'The guv's right you know, we can't fix this.'

Akerman shook his head and was just about to reply when his phone started ringing.

'What?'

'OK.'

'Bring it to DS Sandwell in the main office.'

'What is it?'

'They found more stuff at Murris' flat.'

They walked in to Maidencoombe's office and found him awake but tired and very irritable. Sandwell placed the package on the desk and Maidencoombe took out four passports. One pair belonged to Dennis and Julie Hattmann and the other pair to Reginald and Patricia Wilson but the Hattmann's photographs were in both sets. Sandwell laid another file on the desk with Reg Wilson's photograph on top.

'We dug a bit deeper. They're half brothers.'

'I should have spotted the resemblance sooner, I can see it now.'

'As they were at Murris' flat, it'll look as if he did the blag at Hattmann's.'

'How bloody convenient.'

***

The same day, Vince got up from his bed and pulled back the curtains. He liked the view over Folkestone harbour but thought the top floor room in this holiday hotel overpriced. He put his shoes back on and walked downstairs carrying a carrier bag full of cash. He left the building and walked to an unusually fresh and clean phone box that also overlooked the harbour. He picked up the receiver and dialled. 'Are you OK.'

'More or less.'

'Are you ready? ... Are we gonna do this?

'I'm scared but I'll do it, can't stay here.'

'Get the 10.10 from Victoria, gets here at twelve.'

'Where are we sailing from?'

'Wait and see, it's a surprise.'

He left the call box and wandered around the town until five o'clock, then returned to make some more calls. He started to dial his home number but stopped after a few digits and called his mother-in-law's number instead.

'Steph it's me.'

'Yeah?'

'Has anything happened?'

'Moose and Ron and some other villain have been round here twice. They know you've got Den's money. You'll be lucky if they don't kill you.'

'Is Den still alive?'

'Only just. If he survives he'll be paralysed.'

'Yeah?'

'I knew you'd be pleased.'

'Just keep saying I'm in Margate.'

'Gonna stay down there forever are you?'

'Haven't decided.'

'And what about Julie, you've left her in a mess.'

'Never mind about that, how's the kids?'

'Fat lot you care.'

The beeps sounded and he hesitated for a few seconds before hanging up. He waited a while then he picked up the handset again and called Ron Gooch's yard but only got the answering machine. He tried again ten minutes later.

'Ron?'

'Vince?' For fuck's sake where are you? Jarrett's gonna kill you and Den's been paralysed, shot by one of them bent coppers.'

'I'm in Margate.'

'Moose is trying to persuade Jarrett to get out of the country but he won't till he's found you.'

'Are the regular coppers still after *us*?'

'Don't think so, they haven't been back. One of the bent ones is dead though, Baslow. Shot as well. It was on the news.'

'I didn't see that.'

'The other one's on the run.'

'Fuckin' 'ell.'

'What're you gonna do?'

'I've got a good bolt hole here but I'm goin' on to Spain.'

'With Julie?'

'That's the plan but don't tell anyone. Gotta go.'

Ron put the phone down and looked across at Moose. 'Where is he?'

'Margate, a phone box, like Steph said.'

'If he's saying Margate he's probably somewhere else. Could be in Cardiff for all we know.'

'Says he's goin' to Spain.'

'He's fooled everyone 'till the last min—'

'Says he's takin' Julie with him.'

'So what he really wants, is us to follow Julie while he escapes.'

'Do we tell Russ?'

'Don't know what to do.'

Vince returned to the hotel and spent the whole evening in his room. The next day he got up at eight o'clock, washed and shaved. He went downstairs but decided not to bother with breakfast. Instead, he went to reception and apologised for cutting his stay short. The bemused proprietor accepted his payment without comment. He went back to his room and collected the suitcase, then went downstairs, left the hotel and walked to a row of lock-up garages two streets away. Before arriving at the hotel he had traded his Maxi for a newer Renault so he was disappointed to find that one of the tyres was a bit flat when he opened lock-up number three.

He unlocked the drivers door and leaned over the seat to unlock the door behind. He opened that and pulled up the base of the rear seat and was relieved to find the other bag of cash still present. He put it into his suitcase before moving the car onto an adjacent side street and changing the wheel.

He drove to the outskirts of the town and stopped at a filling station to buy a sandwich and a drink. Although he had set off later than planned he had plenty of time so he decided to use the old A20 instead of the new motorway. When he arrived at Ashford he drove into the town centre and parked near the station. He had an hour and a half to kill so he bought a newspaper and a fishing magazine. Shortly before twelve o'clock he took his suitcase from the boot and walked towards the station where he sat down on a bench overlooking the exit. At midday he heard a train arrive and watched about forty or fifty passengers walk out. The stream of travellers stopped after a couple of minutes and he was about to go into the station to look when he felt a tap on his shoulder. He turned round to see Shirley Smallwood in a bright red coat smiling broadly. 'Like my new look?'

Taken aback, he paused before answering. 'I love it.'

She pecked him on the cheek.

'Where were you.'

'You had the times wrong. Got in twenty minutes ago, been sittin' in a caff. So where're we goin'?

'We're driving to Lydd Airport and flying to Alicante.'

'Thought we was goin' by ferry?'

'Change of plan.'

'Where's Lydd Airport?'

'On the coast, 'bout forty minutes, we've got plenty of time.'

Vince drove slowly along the minor road but stopped a few miles short of the airport and parked in a woodland clearing. 'We need to spread the money about, half each, some in the cases, some in the hand baggage and some in our coats. We'll do it here out of sight.'

'Is that all of it?'

'Only half, the rest is already out there. It was sent out a couple of weeks ago, it's in a bank account.'

They shared out the cash between them and continued on to the tiny airport arriving just as a cargo plane landed. They checked in, much more worried about their false passports being exposed than their cash being found. They handed over their suitcases without problems and the immigration officer barely glanced at their passports. Relieved, they sat in the departure lounge.

'How long you gonna keep stringin' Julie along?'

'As long as I have to.'

'Quite like her really.'

'She's a nice girl,' he said, putting his hand on Shirley's leg, 'but *she* doesn't turn me on.'

Shirley put her hand on top of his.

'I'll call her now.' He walked over to the phone booth beside the cafeteria and looked around before dialling Julie's number. 'It's me.'

'Where are you?'

'I'm at Stansted. I'm flying to Turkey then on to Cyprus.'

'Den's gonna be in hospital for months. The police keep coming back. Ron and that thug Jarrett are looking for you. Moustrianos as well.'

'Are the *police* after me?'

'Don't think so. They haven't asked about you.'

'Stay calm, don't do anything, don't say anything.'

'I can't stand it any more, I need to come with you.'

'It's too dangerous, they'll follow you straight to me.'

'What're we gonna do?'

'I'm working on it, I'll think of something.'

****

Also By JG Neville

Gold is Grief

1984. In the aftermath of a huge bullion robbery, three men are in custody but the bullion has vanished. South London car dealer, Kostas Moustrianos, knows who's got it and sees an opportunity to profit. The men who have it, have other ideas. So do the police.

When the Met appoint a new DCI to coordinate the search, he quickly fixates on the car dealer. But corruption and territorial squabbling hamper the investigation and the bodies pile up.

ISBN 978-1-7395711 3 9 (Paperback)

ISBN 978-1-7395711 4 6 (eBook)

ISBN 978-1-7395711 5 3 (Hardback)

Printed in Great Britain
by Amazon